Behind Barbed Eyes

Davina Kotulski

The opinions in this book represent the viewpoint of the author alone and do not necessarily reflect the opinion of the Federal Bureau of Prisons or the Department of Justice. All characters in this novel are fictional. Any resemblance to real people is purely coincidental, with the exception of the individuals in the helicopter escape.

ISBN: 099783790X
ISBN 13: 9780997837902

Kotulski, Davina.
Behind Barbed Eyes: a novel/ by Davina Kotulski

1. Women in Prison—Fiction. 2. Crime—Fiction. 3. Psychology— Fiction. 4. Spiritual —Fiction. 5. Jewish—Fiction.

Published by Red Ink Press
South Pasadena, CA

Dedication

To the women I worked with at the Federal Correctional Institution in Dublin, California who worked to free themselves from addiction, heal from abuse and be a better version of themselves.

To the men and women who work in correctional facilities who put their lives and hearts on the line when they walk through the prison gates every day.

People, even more than things, have to be restored, renewed, revived, reclaimed, and redeemed; never throw out anyone.

-Audrey Hepburn

Praise of Behind Barbed Eyes

"BEHIND BARBED EYES is a compelling novel that shows the radical power forgiveness has to transform our lives and the lives of others!"—Colin Tipping, Author of *Radical Forgiveness* and *Radical Self-Forgiveness*

"*Behind Barbed Eyes* forces us to examine our own challenges with forgiveness. It reminds us what all spiritual teachers espouse, that unconditional love of ourselves and others, is the universal pathway to true healing."—Dr. Shefali Tsabary, Author of *The Conscious Parent*

Chapter I

Dr. Victoria Thomas raced down the hallway. Thankfully, she realized within the first few days of working at the Women's Federal Correctional Institution how impractical heels were. She had begrudgingly acquiesced to wearing a sensible pair of loafers that allowed her to sprint across the prison compound at a moment's notice.

The new commits sitting in the waiting room rushed to look out the window of the Psych building. They cheered and wolf-whistled as she darted down the wooden stairs and across the compound.

From all corners of the prison, correctional staff members ran in the direction of the prison's recreation yard— a five-acre field with a dirt track and a weight pile. The yard was enclosed in razor wire and accessible only through a metal gate and the back door of the prison's recreation building.

She caught up with Officer Napuna, a solidly built Pacific Islander. "What's happening?" she asked, out of breath.

"102 in progress," he said, sweat dripping from his brow.

102? She couldn't remember what that was.

Mike Russell, the burly prison foreman, stood like a sentry at the metal gate of the rec yard holding it open for staff responding to the emergency. Just as Victoria ran through the threshold of the gate she heard the roar of a motor. The noise was deafening. A sudden solid gust of wind knocked her backward and she struggled to keep her footing. Her long hair blew into her face obscuring her vision.

She could hear Lt. Lopez shouting, "Take cover!"

Officer Napuna dropped to the ground in front of her. "Holy shit!" he yelled.

She quickly dropped to the ground, brushing her hair from her eyes. That's when she saw it.

About forty yards away, a helicopter rose up from the recreation field, hurling sheets of dust everywhere. The rotors spun violently. Like a wasp or some unwanted pest it flew toward them, hovering briefly overhead, then took off.

Victoria got up from the ground and brushed the dirt off her navy pantsuit. It was useless.

"Man down, man down. Control, do you copy?" a frantic voice radioed in.

"Control, copy," a shaky voice responded.

"It's Lourdes, Sylvia Lourdes," she heard Russell yell to Lt. Lopez, a stocky Latino with a shaved head and a permanent sulk.

Victoria knew the name. Inmate Sylvia Lourdes was considered an old timer at Dublin because she had a 50-year sentence for bank robbery.

"You okay, ma'am?" Napuna asked, his pecs visible through his sweat-soaked uniform.

"Yes," she replied, "are you?"

He looked a little pale, but nodded and wiped the sweat from his brow. "Didn't see that coming."

Within moments, two white-coated Filipino physician's assistants drove up to the front of the recreation building in a motorized vehicle the size of a golf cart with a stretcher on the back.

"Let's go!" Lt. Lopez yelled.

She saw Scott Stevenson, who ran the inmate's recreational activities, limp out of the front door of the rec building. He was bleeding from his leg. "Bitch shanked me," he told them.

Officer Napuna, Foreman Russell, and Lt. Lopez lifted Stevenson onto the stretcher.

"Any other wounds?" one of the PAs asked, rolling up Stevenson's pant leg.

"Nope, that's it."

"You're going to live," Lt. Lopez said dryly.

Russell mussed Stevenson's red hair. "I've had worse wounds from a staple gun, Scotty."

Scott gave them a thumbs-up as the PAs drove off with him strapped to the stretcher.

"Okay people, listen up, we're going on lockdown!" Lt. Lopez barked. "We need to get the inmates to their units for an emergency count. After count clears report immediately to the visiting room for your next assignment. And I mean immediately! Don't stop to take a piss or call your family. They'll hear all about it on the news. And don't, I repeat DO NOT discuss this escape with the inmates under any circumstances. Now move!"

Victoria wasn't fond of paramilitary communication, especially commands directed toward her. She was a professional, not a GS-9 correctional officer, like Napuna, who was fresh out of Iraq.

She hurried back to the Psych Building and summoned Brad Shaw, the substance abuse counselor, out of earshot of the inmates. He looked her up and down. "What the hell happened?"

She felt something in her hair and pulled out a twig, noticing for the first time that her hand was trembling. "Helicopter escape on the rec yard. Stevenson got stabbed. He'll be okay though."

Brad's boyish blue eyes turned serious. "What? Where was OSP? Why didn't they shoot?"

"It was crazy," she said, realizing that her navy pantsuit was likely ruined. "They shot a warning shot, but they can't shoot at a moving target. Besides, it happened on the yard. Whoever was in the truck might have missed and shot one of us. Listen, I'll tell you all about it later." Her legs felt wobbly and she wanted to sit down, but couldn't. "We've got to get the inmates to the housing units. Lockdown and emergency count. Then we're supposed to report to the visiting room."

Brad shook his head. "Shit! That means cell feeding!"

"That's not that bad, is it?" she asked. She'd never been through a lockdown, not even in mock crisis training at FLETC, the Federal Law Enforcement Training Center in Glynco, Georgia. She had heard about lockdowns at the men's institutions from other staff members, but she wasn't sure what was real and what was exaggeration. Old timers tended to revel in such stories, which seemed to grow bigger with every telling.

Brad frowned. "Mandatory overtime. Twelve hour shifts. I have a date tonight."

"Yeah," she laughed, "with fifteen hundred inmates."

"I need to make a phone call. I'll lock up and meet you there," he said.

Victoria wanted to call Devin, but didn't because of Lt. Lopez's order. Devin was working late tonight, so she figured he wouldn't miss her anyway. She walked to the room where the inmates awaiting intake were seated and opened the door.

"Ladies, return to your housing units immediately. Let's go."

Two young black women darted past her.

A gaunt, gray-haired white woman looked at her confused. "But I need anti-depressant medications. My counselor said you could help with that." She looked like she might crumble right there in the hallway.

"Yes. Please come back later," Victoria said.

Ms. Garcia, the petite Latina orderly, translated the command to return to the housing units in Spanish. The monolingual Latinas gathered up their belongings and trudged out of the building.

Victoria walked to Unit A/B.

Officer Napuna unlocked the door and let her in. Mike Russell and another male officer Victoria did not recognize reclined in plastic chairs in the TV area of the unit's lobby.

Napuna picked up the phone that doubled as a paging system. His voice echoed across the empty corridor, "Inmates clear the lobbies. Back to your rooms and stand for count." He turned toward Russell and the other officer. "You guys ready?"

"Wait, here comes Shaw," Russell said.

Napuna walked to the door and unlocked it. Brad fist-bumped Napuna.

"What the funk? Sounds like I missed all the action?" He walked over to Russell.

"Yep, this is a Dublin first," Russell joked.

"Don't feel bad," Napuna said. "The rookie here missed it too."

The rookie shook his head. "I was busy handing out toilet paper and maxi pads."

"Is Scotty really okay?" Brad asked them.

"I told you he was," Victoria said, including herself in their conversation, but Brad seemed to intentionally ignore her.

Russell snorted. "He'll be kicking your ass on the basketball court once he's enjoyed his well-earned BOP vacation. Hell, you probably did more damage to your knee playing ball than Lourdes did to him with her sharpened tooth-brush."

Brad laughed. "You're a hard ass, Russell."

Victoria wanted to roll her eyes at this display of male posturing.

"Okay, guys, let's do this," Napuna said. "Rookie, you count. Russell and Shaw, you back. I'll double lock the doors as we go."

"What about me?" Victoria asked, incensed by their total disregard of her presence.

Napuna thought for a moment then unlocked the door to the officer's station. He pulled out a large white plastic bin full of envelopes and placed it on a desk outside the locked officer's station. "Here, Doc, stay here and sort the mail. We'll have to hand-deliver it tonight. Put the letters in alphabetical order and then we'll arrange them by room assignment."

She looked at the pile of envelopes and immediately regretted asking.

"Let's go guys," Napuna said.

Victoria walked over to the desk and picked up a handful of envelopes and began sorting them into piles. Her hands were still shaking. Letter sorting was not something she expected she would be doing when she took the job of staff psychologist with the Bureau of Prisons.

Case Manager King, a voluptuous black woman with dyed blonde hair rounded the corner. "Here, I'll help you with that, Doc." She grabbed a pile from the bin. Despite her long candy apple red fingernails, she was able to sort the letters twice as fast as Victoria.

A voice came over the two-way radio, "All available staff report immediately to the visiting room."

"That's us," King said, picking up the sorted letters and putting them into neat piles on top of the white bin. She locked up the officer's station then walked to the front door of the housing unit, unlocked it, stepped outside and lit a cigarette. "Go ahead, Doc, I'll catch up with you."

Victoria walked briskly to the visiting room. The chairs were arranged theatre-style. A dozen staff members sat scattered in the seats, the majority in the back rows. Victoria took a seat in the second row.

Warden Beshure, a tall, relatively attractive, well-spoken, white man stood confidently at the front of the room. Though new to Dublin, he had taken command easily, learning and remembering the names of each staff member. His eye contact, like his grip, was solid. He was a well-groomed leader, which Victoria appreciated, but she found somewhat intimidating.

Beshure walked toward a podium with a microphone. Captain Brown, a wiry black man who wore his hair closely-shaven and dressed in civilian clothes, followed him. Beshure motioned to his secretary, Ms. Fernando, who sat cross-legged in a plastic chair near the door. She got up and moved carefully across the heavily polished floor, her high heels clicking as she walked.

"We need to install helicopter wire ASAP," Victoria overheard the Warden tell Captain Brown. "Ms. Fernando, work with the financial staff. Put a rush on it. I want a crew in here tonight. We'll need emergency NCIC checks and live fingerprinting. That'll still be cheaper than a lockdown with cell feeding and overtime." Beshure shook his head. "Helicopter wire was a given at the other institutions I worked at, but they said this wouldn't happen at a women's facility."

"Now you feel me, Warden?" Captain Brown took a sip from the paper cup filled with vending machine coffee. Victoria didn't know how he could stand it. Even instant coffee was more palatable than the sludge that came out of the vending machine. "Been trying to get us up to snuff since I arrived from Talladega, but they don't take female convicts seriously. Or maybe this is just a California hug-a-thug thing." Brown was smiling, but she could tell he was pissed and tired of being disregarded, something she sensed he experienced frequently in his life.

The visiting room was filling up quickly. She saw Brad take a seat in the back with the maintenance guys who were cracking jokes and roughhousing. Lt. Lopez made a beeline to the Warden and whispered something to him; Victoria couldn't make it out, but whatever it was, it wasn't good.

The Warden stepped up to the podium and switched on the microphone. "Folks, looks like we're going to be in the funny pages tomorrow. We've had two escapes. Inmate Sylvia Lourdes took a special Con Air flight and it seems one of the campers, Lucille Merriweather, decided it was a good day to take a long walk. We've notified local authorities and we'll need to set up escape posts. Once again all Bureau of Prisons matters are classified. So don't decide to trade your BOP career for five minutes of fame by talking to the reporters in the parking lot tonight."

He paused for a moment and looked sternly at the staff. "Obviously, you're not to discuss this with the inmates under any circumstances. Remember folks, the walls have ears and inmates are listening even when you don't think they are. We realize your families may have questions too, but please remind them you are not at liberty to share. All non-essential staff are to report immediately to the chow hall. We'll be bagging the noon meal, dinner, and tomorrow's breakfast. Plan on being here until we're done."

Victoria took a deep breath, aware she still felt a bit shaky inside. It was going to be a really long day.

Chapter 2

"LET ME OUT!" Bonnie Maldonado's words pierced the silence as she railed against the unyielding metal door. "I gotta get out of here!"

Harris jolted up from the top bunk almost hitting her head on the ceiling. "What the hell wrong with you now?"

Bonnie paced back and forth in the ten-by-seven-foot cramped cell. She could barely make out Harris's figure in the dim fluorescent light streaming in through the small rectangular window of the cell door. She had to get out. "I'm gonna explode!" she yelled.

"Girl, you need to see the goddamned head shrinker! You crazy!" Harris grabbed her covers and pulled them over her head.

Bonnie slammed her body against the door again, pounding her fists until the skin around her knuckles tore and bled. She needed to get out of the room. Her eyes fixed on the empty lobby area on the other side of the cell door. Then she heard the sound of shaking keys moving fast down the corridor.

"Control, back up requested, I need back up in Housing Unit B lower tier," she heard the officer yell into the radio. She squinted, shielding her eyes with her hand against the flashlight he aimed directly at her. She calmed down a bit when she recognized the chubby face peering in at her. It was Officer Randall. He held the flashlight in one hand revealing a circle of sweat under his arm, and in the other, his keys, attached by a long chain to his pants. She could deal with Randall. He wasn't the smartest guard, but unlike some of the others, he didn't seem to feel the need to remind anyone they were in prison.

"What …the hell …is going on?" he wheezed. "What's …the problem?"

Her bloody hands trembled. She swallowed hard, fighting back the lump in her throat as the tears began to form in her eyes. She pulled at her hair. "I got to get out of here."

"Do you need to see the psych or something?"

"Yeah, whatever, just get me out of here!" She felt like a caged animal.

He pulled out his radio again. "Lieutenant, notify Psychology, we have a situation." Randall wiped the sweat from his brow and waited for acknowledgement.

"10-4, en route."

Seconds later, staff ran down the hallway, keys jingling violently on their chains. Her door swung open and two assisting officers pulled her from the cell and slammed her body against the wall outside. They grabbed her wrists and cuffed her hands tight behind her back.

"Let go of me!"

"Pat her down first. Then, take her to the Lieutenant's Office," the shift Lieutenant ordered and then turned and walked away.

Bonnie heard the muffled sounds of the other inmates talking in their cells. A few faces appeared like ghosts from behind the cell doors.

"We've got everything under control," one of the assisting officers radioed into the Control Room.

She felt a hand on the back of her leg, cupping her thigh. Her ears started ringing and unwanted memories exploded in her mind. "Don't touch me!" she yelled and started to kick. "Get off of me!"

The officers grabbed her arms and forced her shoulders to the ground. The smell of cleaner and floor wax filled her nostrils. Someone gripped her hand and twisted her thumbs. Another held her head. Her cheek pressed against the cold tile floor. The memories kept coming.

"You through bucking, Maldonado?"

She heard another officer laugh. She couldn't see him because her long brown hair had tangled around her face. "Last thing we need is a bunch of inmates popping off," he said.

"Let's go." They jerked her to her feet. One held her by the right elbow. The other gripped her left elbow with one hand and the cuffs with his other.

They escorted her out of the housing unit onto the prison compound.

The night air was moist and still. Almost a year had passed since she'd been outside this late at night. She tried to stop and look up at the stars, but the towering overhead lights blocked out the sky, and then there was an immediate painful pressure on her thumb as the officer twisted it, forcing her body forward.

"Keep walking!" he ordered.

"You people take your goddamned jobs too seriously!" she barked back.

Chapter 3

THE PHONE RANG loudly, jolting her awake.

"No," Victoria whined, noting the red numbers on the digital clock—11:11 PM. She nestled deeper into the warmth of her down comforter and her burgundy satin sheets.

"Come on, Vic." Devin nudged her body in the direction of the nightstand. "You know it's for you."

Victoria turned on the light, almost knocking over the empty teacup and the five half-read books precariously housed on the edge of her mission-style oak nightstand. She picked up the receiver.

"What's the inmate's name?" she asked as she searched for a pen and something to write on.

"Bonnie Maldonado, 2-4-8-2-7 dash 0-5-6. Okay, got it. Are you sure this can't wait until morning?" she asked. "I just got home an hour ago, Lieutenant."

She tried to reason with the voice on the other end, but it was useless. " I'll be there in forty minutes." She hung up.

"Damn it. I've got to go in!"

"Sorry, Vic." Devin patted her on the back. It was a condescending touch, but it felt good to feel his strong hand on her body. It had been too long since he had last touched her.

"It's ridiculous they don't pay me extra to be on-call," she grumbled, lifting the comforter higher than necessary hoping to make Devin just a little uncomfortable and to get a glimpse of the man she'd married.

Devin pulled the covers back over his muscular body. "It's ridiculous you want to work some place where you could get stabbed on the job. Start a practice in the financial district, plenty of crazy attorneys. You could charge $100 an hour and $20 for every ten-minute crisis call, but you're the one who wants to save the world, *tikkun olam*, or however you say that in Hebrew. I don't know why you took that job."

"I told you, because I want to help women with drug addictions." She stepped inside the walk-in closet glad she'd told him she was only doing intakes when the escape went down. She quickly changed into a pair of business slacks and a sweater, then grabbed a black leather belt and clipped a metal chain to it. She hastily combed out her brown tangles with the reddish highlights and wiped the sleep from the corner of her green eyes.

"Hopefully, I'll be back soon," she said, knowing she would be gone at least two hours. The federal women's prison was a twenty-five mile drive from their home in Oakland. She kissed her husband goodbye.

"Don't worry, I won't wait up," he said and switched off the light.

She stepped out of her car and felt chilled. It was unseasonably cold for September in the Bay Area. The prison parking lot was mostly empty, with the exception of a handful of trucks and sport utility vehicles. She noted the bumper sticker on one SUV. "Guns don't kill people, people kill people." She shook her head. *That's true, but guns sure made it a whole lot easier,* she thought.

In the distance she saw the lights of the armed patrol truck making rounds just outside the double fences and razor wire that surrounded the prison. She walked toward the flagpole at the front entrance. In the daytime an officer would be stationed there monitoring the comings and goings of staff and visitors, but tonight, the desk at the front entrance was empty.

"Sally Two," she called to the Control Room officer as she stepped up to the sallyport, a corridor with doors on either side in which only one door could be opened at a time.

The lock to the sallyport door released. She entered the sallyport and walked over to a wooden board and turned a one-inch white square around to reveal a red number "27." There were only about fifteen other red squares on the board. This was the way the prison tracked which staff members were in the facility in case of a riot or hostage situation.

The Associate Warden who was taken hostage at the Georgia penitentiary told her during new staff orientation, "They run the place and let us work here." As she looked at the fifteen little squares, representing the lives of fifteen staff members, she realized how true his statement was. She was glad she worked the day shift—the board was at least half full of about 65 red squares. The clock on the wall, visible through the bars, read exactly midnight. She waited for the Control Room officer to unlock Sally One, the door that opened to the prison grounds.

"Sally One," or "the Front Entrance," was one of only two entries into the prison. To the inmates, it was one of two exits, and the only exit that would legitimately lead to their freedom. The other was the rear gate where inmates left by bus to be transferred to other prisons or ended their sentence early by dying and were wheeled out on a stretcher and given the designation "escape by death."

Victoria walked through the sallyport and up to the Control Room window that faced the interior of the prison. It was like a cashier's window at an inner city bank or gas station, made of bullet-proof glass with a sliding metal tray used to exchange keys and radios. A sign on the window read "NO CHIT, NO CHAIN, NO KEYS." Victoria placed her chit, a metal circle, coin-size, with her name engraved on it, into the tray.

"Q-8," she said.

Officer Jones, a black woman with short hair, tossed the keys into the tray and they made a loud clanking noise. "They're waiting for you at the Lieutenant's Office, Doc."

Victoria picked up the keys and fastened them to the chain attached to her belt. All staff had to clip their keys onto chains attached to their belts —to prevent staff from accidentally leaving their keys in the door where inmates could steal them. If one staff member lost a key or a set of keys, all locks in the prison would have to be changed, along with all 270 staff members' key sets. Victoria wasn't sure she was going to need her keys, but she didn't want to have to walk back to the Control Room if she did.

"Thanks," she said, and made her way to the Lieutenant's Office. She found Lieutenant Frank Williams, a big burly man in his forties with a flattop, leaning back in his chair, his feet up on a desk cluttered with paperwork, a pack of Marlboros, a paperback copy of *Slaughterhouse-Five*, a coffee cup, and his burgundy clip-on tie, part of the mandatory uniform for all male correctional staff. It was a clip-on tie so that the inmates could not use it to strangle staff. Female officers were issued burgundy bowties that looked more like something a cocktail waitress would wear than a law enforcement officer. Many of the female officers refused to wear the dainty bowties and had filed a claim with the union to wear the clip-on tie instead. Victoria admired that. For many years females weren't even allowed to work as officers in men's facilities.

To the right of Frank Williams's desk, Victoria noticed the hunched over figure, dressed in a white T-shirt, grey sweat pants, and prison-issue, black steel-toed work boots. Her arms were cuffed behind her back and she was staring at the floor, her stringy brown hair covering her face.

"Lieutenant, may I speak with you for a moment?"

"Sure, Doc." Lieutenant Williams eased his feet off the desk and grabbed a cigarette as he followed her out of his office into the hallway. "Sorry to get you out of bed, Doc, but we don't need any funny business. Things are really tense around here. Plus I've got almost half my staff babysitting the work crew out on the rec yard. We need to get that helicopter wire up before anyone else tries to escape."

Victoria nodded sympathetically. "What happened?" she asked.

"Well," he fumbled for a match, "according to Randall, this one just popped a gasket, started punching her cell door, hollering and demanding to let her out." Lt. Williams delivered the sentence like he had a large audience hanging on his every word. "You know how these convicts are, immediate gratification, can't handle anything."

Victoria stepped back to avoid inhaling the cigarette smoke, annoyed he was ignoring the rules about smoking inside. "What seems to be wrong?"

He leaned in towards her and laughed. "Isn't that your job, Doc?" He took a deep drag off his cigarette. "She wouldn't tell us. Maybe she's just trying to get out of her cell or work call tomorrow." He exhaled, chuckling as he blew. "If you ask me, I think a little diesel therapy would do the trick. We could ship her out tomorrow; smelling fumes from here to Texas usually calms them down."

Victoria held back her disgust at the idea that transferring the inmate would solve her psychological problems. "I'll see what I can do."

"Work your magic, Doc."

Victoria walked into the Lieutenant's office and closed the door behind her. Lieutenant Williams stayed outside to finish his cigarette. The figure in the chair was still staring at the floor, her long brown hair covering her face. Her right leg shook fiercely, causing the chair to squeak. She could see the woman's knuckles were bleeding. She moved the Lieutenant's chair across from the woman and sat down.

Victoria reached into her pocket and consulted the scrap of paper she'd scribbled the woman's name on. "Hi, Ms. Maldonado, my name is Dr. Thomas. I'm a psychologist. Can you tell me what's bothering you?"

Maldonado jerked upright. Her face was sweaty and flushed. Her anxiety was palpable. "I can't handle it! I just can't fucking handle it!" Maldonado burst out.

"Handle what? Can you be more specific? Being on lockdown?" Victoria urged. "I'm sure it will only be another day or so and then it will be back to normal operations."

"No, not lockdown, the shit that happens to me. I can't fucking deal with it anymore!" Her voice was hoarse, like she'd been screaming. Tears fell from her eyeliner-darkened eyes and onto her T-shirt, forming black splotches.

Victoria suddenly felt guilty she couldn't give the woman a tissue. With her hands cuffed behind her back, a tissue would be useless. She decided it would also be too much of a battle to ask the Lieutenant to un-cuff the inmate or to cuff her hands in the front. He'd call her a "Hug-a-thug." She sure as hell couldn't wipe away the inmate's tears for her. There was a strict rule about staff touching inmates. So, she just watched as the tears rolled down Maldonado's face, off her chin, and onto her clothes.

"Why does bad shit always happen to me?" Maldonado sobbed, still avoiding eye contact.

Victoria let Maldonado cry. She leaned in toward Maldonado hoping to develop a rapport with her. "I know this is hard, but can you tell me what's going on?"

Maldonado looked up and flung her head sideways trying to move her wet hair out of the way so she could see. Her eyes met Victoria's. Tears ran down her smudged face. "I can't stop thinking about him. Why? Why?" Maldonado's leg shook again making a loud rhythmic squeaking noise.

Victoria guessed at what was troubling Maldonado. "Are you having problems with your boyfriend?" She had seen this type of behavior so many times before—a prison relationship break up, problems with their kids on the outside.

Maldonado was quiet for a moment. "Yeah," she drew out the word like it was three syllables. "That motherfucker went back to his ex-wife!" Maldonado kicked her leg out banging the Lieutenant's desk with the side of her boot.

Finally, we're getting somewhere, Victoria thought. "Did you just find this out?"

"Yeah, I got a letter today."

Maldonado looked to be in her thirties; Victoria guessed they were close to the same age. She wondered what brought Maldonado to prison. Drugs, money, love? Was she a career criminal or had she just fallen in with a bad crowd? Was she abused, molested, or raped like most of the women at the prison? Her fuck-the-world attitude and poor anger control suggested some sort of violation, which meant a serious drug addiction as well. The prison was full of women who hid their wounds behind a façade of hostility.

Maldonado burst into sobs again, lowering her head to her lap. "I can't take it anymore."

"Just breathe, Ms. Maldonado. What can't you take anymore?"

Maldonado took a deep breath and tried to regain her composure. "I changed my mind. This is fucked up, I don't talk to cops!" She sniffed hard then lowered her head, trying to wipe her face on her pants leg.

Victoria didn't argue. All staff members were correctional workers first, which made her a cop by default.

As casually as she could, Victoria inched her sweater up her arm to peer at her watch. The gold on the watch caught the reflection of the fluorescent light overhead and gleamed brightly. It was already a quarter to one, not the ideal time to start a therapy session. She needed to get up at six o'clock to be back at the prison by 7:30 AM. Not to mention, this woman was clearly too vulnerable for Victoria to begin dissecting her childhood to find out what had gone wrong.

"What do you want to do now?" Victoria asked softly.

"Wish I had thought to hijack a helicopter so I can go find him and kick his ass!"

"What did you do to your hands there?"

Maldonado craned her neck to look at her hands still cuffed behind her.

"Are you planning on doing anything else to hurt yourself tonight?"

"No," Maldonado said, sniffing back her runny nose.

"Are you okay to go to your room or is the suicide watch room better for you?"

"I'm not suicidal! I wouldn't give you assholes the satisfaction." Maldonado tried to fling a wisp of hair out of her eyes by whipping her neck to the side. She was unsuccessful. "Can I get out of these goddamned cuffs?"

Victoria wondered what Maldonado was hiding, but didn't want to press it. *If I push right now it would only cause more walls to come up*, she thought. She needed to build rapport if Maldonado was going to tell her anything and rapport took time, more time than she had tonight. Maldonado seemed calmer and more in control of her emotions, but Victoria wanted to make sure. She wouldn't be able to forgive herself if, in her own desire to return home, she overlooked some important detail and Maldonado killed herself. "Just one less inmate to count!" the lieutenants would joke, as they often did, but Warden Beshure would have to take swift action for an oversight like that with yesterday's escape all over the news.

"Are you sure?"

"I'm sure, I'm okay now."

"I'd like to meet you in the morning. Are you all right with that?"

Maldonado nodded.

"Ms. Maldonado, I know it's been a hard night, I'm glad you reached out."

Maldonado wiped her nose on her knee and got up from the chair.

There was an officer standing outside the Lieutenant's office waiting for Victoria's direction on what to do with Maldonado. She got up, opened the door and called to him. "You can take her back to her housing unit now."

Maldonado stepped into the hallway and faced the wall. The officer removed her cuffs from behind, but re-cuffed her hands in the front and escorted her outside.

Victoria followed. "I'll see you in the morning, Ms. Maldonado. Get some sleep."

Maldonado pulled a cigarette from the pocket of her sweatpants and put it in her mouth. She turned toward Lieutenant Williams who was standing in the outside doorway smoking. "Hey, L.T. can I get a light?"

Lieutenant Williams looked at her with disgust, threw his cigarette on the ground and crushed it out with his boot.

"Let's go, Maldonado." The officer grabbed Maldonado's arm and escorted her towards the housing unit.

Victoria followed Lieutenant Williams into the office.

"Well, Doc, what's the deal with that one?" he asked.

Victoria, uncomfortable with the prison's porous confidentiality system in which the system, not the inmate, held the privilege of confidentiality, hesitated before answering. "Sounds like a break up with her boyfriend."

Lieutenant Williams leaned back in his chair and put his feet back up on the desk. "Can you blame the guy?"

"Maybe." Victoria gave him a serious look. "Goodnight, Lieutenant."

Chapter 4

THE YARD OFFICER unlocked Bonnie's cell door and removed the cuffs from her wrists.

"Try to keep your shit together for the rest of the night." He said after he locked her in the cell.

"Fuck you, asshole," she muttered under her breath.

Bonnie walked to her locker and took out a paperclip. She removed the batteries from her alarm clock and jerry-rigged the paper clip with the battery until it sparked. She held a cigarette in her lips and inhaled repeatedly to catch the spark, until finally the cherry glowed red-orange. She still felt like punching the wall. She was pissed at Gary for going back to Carolyn and because he'd made her cry in front of a cop. Dr. Thomas seemed harmless, but she was still a cop and talking to a cop would just bring her more problems. She took a drag off her cigarette.

Harris leaned over the bunk. "You okay, girl?"

"Bitch, I thought I made it clear I don't talk to you." Bonnie took one last, long drag off the cigarette then flushed it down the toilet and slipped into bed.

"Deal with that shit on your own time so I can get some sleep," her cellmate barked.

Bonnie pressed her face to the wall. The cold cement felt good against her bruised cheek.

Chapter 5

VICTORIA LOOKED AT the clock on her car radio—7:28 AM. She was cutting things close. She parked the car, grabbed her coffee cup, and walked briskly to the front entrance of the prison.

"Good morning." Victoria greeted Christy, the front entrance officer, a cheery woman who donned outrageous earrings every day—today handcuffs, yesterday, flamingos.

"Another beautiful day in paradise," Christy said, popping her gum and smiling.

Victoria passed through the sallyport and on to the prison grounds. She noticed the dew glistening on the silver razor wire.

At least once, Devin, in his poetic voice that had made her fall in love with him, quoted Audre Lorde to her. "The master's tools will never dismantle the master's house." But Victoria argued that being on the inside allowed her to ensure that inmates were getting psychological care, something she would have no control over if she were "outside the master's house."

Victoria tried to bring her professionalism to the prison and looked more like a power executive than a prison psychologist, dressed in a royal blue designer suit and carrying a black satchel. That was until she set down her coffee cup on the ledge outside the Control Room and struggled to free the chit from the chain attached to her belt.

"Good morning, Mr. Tracy. How are you?"

"Morning, Doc." The officer, a slight fellow who barely looked twenty, plopped her keys in the tray. "Doing okay for a Wednesday."

She fastened the keys to the chain and caught a glimpse of Warden Beshure talking to the landscape foreman. He waved and walked in her direction. She smiled self-consciously. "Good morning, Warden."

"Good morning, Victoria." He extended his hand. His grip was solid. "Everything going well, I hope?"

"Yes, sir," she said, embarrassed by her sweaty palms.

"Heard we had a situation last night?"

"Yes, an inmate received a Dear Jane letter and was having a hard time processing the loss." Victoria felt nervous around the Warden. His opinion was more important than anyone else's— wardens were the five-star generals of prisons. Warden Beshure had a reputation for being firm but fair, unlike the previous warden who had "his boys," and not only looked the other way when they got into trouble, but promoted them to take the heat off.

"Dr. Scarsdale told me he doesn't have any paperwork from you yet."

"Off to do that right now, Warden," she said, trying to hide her disgust with her boss. *Bob should have known I'd do my notes in the morning,* she thought.

"Excellent, Dr. Thomas, keep me posted." He smiled. "And did you hear the good news, Doc? They caught inmate Lourdes and her helicopter pirate last night. It turned out to be Rodney McGuire."

"The inmate who escaped last month during transfer?"

"Yep, he came back for Lourdes. They were going to live happily-ever-after in Mexico, but she insisted he stop and buy her an engagement ring. They nabbed them at a jewelry store outside a mall in Sac."

"That's amazing!" Victoria said.

"That's a convict for you," he laughed. "Lourdes already had 50 years for bank robbery, but McGuire only had a month left on his sentence. Now he'll be charged with his own escape, air piracy and helping an inmate escape."

"Wow," she shook her head. "That's some chutzpah."

"We're going back on normal operations at 8:30 AM, but the yard will remain closed. Doc, get me that report as soon as you can."

"Yes, sir, I will."

Victoria took off at a clipped pace towards the Psychology Building, hoping to get the paperwork to Scarsdale before he had a chance to ask for it.

In the distance a team of outside workers installed forty-foot tall poles with a crane and connected wire to each existing light pole on the rec yard. It looked like the understructure of a circus tent.

The "Psych Building," as the inmates called it, a simple modular trailer, was dark when she arrived. Her office was at the end of the hallway, directly across from Brad Shaw's. Brad wasn't a psychologist, but he ran the Bureau's alcohol and drug program. There was an empty office that belonged to a psychologist who left on maternity leave during Victoria's first year and never returned. Bob Scarsdale, the Chief Psychologist, wanted to hire another psychologist, but it was a hard position to fill. Few psychologists wanted to work in prisons and those who did rarely wanted to work with female inmates.

Scarsdale's office was in the Chapel, which was closer to the prison's entrance. He shared a secretary part-time with the Religious Services Department.

Victoria opened the door to her office and set her bag on the floor and her coffee cup on the desk. Her office was clean except for a few stacks of paper. She had an oak bookshelf filled with psychology books—some pop, others more academic—and a few on substance abuse. She also had two thinly upholstered Prison Industries Corporation chairs, an old desk chair, and three plants she watered every Monday morning when she arrived.

She hesitated for a moment, enjoying the silence. In about thirty minutes, the empty hallway chairs would be overflowing with inmates needing things. This would be the last moment of quiet until she was in her car driving home at the end of the day. She picked up the beige phone and dialed in the code for the paging system.

"Attention on the compound," her voice echoed throughout the prison grounds. "Inmate Maldonado, please report to the Psychology Building."

She wrote "Maldonado, Bonnie 24827-056," across the top of a new file folder. Then she took out a legal pad and jotted down her observations of Maldonado's behavior last night and her initial diagnostic impressions:

Thirty-something year old white female with explosive temper and self-injurious behavior, denies current suicidal gesture, but endorses some suicidal ideation and self-hatred. Recent stressor-break-up with boyfriend. Diagnosis-Rule Out Borderline Personality Disorder.

Inmate Maldonado peered awkwardly through the window of Victoria's office door. Her stringy hair still covered her face, but she had touched up her eyes with thick black eyeliner. She was wearing the standard-issue khaki uniform with her shirt untucked. The uniform hung on her body, which was not uncommon, since all the uniforms were men's uniforms considered "unisex."

"Please come in Ms. Maldonado."

Maldonado sat in the chair to the side of Victoria's desk and examined the ceiling. Victoria studied her new patient, struck by the stench of cigarette smoke on Maldonado's clothes.

"You seem better today," Victoria said, trying to meet Maldonado's eyes.

"I was just pissed off when I got that letter. Anyway, I'm cool now. So, I'm going to go."

"We can talk about how to deal with those feelings when they come up again."

Maldonado got up. "No, that's okay."

Victoria wasn't going to give up that easily. "It seems like this breakup is really hard on ..."

Maldonado interrupted her, "Look, I don't need to see a fucking head shrinker. I got this." Maldonado got up from the chair and rushed out the door.

Victoria felt deflated. She ran her fingers through her hair and rested her head in her hand. She thought about Joanne. It unsettled her. She took a sip of her now lukewarm coffee and looked up to see the petite Latina orderly standing in the hallway with a plastic bag in her hand.

"*La basura, Doctora?*"

"Yes, please come in Ms. Garcia," she said, hoping that her frustration hadn't shown.

Ms. Garcia knelt by Victoria's chair and gingerly eased the garbage can out from under her desk. Even though all of the inmates had jobs, it unnerved Victoria to see Latinas cleaning offices and black women sweeping walkways and tending to the landscaping. It wasn't hard to imagine the prison as an antebellum plantation. Even the Prison Industries Corporations (PIC), the inmate operated factory that the government profited from, seemed at times like a sweatshop.

Victoria finished her report on Maldonado for Scarsdale and made a photocopy for Warden Beshure. Then she grabbed a pocket-seized notepad, locked her door, and walked towards the chapel. She was relieved to find Scarsdale's office empty. Cassandra, his secretary, was in her office brushing her blonde hair.

"Hi Cassandra, do you mind giving Robert a copy of this and taking a copy to Warden Beshure? I need to do SHU rounds."

Cassandra put the brush down. "Sure, I've got to run some other things up to Warden Beshure's office anyway."

"Great thanks," Victoria said, pleased to avoid another anxiety-provoking meeting with the warden. Victoria handed her the paperwork and hurried toward the chapel's exit. On her way to the Special Housing Unit she flagged down the yard officer to unlock the SHU sallyport door.

Victoria was not fond of SHU rounds but they were a mandatory part of her job every four weeks. The SHU, also known as 'the hole,' housed inmates who got in trouble for fighting, stealing, doing drugs, making hooch, or having sex. SHU inmates were locked down twenty-three hours a day, only getting out of their cells to go to the rec cage. Some considered it a vacation from work and enjoyed the slower pace, but a few couldn't take the isolation. The SHU was where most of the prison suicides took place, and inmates knew staff feared a suicide on their shift and used the threat of suicide to get out of doing SHU time, to get a phone call home to their family, or to get a cell move. Some threatened to kill themselves to manipulate the psychologist into getting other staff to do things for them. Victoria knew the majority of inmates in SHU didn't want psychological help—they wanted sleeping medications. Still, she had to be vigilant, distinguishing malingerers from the truly suicidal.

Once inside the sallyport, she waited for five minutes for Officer Landers to unlock the grill gate. "Where do you want to start first, Doc?" he asked.

Victoria took a pen out of her pocket and signed the logbook. "AD is fine."

Officer Landers opened the door to Administrative Detention, the side of the SHU which housed women accused of rule infractions, but had not yet been found guilty. Victoria walked the hall, looking in through the small rectangular windows on the cell doors and calling out, "Does anyone need to speak to the psychologist?"

The first three cells were routine—bodies cocooned in blankets barely shaking their heads then slipping back under their gray wool blankets.

In the next cell, a white woman with cornrows in her hair stood on the top bunk facing the outside window with its thin allowance of daylight and yelled at someone out on the yard. She ignored Victoria's presence altogether. "Latasha, go find Smokey!" the woman shouted.

Her roommate, a short Native-American woman with a bad complexion, approached the door. "I need to see the psych," she said.

"How can I help you, Ms…" Victoria looked for the inmate's name on the plastic placard on the outside of the door.

"It's Six Toes," the inmate said. "Got anything on how to manage anger?"

Victoria jotted down the cell number on the notepad. "I'll see what I can get for you Ms. Six Toes."

Six Toes lowered her voice. "If you got anything on dealing with negative thoughts, that'd be good too."

Victoria nodded and continued down the hall where she found a woman pounding on the cell door window.

"Listen," the inmate barked, "I don't need to see no psych, but I told that damn officer three times already that I done broke my tooth on this nasty-ass food and I need to see the dentist." She opened her mouth and showed Victoria her chipped tooth. It looked bad.

"Officer Landers, Inmate…" Victoria yelled down the hall as she read the name on the paper outside of the cell door, "Jenkins is requesting to see the dentist. She has a broken tooth."

"Thanks, Doc." Landers didn't look up from his paperwork. "I told her I'd call when I have time. I'm doing classification and room moves right now and after that I'm heating up their food trays. I'll get to it when I can. She can always write a cop-out." He replied dryly, referring to a form used by inmates to make formal requests to staff.

Jenkins rolled her eyes. "I already asked that fool for a cop-out and he say he don't have none!"

"I'll contact Health Services and let Dr. Huang know," Victoria assured her.

"I hope you do, cause if you don't, I'm adding your name to the BP-9 I file on that asshole."

"Ms. Jenkins, I just told you I would let Health Services know."

"Maybe if you people did your jobs right, that bitch wouldn't have gotten away. That's right, I said it. These COs are all a bunch of punk-ass light-weights."

Victoria took a deep breath and walked to Disciplinary Segregation, the side of the SHU that housed inmates who were formally charged with breaking prison rules.

"Anyone need to see the psychologist?" she called out as she walked the hall. Someone yelled from a cell at the end of the corridor. Victoria cracked open the door from the Disciplinary Segregation Unit. "Officer Landers, can you open a food slot so I can talk to one of the inmates?"

Officer Landers got up from his paperwork and walked down the hallway to unlock the food slot. It fell open with a thud.

"How can I help you?" Victoria leaned down to hear the inmate's response. The inmate pressed her face to the opening; her breath was sour.

"I'm having trouble sleeping and want to get back on Elavil."

The stench of the toilet and rotten food scraps caught in the food slot filled her nostrils. Victoria started to gag. She held her breath and jotted down the inmate's name as quickly as she could then got up and slammed the food slot closed. This was taking longer than she had anticipated.

Victoria hurried on to the next cell window. "Does anyone here need to see the psych?" she asked, mortified to find a woman sitting on the toilet urinating.

"Excuse me!" the woman growled.

Victoria turned around abruptly.

A skinny white woman peered through the window of the adjacent cell. "Can I talk to you out there?"

Victoria looked at her watch again. It was 9:15 AM. *There's no way I'm going to make it out of the SHU on time for the trauma group now,* she thought.

"Is this an emergency?" she asked, hoping the answer was "no."

"Yes, it's really important."

Victoria walked back down the hall to Officer Landers's desk. "There's an inmate who wants to come out. She says it's an emergency."

Officer Landers's chair scraped the floor as he got up from his desk for the third time and walked into the key room. He took three pairs of handcuffs out of the locked cabinet and walked to the cell.

"Which one of you wants to come out?"

"I do," the young, skinny woman said. He opened the slot and the inmate backed up to the door and put her wrists through the food slot.

"Okay, I need the rest of you to step over here and cuff up." Landers handcuffed the women's other roommates and then locked the food slot. "Okay, now step away from the door while I bring Vogler out." Landers opened the cell door and Vogler backed out slowly and then stood and faced the wall while Officer Landers locked the door behind her.

"Stay there," he ordered Vogler and unlocked the food slot a second time. "Ladies, come on back so I can remove your cuffs."

Victoria stared at her watch. The minute hand ticked past 9:25. Officer Landers removed the cuffs from the woman's roommates, shut the food slot a third time, gathered the handcuffs and escorted inmate Vogler down the hall to an interview room. Victoria, completely exasperated and late for her women's trauma group, sat down opposite her, noticing for the first time the reddish-purple bruise under the inmate's right eye.

"How'd you get that shiner?" Victoria asked Vogler, who appeared to be in her early twenties and looked like she should be on a college campus rather than in a prison.

"That's what I wanted to talk to you about. Can anyone else hear us?"

Victoria looked at the door. "I don't think so. Officer Landers is down range and these walls are pretty solid. Do you want to tell me what happened?"

"This girl I work with thought I was trying to get with her man."

Victoria smiled. "Well, not like you can do anything while you're in prison."

"He's staff. She got crazy on me thinkin' I was trying to take him from her."

"So she hit you," Victoria said, trying to hide her embarrassment.

"Yeah, and I hit her back and now I'm going to lose my good time." Vogler lowered her voice. "If I told you who he was, can you help me keep my good time?"

"So they were involved in a relationship?"

"He told her he's going to leave his wife for her when she gets out."

"How do you know all that?"

"We were friends before this went down," Vogler said.

Victoria nodded. "I see. I can't make any promises, but I'll see what I can do. Who is he?"

"He works in Maintenance."

"You said you were going to tell me who he is."

Vogler shook her head and leaned back in her chair. "Hell no! I'm not just gonna tell you who he is then have her and her friends kick the crap out of me. I need a guarantee that if I tell you I'll keep my good time. I was supposed to leave next month. This will probably cost me 90 days good time."

"I'll see what I can find out." Victoria said. She opened the door and called for Officer Landers.

"Did Sylvia Lourdes really escape in a helicopter?" Vogler asked.

"I can't discuss that."

Landers took Vogler by the arm. "Let's go."

"Mr. Landers, would you mind letting me out first? I'm late for my group."

"Sure," he said. "Vogler face the wall."

Vogler turned and faced the wall. Officer Landers opened the sallyport's inner door and radioed to the yard officer to come and unlock the outside door. By the time the yard officer opened the final door, she was already fifteen minutes late to her women's trauma group. Still, she knew she first better talk to Captain Brown about what inmate Vogler told her. She walked to his office and knocked.

"Come in," he called out.

Victoria opened the door and walked in. The walls of Captain Brown's office were covered in thick wooden plaques with titles like *Correctional Worker of the Year 1985* and *Supervisor of the Quarter 1991*.

"What can I do you for, Doc?" he asked, sorting papers on his desk.

She told him what inmate Vogler had said.

He pursed his lips, took a deep breath, and shook his head. "Inmates lie, Doc."

Victoria felt like a shamed child. "I realize that, Captain."

"Sounds like she doesn't want to lose her good time and she's inventing a story so we won't take it from her." He smirked. "We don't make deals with inmates, Dr. Thomas. If we start doing that they're gonna be runnin' us more than they already do."

Victoria pressed on. "Couldn't there be some veracity to her story?"

"Veracity," the Captain repeated and shrugged his shoulders. "Listen, Doc, write up a report and I'll forward it to the Warden, but there's not a lot we can do if we don't have a name."

"She said it was someone from Maintenance."

Captain Brown laughed. "Could be one of ten guys. I'm not putting 'em all under investigation. You know how that would affect morale? Hard enough to get skilled workmen in here for these wages, I'm not gonna jeopardize losing anyone. Can't run a prison if we got buildings falling apart, or if the heat or plumbing is broken cause we wrongly accused somebody and they got pissed and walked off the job. I need a name."

Victoria glanced at the clock on the wall. It was almost 10:00 AM. "I'm late for my group," she said and quickly excused herself.

Chapter 6

BONNIE SIGHED, RELIEVED to be out of the Psychology Building and away from that shrink. *No way in hell I'm gonna let some shrink anal-ize me*, she thought as she walked to the cigarette lighter mounted on the side of the building, pulled a cigarette from the pack in her shirt pocket, and leaned in to light it.

One of the yard orderlies, a short, heavy set, Korean woman sweeping the walkway came up to her. "Ain't you Maldonado? They were calling you to the Psych Building."

Bonnie took a long drag off her cigarette. "Mind your own fucking business," she said and flicked the cigarette butt on the ground where the woman was sweeping. She could hear her father's voice echoing in her head, telling her how weak she was.

She walked to the punching bag by the weight pile on the rec yard and cursed at it like it was Gary standing in front of her.

"You motherfucker, Gary. I held my tongue, made sure none of you took the fall, and this is the shit you do for me! Fuck you!" She swung at the bag, tearing open the fresh cuts on her knuckles.

Out of the corner of her eye, she saw Tennessee walking around the dirt track with her girlfriend. Bonnie waited for them to circle in her direction, she didn't want to run up on her and seem desperate.

Tennessee was a lean, wiry woman with feathered dirty-blonde hair and blue eyes. Tennessee's girlfriend, Melanie, looked like a carbon copy of Tennessee except younger with strawberry blonde hair. Melanie wore her altered prison uniform tighter around her chest and ass. Both had hung with the Aryan Brotherhood before they came to prison. Tennessee stopped when she saw Bonnie, Melanie kept walking.

"Looking pretty shitty, Slick," Tennessee said. "Need a little somethin' somethin'?"

Bonnie nodded then cracked her swollen knuckles.

Tennessee looked around to make sure no one was watching, then pulled a pinky-sized bag of white powder from her bra and slid it into Bonnie's palm like they were low- fiving. "Melanie will send you my commissary list. Pay me next time your unit shops."

She knew from Gary's letter she was going to have trouble getting money to buy what Tennessee wanted, but right now she didn't care. "Yeah, no problem," she lied.

"All right, Slick, enjoy."

Bonnie tucked the bag in the seam of her shirt and headed to her housing unit. She stopped at a trash bin and fished out an empty Coke can. In her cell, she took out a syringe hidden in the frame of her bunk bed. She crushed the pop can, making a bowl-like area in the middle, tapped the white powder into it then spit on the powder to moisten it for cooking. She took a cigarette and tore a pinch off the filter.

"Now for some fire," she said, and reached for the paperclip on top of her locker, using it and one of the batteries from her alarm clock to catch a piece of paper on fire. She got a good flame going under the pop can and the dope began to liquefy. She cradled it in her shirt to keep from burning herself. Then she rolled up her shirtsleeve, took off her white prison belt and tied it around her left arm, and stuck the tip of the syringe into the filter. She carefully pulled back the plunger, soaking the liquefied heroin into the syringe. "Sweet oblivion, here I come," she whispered and edged the needle into a vein, careful not to miss. She didn't want any more track marks; she already had enough from her first times shooting up after Tim's death.

She could feel the dope begin to work its magic. She fought the nod long enough to pull the needle out of her vein and hid it and the can under a pile of dirty clothes underneath her bunk. Then she closed her eyes and let go. Everything was good again.

"Get up, Maldonado. It's 4:00 o'clock. Count time," Harris said.

Bonnie lay there nodding out.

"What's wrong with you?" Harris asked. "The CO gonna be in here any minute and if you ain't standing by the time they come ... "

"Fuck the fuck off," Bonnie said, her words slurred.

"Look, bitch. You better get your ass up. They ain't putting up with no bullshit right now, that Spanish Mommy fucked it up for all us. I don't want my room shook down 'cause you don't want to get with the program." Harris grabbed Bonnie's arm and jerked her to her feet just as Officer Berger poked her head into their cell to count them.

"She all right?" Berger asked.

"She had a rough night. Her old man dumped her."

"Don't squeal my business to the pigs!" Maldonado half-lunged half-fell towards Harris. The room spun and she tried to steady herself against the frame of the bunk bed.

"You ain't right!" Harris looked at her disgusted and backed away.

Berger's brown hair was cropped short and she wore a blue pen behind her right ear. Berger grabbed the pen and pulled a pad of paper from her shirt pocket. "I'm writing you up for failure to stand count and insolence. Where's your card?"

"Over there." Bonnie motioned to the prison ID card on top of her locker.

Berger picked up the card and jotted notes in her notepad, then put her pen back behind her ear and stuffed the pad into her pocket. "You're coming with me, Maldonado. Let's go!" Berger grabbed Bonnie by the arm and led her to the Lieutenant's Office.

This time Bonnie didn't fight; the fight disappeared when she pushed the needle into her arm.

There were tricks to keep the cops from knowing you were using. In state, when she was paged for a random urine analysis, she'd insert a masking-tape covered aspirin bottle-full of "clean piss" into her vagina. The officers would escort her into the bathroom and wait for her to pee. As soon the officer looked away, she'd poke a hole in the tape with a straightened paperclip she'd kept in the lining of her waistband and the pee would come streaming down into the cup. But now, she had nothing.

"I just went before count," she lied.

A dirty UA would land her in the Hole. She didn't want to go to the Hole. The thought of being locked in a cell twenty-three hours a day made her feel panicky. There would be nothing to do but think. She might miss a letter from Gary, saying he'd changed his mind. She hoped for a miracle—maybe somehow the drug hadn't hit her system yet.

"I don't have all day, Maldonado! Pee or you're going to SHU." Berger turned on the faucet and waited for Bonnie to urinate.

Bonnie took a deep breath and then peed into the cup.

Officer Berger reached out her gloved hand for the urine sample. Bonnie thought about "accidentally" spilling it, but that would be too obvious.

"You can go, Maldonado. I'm gonna drop refusing to stand count, but I'm still writing you a shot for insolence."

"That's bullshit!"

"Do you not know the definition of insolence?" Berger shook her head. "Go before I put your ass in the SHU."

Chapter 7

VICTORIA LOOKED AT her watch. 3:45 PM, usually the time she headed for the front entrance. She got off at 4:00 PM, but with waiting in the key line and having to walk through all the different sallyports, not to mention if an inmate stopped her on the yard, she rarely made it to the parking lot by 4:15 PM.

She was exhausted and still processing yesterday's escape. It was hitting her how serious it was. She couldn't think about it yet, she had to get that report to Captain Brown. She stuffed it into an envelope, marked it confidential, and walked to his office.

"He's gone home," the evening watch shift lieutenant told her. "I'll make sure he gets it." He took the envelope from her.

She wanted to take it back from him, but she knew she needed to choose her battles wisely with the correctional staff. "Okay, good night."

"Devin?" Victoria walked through the house searching for Devin. She hoped to find him in the kitchen fixing dinner. Instead, she found him sitting at the computer in their shared home office. "What are you doing?"

"Just finishing up some paperwork," he said, not looking up from the computer.

"How much longer?" she asked already impatient.

"Listen, you went to work in the middle of the night and you're an hour late."

"I'm on call."

He gave her a look. "Give me about ten more minutes."

"Fine," she said and walked to the kitchen. She boiled a pot of water and opened a jar of spaghetti sauce and poured it into a saucepan. It was all she had the energy for tonight.

Devin entered the kitchen and looked at the pots on the stove. "Spaghetti?"

Victoria bristled. "Devin, I've had a long day!"

He turned off the stove. "Let's go out, baby."

"Fine, I'll eat this for lunch tomorrow." Victoria drained the pasta, poured it into a Tupperware container, and dumped some sauce on the top.

They drove in silence to the restaurant, a seafood place in Jack London Square.

"Remember the first time you took me here?" she asked as they walked in.

"I remember that sexy black dress." He smiled. "What a hottie you were."

"Were?" she asked, sitting down at the table.

Devin took his seat. "It's been forever since I've seen you in a dress."

"Wearing a dress in a prison isn't smart. If you want me in a dress take me somewhere special."

"This isn't special?" he asked.

"It's not a weekend getaway."

"Let's hit the wineries Columbus Day weekend," he said.

Victoria reached across the table to touch his hand. For a moment, she thought she felt him flinch when she touched him. *I'm just imagining things,* she told herself.

Chapter 8

"CAN'T BELIEVE I make three cents an hour fixing toilets and painting walls. I used to make serious cash on the outs. How about you, Jessie? Bet you made bank moving dope."

Jessie, a short scruffy looking woman with a Texas accent, shook her head and laughed, making her mullet flip back and forth like a horse's tail. "Nah, I got busted my first time. Hey, y'all hear that?" she asked, patching up the wall around the toilet near the cell door.

"Hear what?" Bonnie asked continuing to paint the cell's windowsill.

"Your name, darling, they just paged your ass to the Lieutenant's Office."

Bonnie dropped the paintbrush in the tray. White paint splattered on the concrete floor and onto Jessie's black boots. "I'm fucked!"

Jessie eyed the paint on her boots for a moment, looked up at Bonnie and then went back to painting.

"Sorry, gotta go."

Inmates were like vultures. Anytime somebody went to the SHU, they would rush that inmate's cell and pick the place clean.

Bonnie wasn't going to give them the chance. She took her radio and headphones out of her pillowcase and took all her important papers and locked them in her locker. She hid a pack of cigarettes inside the heating vent in the ceiling where no one would look. She left her prison uniforms hanging on the rack above the toilet with Harris's. She didn't care about the uniforms.

Unlike Harris, who had covered her bulletin board with pictures of her kids, Bonnie's was empty. *The only good thing about this,* she thought as she made her way to the Lieutenant's Office, *is it's going to buy me some time to pay back Tennessee.*

"You're becoming a real regular here, Maldonado. Come in and sit down."

Bonnie slouched in the chair and studied the paint on her hands, avoiding eye contact with Lieutenant Lopez.

"Maldonado, you're going to SHU for a dirty UA. You will remain there until you meet with the hearing officer who will determine your exact length of stay. Is that clear?"

Bonnie moved her finger along the paint splotches on her khaki pants.

"All right, get up. Go with Officer Berger. She'll strip you out."

The first week was the hardest. Eat, sleep, and piss, that's all there was to do in the SHU. She wanted a fix, but the extra security and isolation of the SHU made it almost impossible—impossible for her anyway. There was no way she was going to give Officer "Dark and Lovely" Hamilton a blowjob. She had overheard some of the women talking in the rec cage that if they wanted dope, he would hook them up if they sucked him off. She wasn't going down that road.

She'd gotten into a routine to make the time go faster. She woke up when Landers opened her food slot to "slop them" as he called it. After breakfast, she brushed her teeth and showered— except on weekends—when she did neither. After her shower she dressed in the yellow SHU smock and pants and played solitaire. At 11:15 a.m., she ate the reheated lunch Landers brought them. At 2:00 p.m., after the officer shift change, she exercised like Tim had when he was down—100 pushups, 100 sit-ups, 100 squat thrusts, 100 leg lifts, and then 100 laps around the cell, which drove most of her roommates crazy. They preferred to sleep all day and asked to be moved after a few days of being celled with her. None of them had the guts to say anything to her, except a stud broad named Lindsey Grinder who was in for a 205—sex with another inmate.

"Damn, can't you freakin' be still, Maldonado?" Grinder blurted from her bunk.

Bonnie gave her a dirty look. "What's your problem, you got something against looking good?"

Grinder cocked her head to the side like a parrot. "Didn't know you were gay for the stay? Thought you were straight."

"I am, Grinder."

Bonnie continued circling the cell and counting on her fingers to make sure she got 100 laps in.

"So, what gives?"

"I'm doing what any self-respecting white girl would do in the Hole. I'm not letting myself go soft. Looks like you could use a little toning yourself." Bonnie dropped to the floor and began doing sit-ups.

Grinder shook her head. "You're crazy, Maldonado." She pulled the covers over her head.

4:00 PM was count, followed by a dinner tray at 4:55 PM. After dinner she put on a T-shirt and sweatpants, not the floral-patterned nightgowns they issued female inmates, then she lay on her bunk playing solitaire until she fell asleep.

Twice a week, Chaplain Edwards, a clean-shaven, fair-haired man in his early forties, came to SHU for church chats. He always had a solemn look on his face, which made Bonnie want to annoy him and make him lose his cool.

"Religious people are a bunch of hypocrites. Anybody would get over if they knew they wouldn't get caught," she told a new commit, a mousy brunette, locked up for smoking out of bounds.

"Why do you say that?" she asked.

"The chaplain at WCC in Oregon gave extra phone privileges for blowjobs. One time, a lieutenant paged a woman to the chapel because her son was in the hospital and the chaplain wouldn't let her call the hospital until she jerked him off."

"That's disgusting!"

Bonnie shook her head. "That's a preacher!"

Chapter 9

Victoria sat at her desk writing treatment notes. The phone rang.

"Hey, Doc, it's Russell in Maintenance. I heard you saw Vogler. Is she okay? That was some fight. She and Hafner really got into it. Haven't seen these inmates go at it like that for a long time. Hafner clocked her good. Did she say why she done it?"

Victoria felt uncomfortable with his questions and didn't answer. She didn't want to disclose anything, not only because she respected client confidentiality, but because what Vogler had told her was now the subject of an investigation. "Just some sort of disagreement between the two of them," Victoria said.

"You got a tough job, Doc, trying to understand these inmates. I don't envy you."

"It's certainly never boring," she said, trying to be friendly enough, but not wanting to encourage the conversation further.

Russell laughed. "That's for sure, Doc. Listen, me and the wife are hosting a barbeque Columbus Day. Bring your husband by, give folks a chance to get to know ya."

"Thank you, Mr. Russell, but we're out of town that weekend." She was glad it was the truth and she hadn't needed to search for an excuse.

"Well, then I hope you'll join us for Super Bowl Sunday. Scarsdale and Shaw usually come. I know it's a ways off, but a lot of us want to get to know you better."

"Only if the 49ers are involved," she joked.

She knew Devin wouldn't go for that. Once she'd mentioned the Christmas party and he'd barked, "The last thing I'd want to do is hang out with prison guards."

"Have a good day, Doc."

"You too," she said and hung up the phone feeling unsettled by the conversation. Within minutes the phone rang again, startling her. "Psychology Department, Dr. Thomas speaking."

"Hi Victoria, it's Francis."

"Hi Francis, what's up?"

"My blood pressure for sure. I can't get these physician's assistants to stop screaming at the diabetic inmates when they forget to come get their insulin. They think yelling at someone is an effective method of getting patient compliance."

"Oh, my God," Victoria shook her head. "I thought I had it bad."

Francis was the only person at the prison Victoria felt she could be candid with. They both swam against the current with their desire to help the inmates, not just warehouse them.

Francis's voice became more serious. "Victoria, I'd like you to do a training for them about rapport with patients."

"You'll have to ask Scarsdale. He takes chain of command pretty seriously."

Francis sighed. "Endless bureaucracy!"

Victoria twirled the telephone cord around her finger. "I just had a weird phone call with Russell."

"Mike Russell, the foreman?"

"Yeah, you know him?" She trusted Francis, but she didn't want to offend her.

"Not really. Why?"

"He called about an inmate on his work crew. That's not unusual, but then he invited me over for a barbeque." Victoria wanted to tell Francis about inmate Vogler and that she thought Russell might be the guy Vogler was talking about, but because of the investigation, she didn't.

"He and Scott Stevenson in Rec are always throwing big parties. Last month, it was a weekend bus trip to Reno. PA Flores is still talking about how much fun she had."

"But why is he inviting me now?"

"Maybe they want to see what you're like when you let your hair down or somebody is into you."

"I never let my hair down. Besides I'm married, Francis."

Francis laughed. "Said no adulterer ever. Forgotten about your three weeks at FLETC?"

Victoria thought for a moment and then remembered her training at the Federal Law Enforcement Training Center, in Glynco Georgia. "Right, my slutty roommate." Victoria shook her head. "And she wasn't the only one. Several other married classmates hooked up with people from other prisons and law enforcement agencies."

"So you're going?" Francis let out a nasal laugh.

"Yeah, right. We'll be in Sonoma that weekend. I better go. I need to catch up on notes. Let me know what Bob says."

Chapter 10

BONNIE HEARD A knock on her cell door. She got up from her bunk and looked out the cell's window. She saw a muscular, dark skinned officer with a shaved head.

"Times up, Maldonado," he said.

"Already?" Bonnie was unable to contain her sarcasm.

"Good thing too, you need some sunshine, look at how pasty white you are."

Bonnie stepped out of the cell and looked at her arms. *I'm from Portland, asshole, my arms don't look any different than they always looked.*

"Here's your property." He handed her an army-issue green duffle bag filled with the few belonging she had locked in her locker. Even though the inmates had lockers with combination locks, the staff had a master key.

"You travel light," he joked.

Most women's bags were stuffed to the gills with yarn, crochet needles, hand-knit blankets, stuffed animals, face cream, body lotion, perfume, coffee, and cans of sardines. The contents of their lockers filled three bags, while hers filled only one. Bonnie's bag contained mostly just the basics; hygiene items, gray sweat suit, tennis shoes, her three prison-issued uniforms and under clothes, work boots, and a few partially crumpled Cup of Noodles. The only extras were a black eyeliner pencil and some eye shadow.

She slung the bag over her left shoulder, avoiding eye contact with him. She felt stronger that she didn't need things or people.

"Don't forget to show up for work call this morning," he said, and unlocked the inside door to the SHU sallyport.

She walked inside. A black female officer, stood on the other side of the sallyport waiting for the door to lock. "All right Maldonado, I'm taking you to your housing unit." The officer did not grab her by the elbow and physically escort her like many of the male officers did. Instead she walked alongside her. Bonnie was glad. She hated to be touched.

It felt good to be outside. The weather was noticeably cooler than it was in September when she'd gone to the SHU. Summer was long gone. The trees were beginning to lose their leaves. She took a deep breath then exhaled the last of the stale re-circulated SHU air from her lungs.

A few women she'd worked with at Maintenance were digging a trench near the chow hall. She nodded at them and continued to her housing unit. The officer radioed the unit officer to unlock the door. She hurried by him to the Unit Counselor's office.

"Can you move me to a new room?" She asked Counselor Riley, a bald headed white man in his fifties.

Counselor Riley gave her an irritated look. "Why?"

"I want to cell with a white chick."

"Maldonado, learn to play with others or go back to the SHU."

"Better the SHU than the zoo," she muttered.

She walked back to her cell. Harris was on the top bunk, but Harris's stuff—Ebony and Jet magazines, a sweat suit, and pair of tennis shoes covered her bunk. She knocked it all onto the floor.

"What the fuck, Maldonado? You don't need to throw my shit on the floor." Harris got down to pick up her things. "I'm sorry they took you to the bucket."

Bonnie heaved off the green duffle bag, dropping it on the newly emptied bunk.

She climbed the locker and reached into the heating vent. Her cigarettes were still there. Pleased, she climbed down and went outside to smoke for the first time in sixty days.

"Mr. Lee, I'm back. Miss me?" Bonnie asked her work supervisor at Maintenance.

Even though Mr. Lee was Chinese, he was a decent boss, unlike Kovach, a guy she'd worked for in state prison.

"I hope you enjoyed your two month vacation." He smiled, his teeth perfect. "I need you and Beltran to fix a sink in the G Unit."

Bonnie and the young, Hispanic inmate walked to the unit.

"You just out hole, eh?" Beltran's accent was thick.

"Fucking learn English, you're in America," Bonnie said, ignoring her question as they walked.

"I heard there's rats in there?" Beltran crinkled her face like she smelled something nasty.

"The only rats in there are the snitches who don't want to get their asses kicked."

"Wad you means?" Beltran asked.

"Damn you're a new fish, your back still wet? Protective custody. Snitches beg to get locked up for their own protection. They aren't real rats."

"Oh," Beltran nodded, but Bonnie wasn't sure she understood.

"Where's this broken sink anyway?" Bonnie asked, entering the housing unit.

Beltran pulled out the paper in her pocket and looked at it. "Room G242."

As she tinkered with the sink, she wondered what would have happened if she had listened to Mr. S, her favorite foreman at Oregon Women's Correctional Center, and tried to get trade-work, instead of being a waitress after she was released. Mr. S was the only one who had ever believed in her.

Pamela, the head clerk for the foreman in Maintenance, walked in and pushed Beltran out.

"Give me that. I'll show you how it's done." She grabbed at the wrench in Bonnie's hand.

Bonnie jerked her hand back and then without thinking, swung it forward clocking Pamela square in the forehead drawing blood. Pamela, disoriented for a moment, rubbed her head. "You're fucking dead bitch!" She screamed and grabbed a thick handful of Bonnie's hair and punched her repeatedly in the mouth.

The two scuffled wildly. Inmates gathered in the doorway cheering on the battle. Within minutes, staff arrived, cuffed them and took them to the Lieutenant's Complex.

"Maldonado, what's wrong with you?" Lieutenant Williams sat behind his desk tapping a cigarette on the cover of a pea-green linen covered logbook with the letters S.H.U. hand-written in black ink. "They just let you out after two months and you're back again. You didn't even make it a day!" He shook his head.

Bonnie flicked her head to the side to get her hair out of her face and licked the blood from her split lip. She didn't want to make things worse by cussing him out, so she sat in the chair, her hands cuffed behind her, and said nothing.

Lieutenant Williams motioned for the officer in the hallway.

"Yeah, boss?" the officer said, looking at Bonnie with disgust.

"Officer Tracy, take Calamity Jane here back to the bucket."

Chapter 11

VICTORIA TOOK A sip of her coffee and stared out the window, watching the women coming out of the Maintenance building with landscaping equipment. They were like rowdy teenagers, rough housing with each other, singing and screaming at the top of their lungs, and swinging the tools around like they were toys.

She was not in a very good mood this morning. Devin's mother had gotten sick and ended up in the hospital with diverticulitis, so they had to reschedule their trip. Between her on-call schedule and Devin's work schedule they wouldn't be able to get away for another long weekend until February.

Brad half opened the door. "Cassandra wanted me to tell you to call her."

"Thanks," she said, picking up the phone and dialing. "Brad said to call you?"

"The Warden would like you to come up to his conference room at 10:00."

Victoria looked at her day planner. "I'm going to have to cancel a group. Can you tell me what this is regarding?"

"His secretary didn't give me any additional information."

"Okay, thanks." Victoria hung up the phone. Her mind raced. Had she forgotten to do something she'd said she would do? Had she broken some policy? She couldn't think of anything she'd done wrong. Still, it made her nervous.

At 9:55 AM she took a deep breath and knocked on the Warden's conference room door. She tried to reassure herself that it was probably just a routine check in.

Lt. Williams opened the door. Captain Brown was sitting at the conference table across from an attractive blonde woman in a tailored business suit. He motioned to Victoria to sit. "This is Agent Lisa Smith."

"FBI?" Victoria asked, sitting down in a dark leather chair.

"Don't be intimidated, Doctor." Agent Smith smiled. "You're not in trouble."

"Well, we hope not," Lt. Williams laughed.

"You're in good hands, Doc." Captain Brown got up from his chair. "We'll be in touch, Lisa." He waved goodbye and walked out.

"Do you need any coffee or anything before I leave, Lisa?" Lt. Williams asked.

"Nope, Frank, just come get me in an hour."

"Will do," Lt. Williams smiled. "Thanks for helping us get the bad guys, Doc."

"Is this about the report I turned in?" Victoria asked when they were alone.

"Yes." Agent Smith opened the cover on her laptop and glanced at the screen. "You state that inmate Vogler told you an inmate was having a sexual relationship with a male staff member in Maintenance."

"That's right."

"Before we begin you'll need to take an oath and when we're done you'll sign an affidavit affirming the truth of your statements."

"That's not a problem," Victoria said.

"Please repeat after me. I, please state your name, affirm that what I am about to share with Agent Lisa Smith is accurate and true to the best of my recollection."

Victoria repeated, "I, Victoria Thomas, affirm that what I am about to share with Agent Lisa Smith is accurate and true to the best of my recollection."

Victoria reiterated the contents of her report while Agent Smith took notes on her laptop. When she was finished, Agent Smith handed her the affidavit. Victoria read it over. Everything looked accurate.

"There's one more thing. It seems odd to tell you but…" Victoria hesitated.

"What is it?" Agent Smith asked and continued typing in her laptop.

"I got this call from the foreman, Mike Russell, right after I turned in that report. He invited my husband and me to a party at his place. We've never even spoken before."

"Do you think he was just being social?" Agent Smith said.

Victoria signed the affidavit. "Perhaps he was," she said, "but he asked about Vogler."

Agent Smith looked up from her laptop and directly at Victoria. "Let me remind you that you have signed an affidavit not to discuss this with anyone else. Do you understand?"

Victoria nodded and got up to leave.

"Thank you again, Dr. Thomas." Agent Smith smiled.

"You're welcome, Agent Smith." Victoria let herself out.

Chapter 12

Chaplain Edwards stopped in front of Bonnie's cell in the SHU. "Ms. Maldonado, didn't you just get out?"

"Do you think I have bad karma?" Bonnie's face lit up with amusement.

Chaplain Edwards responded with the earnestness that drove her crazy. "I'm not a Buddhist, Ms. Maldonado, but many Buddhists believe in karma and intention. I'll bring you a book tomorrow and you could read about it."

The next day Chaplain Edwards asked Landers to open Bonnie's food slot and handed her a book *The Miracle of Mindfulness*. "I hope this helps, Ms. Maldonado."

"Hey, why not, dude. I've got nothing but time. Just chillin' like a villain."

She went to toss the book on the floor, but was caught by the writing on the back cover: "Mindfulness is a technique in which a person becomes intentionally aware of his or her thoughts and actions in the present moment." *Well shit, I've got nothing else to do in the present moment,* she thought and cracked the book open.

"Hey Chaplain, what's this Thick Nut Hut's obsession with breathing?" she asked the Chaplain the following week when he returned.

Chaplain Edwards looked surprised. "You read the book?"

"Sort of." Bonnie pressed her face against the small window on the cell door.

"Hang on just a second." Chaplain Edwards got up from his stooped position, asked Officer Landers for a chair, then rolled it over to Bonnie's cell and sat down. "Ms. Maldonado, my understanding is that Thich Nhat Hahn is saying that focusing on your breath anchors you in your body and in the moment."

Bonnie took in his explanation. "Like living for the moment? That's what I was doing by not having a job and not making any plans, just going with the flow."

"Not exactly," he said carefully. "More like not being stuck in the past or living for the future, being fully present in the now."

She cracked her knuckles. "That's what I said."

She thought about handing him back the book, but then she decided to take a risk. "Like what he means about washing the dishes and feeling the warmth of the water on your hands, instead of rushing so you'll be done?"

Chaplain Edwards leaned in. "Yes, actually being aware of your senses and fully being in that moment, whatever it is you're doing."

"The part about when you eat you should look at your food, naming it as you eat it sounded crazy. But," she cocked her head to the side, "I have a lot of time to kill in here, so I tried it. I set my food-tray down and looked at the carrots and said *carrots*. Then I took a bite, closed my eyes and concentrated. It was weird. They tasted better. I did it with my fruit salad too. Just stared at it for a while. Then I ate a peach. It felt slimy on my tongue, but sweet. I tried it with the fish sticks and that was just nasty, could have done without that."

"That's very interesting, Ms. Maldonado."

"Yeah, it was interesting." She tried to read him. Was he trying to stifle a laugh? *Fuck you,* she thought. *You think I'm stupid. I ain't got nothing better to do!*

"I'm glad you found the book useful, Ms. Maldonado."

"Like I said, Rev, it's pretty boring up in here. I'm sure an algebra book would be just as interesting." She felt her cheeks turning red.

Chaplain Edwards stood up. "We can talk more next week if you like." He waved goodbye.

She heard Dr. Thomas in the corridor and quickly got in her bunk. She pretended to be asleep as the shrink walked by her cell. She had nothing to say to her.

Bonnie spent the week studying the mindfulness meditations in the book and naming and tasting her food. She was excited when she heard Chaplain Edwards two cells down talking with a Muslim inmate in his calm prison chaplain tone.

"Ms. Jordan, I'm sorry, it's the best we can do for your Ramadan worship needs."

"My attorney will be calling the Warden. You're violating the Religious Freedom Act. Even though I ain't a Christian, I have rights, Chaplain."

"Try to remember, Ms. Jordan, I have thirty-three other religious groups I minister to and we're doing our best to accommodate you during your stay in SHU."

Bonnie was surprised that Chaplain Edwards kept his cool, even though his calm tone sounded somewhat forced. Some staff yelled back at the inmates, some even cursed. Bonnie wasn't above swearing at a cop, but thought staff should hold themselves to higher standards. *They were paid to be here after all.*

Bonnie pounded on her cell door. "Hey, Chaplain, can I talk to you?"

He motioned to Officer Landers. "Could you unlock the food slot?"

Officer Landers unlocked the food slot and rolled a chair over for the Chaplain.

"How can I help you, Ms. Maldonado?"

"I don't need any help, Chaplain. Just had a question about this monk stuff. What does he mean by breathing in anger and breathing out anger?"

Chaplain Edwards hesitated a moment before speaking. "He's suggesting that when we feel anger or sadness, for example, instead of reacting, we should breathe and observe what we're feeling until the feeling goes away. In this way, we don't always have to act on our emotions, which as you have likely experienced, can cause problems."

"True that." Bonnie nodded. "If I feel angry I just cuss out the person who pissed me off or hit 'em. If I can't hit them, I hit a wall or something. It all happens so fast I don't know if I could stop it."

"Perhaps this could help you manage your emotions?" Chaplain Edwards mused.

"You might be better than that lady shrink they have here."

"I better get going. We can talk some more next time I make my rounds," he said, closing the food slot.

Bonnie lay on her bunk and stared at the wall. The concrete blurred and morphed into faces and memories. She remembered sitting at the dining room table with her family. She had accidentally knocked over her milk glass and it spilled into the casserole dish. Her father was so enraged he reached across the table and slapped her hard across the face and sent her to her room. She was seven. She'd sat on her bed feeling sad and angry. She picked up her pet gerbil to play with it. It crawled across her hands one to the next. She began to squeeze it. It struggled. She continued to squeeze it, harder and harder, until it died in her grip. The memory troubled her.

She had never "observed" how she felt like Chaplain Edwards was talking about. She'd always reacted —killing the neighbor's dog because she was angry at her father and couldn't kill him, getting high when she felt sad or lonely, carving "fuck off" into her arm with a paperclip after she'd fought with Gary.

She suddenly felt ashamed that she hadn't known another way. She looked down at the faint scar on her arm and traced the barely visible words "fuck off," on her arm. It made her want to cry and hit something. She wrapped the gray wool blanket around her shoulders and closed her eyes. She began breathing in through her nose and out through her mouth. *Breathing in emotion, breathing out emotion.* She repeated the words in her mind as she breathed in and out. She noticed her breathing begin to slow and the thoughts racing through her mind gradually disappeared. Her body felt warm and relaxed. The bad feelings were gone.

Chapter 13

"CUFF UP, MALDONADO, they're giving you another chance to be a good citizen on the compound. Don't blow it with your Taxi Driver routine!" Officer Landers joked.

Bonnie put her hands through the food slot so he could cuff her. He escorted her to a room with a female officer wearing handcuff earrings.

"Officer Hopyard's going to strip you out and give you your property," he said.

The officer popped her gum. "Turn around and let me get those cuffs off you."

"What about taking off your cuffs," Bonnie said, glaring at the officer's earrings.

"You don't like my earrings, huh?"

"Not so much."

"To each his own," she said and removed Bonnie's handcuffs. Bonnie felt the key scrape her wrist as she removed them. She assumed it was intentional.

"Disrobe please," Hopyard said.

"Your pleasure," Bonnie said, reluctantly removing the bright yellow smock and pants and standing naked before the officer.

"You know the drill," Hopyard said, continuing to loudly pop her gum.

Bonnie stuck out her tongue and lifted it up to show Hopyard she didn't have any contraband in her mouth then turned her palms face up.

"Good, turn around." Hopyard make a circular movement with her finger.

Bonnie turned around, brought her hands to her head and pulled her ears forward, then lifted up one foot, then the other, to show that she wasn't hiding anything on the bottom of her feet. She bent over as fast as she could, spread her cheeks, and coughed.

"Okay, we're good," Hopyard popped her gum again.

I'm glad it was good for you! She wanted to say. She hated being strip searched, but still preferred this to being felt up by a male guard under the guise of a pat search—that made her want to kill somebody.

Hopyard walked over to a wall lined with metal shelves of stacked clothing and plastic bins of shoes. "What size underwear do you wear, Maldonado?"

"Six."

"Cup size?"

"Wasn't it obvious?"

Bonnie put on the underwear as fast as she could.

"Here you go." Hopyard handed her a medium-sized white sports bra. Then dropped a pair of blue slip-on tennis shoes on the floor in front of her.

"I guess there are advantages to being abandoned by your parents. I feel sorry for the poor bitches who go through this bullshit every week for visits."

Hopyard handed her a folded pair of khaki pants with an elastic waistband and a matching khaki button up shirt. "Interesting philosophy, Maldonado."

"I don't expect you to get me."

"Change your attitude Maldonado or you can change right back into a clean yellow smock and stay around another month and see my entire collection of earrings."

"Not that interested, thanks."

As soon as Hopyward let her out of SHU Bonnie headed straight to Maintenance hoping to get her old job back.

"Look who it is?" Mr. Lee said, looking up from the paperwork on his desk.

"I'm ready to get back to work. I about died of boredom in there."

Mr. Lee scratched his head. "Sorry Maldonado, I can't put you back on my crew."

"Why?" she asked incensed.

"After your last stunt you think they're going to let you handle tools again?"

"Damn it!" she yelled and kicked the doorframe.

"I'm going to have to ask you to leave, Maldonado. Open movement is about to end and I can't have you back here."

"But I'm a hard worker."

"Good luck," he said, avoiding her eye contact.

Stunned, Bonnie left the Maintenance Building in a huff. She walked to the Chapel. Chaplain Edwards was in his office. A petite

Asian inmate was on the telephone crying. Chaplain Edwards waved at Bonnie, then got up and stepped outside of his office.

"You're out," he said. She thought it sounded almost like a question.

"Looks like it."

He looked at her curiously. "How can I help you?"

"Chaplain, I want to accept the Lord, Jesus Christ into my heart." Bonnie tried to hide a smirk.

Chaplain Edwards looked skeptical. "Really?"

"No, I want a job, but I figure I could learn something about God's miracles working here." She gave him a rare smile she hoped would seal the deal. She knew Chaplain Edwards was always willing to give someone a try. He unknowingly hired "bible thumpers" who used their access to outside volunteers to bring in contraband.

Chaplain Edwards clasped his hands together, "We might have something for you to do. Get your job change signed and you can start tomorrow."

"Maybe you can teach me how turn water into wine." Bonnie laughed and walked out of the Chapel. She made a beeline to the rec yard to find Tennessee.

Tennessee was at the weight pile. She set down the barbells and removed her sunglasses from her eyes and propped them on the top of her head. "You owe me money, Slick."

"That a new tat?" Bonnie asked, noting the black four-leaf clover on Tennessee's arm and hoping to change the subject.

"Yeah, Melanie and I got matching ones. You want something?"

Bonnie nodded. "Just got out of SHU. I'll pay you when I get my first paycheck."

"Okay, Slick, I'll hook you up."

Chapter 14

VICTORIA TURNED IN her keys at the Control Room and waited for the officer to open the sallyport doors. Today was a good day to go out for lunch and get away from the prison. Francis dropped a bomb on her by telling her she was going to take early retirement rather than stay on until she was 57. The thought of being at the prison without Francis depressed her. It was going to be hell. Francis had repeatedly helped her manage Bob's coldness and criticism and Brad's attempts to win an award as leading sycophant.

She drove to a Mexican restaurant and ordered a plate of chicken enchiladas. She didn't care that her lunch was going to take more than the thirty minutes the prison staff were allotted for their unpaid meal break. Usually she followed the rules, but today she disregarded the proverbial ticking clock, she needed to be out of the prison.

Mike Russell had left her another message about getting together. She didn't call him back. *How many excuses can I make up about why I won't ever go to one of his weekend barbeques?* She thought.

Agent Smith never re-contacted her and reporting something so seemingly insignificant as Russell's invitations to Captain Brown would not win him over in any way. She dipped a chip in the salsa and stuffed it in her mouth, hoping to take away the sick feeling in her stomach.

Chapter 15

BONNIE SAT ON the floor reading a book on Vipassana Meditation from off the book cart. Sandy Jean, the head orderly, an older white woman with coke-bottle thick glasses and gray thinning hair, gave Bonnie a severe look.

"You've been sitting there doing nothing for the better part of an hour." The old woman's voice rose. "I suggest you read on your own time."

Bonnie ignored her, but looked at the clock. To her amazement forty-five minutes had somehow slipped by.

Chaplain Edwards walked in. "How are things going, Ms. Maldonado?"

Bonnie snapped the book shut. "Good Chaplain."

She quickly returned to shelving books, but as soon as he was out of sight she found another interesting book on Buddhism and sprawled out on the floor again flipping through it. It was like a new addiction.

Karen, the only chapel orderly she actually liked, a red-headed white woman walked in. "Did you hear? Alison Green tested positive for HIV," Karen whispered to Bonnie.

"Doesn't she…?"

"Buy from Tennessee," Karen interrupted. "Yeah. People are freaking."

"Fuck, I just used one of her rigs, but I swear I saw her pull it out of the plastic."

"She may have just re-wrapped it." Karen gave her a serious look. "Get tested."

"Fuck that, I don't want to know."

"Suit yourself."

"Did you say shoot yourself?" Bonnie laughed. "I think that's the lesson here."

"You're crazy, Maldonado."

"It's been foretold."

Karen walked off and Bonnie opened the book again and thumbed through it. Her eyes fell on the part that talked about craving and about the suffering that craving caused. Dope always numbed her, but the cravings were unrelenting. She hated them. She'd wanted to quit for a long time, but the urges always won and she always went back.

The next day she knocked on Tennessee's door.

"My favorite customer," Tennessee said, and handed Bonnie her commissary list.

"Give me the good stuff cause I'm taking a break. Can't keep giving all my money to the Bank of Tennessee."

Tennessee laughed. "First working in the chapel, now this? You need to see the shrink about your identity crisis."

Bonnie's face reddened. "I don't need to see no fucking shrink!"

"Maybe an anger management class," Tennessee murmured.

Bonnie got up from the bed to return the commissary list to Tennessee.

"Chill out, Maldonado, I'm just playing." Tennessee sat on the bottom bunk opposite of where Bonnie had been sitting and prepared the needle.

"That better be clean." Bonnie sat on the bed again next to Tennessee.

"Stop tripping! Do you not see the wrapper I just took it out of? Melanie's got connections in Health Services. We're not going to fuck over one of our own."

Tennessee handed her the needle. Bonnie sat down and gently edged the needle into her vein. "This is the last time," she said.

"No, it ain't," Tennessee whispered in her ear.

The next morning as Bonnie walked to the Chapel she told herself that this time she really was done, but by the following afternoon she felt nauseous. She knocked on Chaplain Edwards's door. He motioned for her to come in.

"Chaplain Edwards, I feel sick. Can I go back to my room and lay down?"

"Yes, you don't look well. You probably have a cold. A lot of people are getting sick from the weather change."

"Thanks Chaplain." Bonnie shut his office door and walked to the housing unit. As soon as she got to her room she collapsed on the bed shivering, her clothes soaked with sweat.

"You dope sick?" Harris asked.

Bonnie ignored her.

"Crazy cracker." Harris slammed the metal cell door behind her.

Bonnie felt like her head was going to explode from the noise. She tried to bury it in the pillow. Her body trembled with fever and chills. *Why didn't I just leave it alone after kicking in the SHU?* She cried. Her head throbbed. There was a loud knock on the door.

"What?" she yelled.

The door cracked open. Tennessee came in. "Oh Slick, you look like death warmed over. I got something for you. Hang on. Mel, pin for me."

Tennessee sat down on the edge of Bonnie's bed and took out a needle. "Consider it a gift. I hate seeing my own kind suffer." Tennessee grabbed her arm.

Bonnie sat up and rolled up her shirtsleeve. She could almost taste it. Right now she didn't care that the needle hadn't come out of the plastic wrapper. She just wanted it. She held out her arm to Tennessee.

"That's right, baby girl, don't fight it," Tennessee said.

Suddenly Bonnie felt a wave of rage rush through her body. "What the fuck did you just say?"

"I said, relax, baby girl."

Bonnie shoved Tennessee off of her. "I ain't your fucking, *baby girl*. Get the fuck away from me!"

"Hey, slow down, Maldonado, I'm helping you out here." Tennessee regained her balance.

"No, fuck you! I don't need your fucking help. Get the fuck out of my room." Bonnie grabbed her plastic coffee cup and hurled it at Tennessee. It missed her head by inches, but hit the door.

Tennessee calmly picked it up and set it on her locker. She pointed her finger at Bonnie, like it was a loaded gun. "I'm gonna let that go cause you're sick. But you'll be back, Maldonado, you fucking junkies always come crawling back."

A few days later she went back to work. She'd slept most of the days, staying in her room, skipping meals, only getting up for count or an occasional smoke. She was amazed she'd somehow made it through.

She stood in Chaplain Edwards's doorway. "Good morning, Chaplain. Need your trash emptied?"

He looked up from the papers on his desk. "Good morning, Ms. Maldonado, glad to see you. Sounds like you had a nasty cold. Feeling better now?"

"So much better, Chaplain," she said, smiling as she emptied his trashcan. She felt lighter, cleaner inside. It was hard to understand it.

"Can I ask you a question, Chaplain Edwards?"

"Sure."

"That Buddhist guy talks about not getting attached to good or bad times 'cause everything changes."

Chaplain Edwards dropped his pen and turned his chair toward her. His face was pleasant to look at. He had kind eyes and looked almost boyish at times. He sat back and folded his fingertips together at his chin. "Reminds me of something they taught us back in seminary called Witness Consciousness where you stand back and watch your life like an observer would. It's a way to stay neutral about what happens in your life."

"I don't get it. Good stuff is good stuff and bad stuff is bad stuff right?"

"Maybe, but maybe not."

"That's too deep for me," she said. "What are those?" she asked, noticing a stack of flyers on his desk.

"We have a speaker coming in tomorrow. Can you hand these out in the housing units?"

"Sure," she said and took the flyers from him. Bonnie glanced at the flyers and saw the words "Victim Witness Program" on them. She wondered what that was.

Later, after she'd pinned them to the bulletin boards in the housing units, she sat outside smoking. She liked the evening best, things seemed freer at dusk, as the light disappeared and the shadows hid the fence line. The chatter of inmates talking as they walked the compound together and the soft melodic singing of a group of Mexican women on the rec yard triggered a swell of loneliness. She took a drag off her cigarette. *I didn't come to prison to make friends,* she reminded herself, trying to push the feelings back down. *Don't let anyone get close to you and no one can hurt you.* Still, a part of her wanted to believe that people could have relationships where neither person was trying to get one up on the other, where both people really loved one another, but even wishing made her feel stupid.

She crushed out her cigarette and walked to the housing unit. As she rounded the corner to the B-side, she almost bumped into two inmates coming out of one of the cells.

"Watch where you're going, Maldonado."

"Sorry about that," Bonnie apologized.

The two women exchanged surprised glances. One started to laugh. "She's turning into a punk." She heard the other one mutter as she continued walking down the hallway to her room.

Chapter 16

MORNING COFFEE IN hand, Victoria stopped by her office to drop off her bag. On a whim, she fished into her desk drawer for a calculator. At eight hours a day, forty hours a week for the close to two years she worked there, Victoria had already served the equivalent of a *six and a half month* prison sentence. By the time she retired with thirty years in, she would have served a total of seven years and one month behind bars. *Thank God, I'm on the "installment plan" and get to go home on nights and weekends, rather than having to do all my "time" at once,* she thought. She got up from her chair, locked the door behind her and walked briskly to the chapel. The Religious Services Department was bringing in a speaker from Victim Witness to talk to the inmates about being a crime victim and had invited the Psychology Department to co-sponsor the event.

Chaplain Edwards motioned her into the chapel's sanctuary. "Dr. Thomas, thank you for making time to attend our important program today."

Victoria had always found Chaplain Edwards intelligent and well-meaning, though a bit pretentious. Dr. Scarsdale, Counselor

Shaw, and a few other staff members sat in the back rows. She walked towards them.

"You're cutting it a little close, don't you think?" Scarsdale looked at his watch and then at her cup of coffee. It felt like Scarsdale was always finding fault with her. When she first met him and commented on the fact that his last name was the same as the town in New York she'd grown up in, he seemed completely uninterested.

Brad lifted his briefcase from the chair. She thought she saw a smirk on his face.

"There's an extra seat here," he said.

She sat next to him and scanned the room. She recognized a few of the inmates. One woman looked familiar, but she couldn't quite place her, then it came to her. *Maldonado.* She hadn't seen inmate Maldonado for several months. Maldonado looked in her direction, but then abruptly averted her gaze. *She's obviously still embarrassed, but coping better,* she thought and then turned her attention to the podium, anticipating the introduction of the guest speaker.

Chapter 17

BONNIE WAS SURPRISED at how transformed the chapel was—chairs were set up, the podium was in place, Chaplain Edwards had even purchased two bouquets of flowers.

"Ms. Maldonado, can you please go to the closet and get two vases for these." He set the flowers on a chair. "I'd like one placed on each side of the podium."

Bonnie walked by a handful of inmates sitting in their seats waiting for the guest speaker. Most of them either worked in the chapel or were regulars to any event held there. A few headshrinkers from the Psychology Department sat in the back row, including Dr. Thomas, the psychologist she'd spoken with after she got Gary's letter. Her face reddened and she felt a rush of adrenaline through her body. She quickly retrieved the vases, stuffed the flowers in them, and moved toward the front of the room to avoid contact with her.

As she was placing the vases next to the podium, Chaplain Edwards ushered in the guest speaker, a woman in her early thirties, with curly auburn hair and blue eyes. Bonnie had hoped to leave before the lecture started and get back to the library, but a rush of women had filled the seats, and Chaplain Edwards was beginning his introduction. There was no way to make a quick exit without being rude and offending Chaplain Edwards. Reluctantly, Bonnie found an empty seat near the front and sat down.

"Please welcome Ms. Amanda Masterson." Chaplain Edwards shepherded the woman towards the podium.

Ms. Masterson stepped behind the podium and cleared her throat. "Good morning ladies," she paused, "and gentlemen." She smiled at the male staff members in the back row. Ms. Masterson was dressed in a chocolate brown sweater and beige pants. She wore light make up.

"Four years ago on a July evening, I was waitressing the late shift at Blossom's Diner." She took a deep breath and continued. "It was about midnight. The place was dead. I had one hour left on my shift and then I was going to pick up my kids, Kyle and Kaylee, from my mom's house and take them home. I hated working nights but we needed the money." She paused and took a sip from her bottle of water.

Bonnie noticed Ms. Masterson's hands trembling. She didn't want to stay and listen, but she couldn't leave now. She felt her stomach churn.

Ms. Masterson spoke again and her voice quivered. "I heard the door open and turned around to get some menus. A large man in a flannel shirt started yelling at me. I could barely understand him, but when I saw the gun in his hand, I understood. There was another guy in a baseball cap. He walked behind the counter to the kitchen. He pointed his gun at the cook and the dishwasher and told them to get down. They dropped to the floor. The man in the flannel shirt yelled at me to open the cash register. I was so scared."

Ms. Masterson stopped speaking and took another sip of her water. She glanced into the audience. Bonnie averted her gaze and stared at the floor.

"My hands were shaking...I was crying. I was so nervous. I finally got the register open then I heard a loud commotion coming from the kitchen. The guy in the baseball cap was kicking Billy, the dishwasher. He kicked him unconscious."

Bonnie looked around the Sanctuary. The room was packed. The inmates seemed hypnotized by the speaker. Bonnie shifted in her seat, she felt sick to her stomach. For the first time in weeks she wanted to get high.

"They took me and the cook, John, to the staff room. He was 23. He tried to look brave for me. The man in the ball cap tied us up in the break room. He took my purse and John's wallet and started pulling out credit cards and money and gave it to the larger man. Then he attacked me." She paused and took a deep breath. "He started grabbing my breasts. He stunk like whiskey. The larger man dug through my wallet, but when he saw the picture of me and my kids he changed." Ms. Masterson looked around the room at the women.

"He asked me why I was working so late, as if I was out past my bedtime. 'I've got to feed my kids,' I told him. 'Where's your old man?' he demanded. I yelled at him, 'Hell if I know.' He was concerned about my children but holding a gun to my head and letting the other guy....'' Ms. Masterson stopped to take another sip of her water. She touched the cross she wore around her neck and began speaking again. "The other guy got angry. 'Who cares about this bitch's sob story?' he yelled and shot John in the head."

Someone in the row behind Bonnie gasped. She felt a quake move through her body and instinctively crossed her arms across her chest and slumped in her seat.

Ms. Masterson looked up to the left and continued speaking. "My hands were tied. I couldn't even wipe the blood out of my eyes. I knew I was going to die, but then the larger man pushed the other guy out of the room. I don't know how long we, I mean, I, sat there, after they left. When the police arrived they said I just kept saying, 'I needed the money.' John is dead. Billy is brain damaged. He doesn't even recognize me."

Bonnie stared straight ahead. She could hear the sound of weeping. Chaplain Edwards passed around a box of tissues.

"I never went back to work. Every time I go into a restaurant, I can't catch my breath. I feel like I'm having a heart attack. We moved out of our home and into a tiny apartment cause that's all I can afford with my disability check. Me and Kaylee share a room, Kyle sleeps on the couch. He's always fighting and angry. Blames himself for not protecting me. He was six. I still have nightmares. Wake up crying."

One of the inmates sitting in the second row got up and handed Ms. Masterson the tissue box.

"Thank you, sweetie," Ms. Masterson said. She took the box and pulled out a couple of tissues and blew her nose. "Those two men took more than my money. They destroyed my life and robbed my children."

Ms. Masterson looked into the audience trying to make eye contact with the women in the first row. Bonnie looked away.

"I believe they were like you, confused. Someone hurt them. Maybe they were trying to make their lives better, but the way they chose to do it hurt others. Hurt people hurt people. Do you want to continue hurting people for money, for drugs? Is it worth it to destroy your life, your family, and the lives of others? Think about your own children. You think they can sleep peacefully without you there? Who's with them when they have nightmares? Make a new choice. Please get help and make a change. Thank you for listening." Ms. Masterson smiled and bowed her head.

The inmates around her began clapping. Bonnie held her hands in her lap. They were shaking. She felt tears stream down her face and promptly wiped them away.

Inmates shuffled out of the chapel in an unusual silence. Bonnie wanted to leave too, to smoke, but she had to stay and clean up. She started stacking the extra chairs and could hear Ms. Masterson talking with the staff on the other side of the room.

She waited until the staff members were gone then crossed the room towards Ms. Masterson. She didn't know what she was going to say, but something pushed her on. Bonnie's voice trembled as she spoke. "You aren't mad at the men who did that?"

Ms. Masterson looked into her eyes without blinking. "For many years I was, but then, I realized the larger man didn't want to hurt me, maybe because I was a woman, or a mother, maybe I reminded him of someone, I don't know. I believe he didn't want to hurt anyone. He was just desperate and needed help. Maybe he even needed love."

Ms. Masterson moved closer and gently put her hands on Bonnie's shoulders. Bonnie flinched at the woman's touch.

"Look inside yourself. Crime is not the answer. Drugs destroy your life and other people's lives. Love—that's the only answer."

What was this woman talking about? She sounded like a cheesy song. Bonnie wanted to get away, but the woman tightened her grip on her shoulders so she couldn't.

"I know someone hurt you. Before you were a criminal, who were you?"

Bonnie stood silent. The question didn't make any sense.

"Ms. Masterson, I can escort you out now," Chaplain Edwards interrupted.

"Think about what I said, love, only love."

Bonnie watched her as she walked out of the chapel. She felt raw inside.

Chapter 18

Victoria sat at her desk and took a bite of her nuked frozen lasagna, something about what the woman from the Victim Witness Program said made her think about Joanne. Victoria wondered if Joanne would have eventually resorted to crime or prostitution to pay for her habit if she'd lived. She'd already demeaned herself with the guys she slept with, mostly drug dealers or sleazy older married dudes, nothing like the guys she dated before she dropped out of college—scholars and athletes, men she aspired to settle down with. The only thing these guys were good providers of was cocaine, and then eventually the meth and crack she couldn't live without.

Victoria's thoughts were interrupted by a knock on the door. Francis, dressed in her white physician's coat, stood outside holding a Tupperware container full of leftovers.

"Mind if I join you?" she asked.

"Come in," Victoria said and cleared some files from her desk hoping that Francis wouldn't notice she was upset. "What's for lunch?"

"*Lumpia* with shredded pork and vegetarian black bean chili."

"That's an interesting combo."

"Would you like some?"

"No thank you. I just nuked my lunch. You can put your food here, please sit down."

Francis sat down and began eating. "So, what'd you think of the speaker?" Francis asked her mouth full of chili.

"A little dramatic, but the inmates seemed responsive." Victoria took another bite of lasagna, noting it was still cold in places, but continued to eat it anyway.

"They need drama to hold their attention. That's why they love Jerry Springer. I still can't believe the new administration let her in."

"Why, what do you mean?" Victoria asked.

"They're not fond of restorative justice programs, or alternative medicine. I was trying to get an acupuncturist in to help the women with their addictions. A simple needle in an earlobe, they can't cope with that. Last month they did away with the HIP DIP?"

"What's the HIP DIP?" Victoria laughed.

"It used to stand for Health Promotion Disease Prevention. It supported educational pamphlets for the inmates, like how to avoid HIV, which seems to be growing in our population. Can't believe how many new diagnoses we've had," Francis sighed. "They've replaced it with the Health Prevention Disease Promotion Program!"

"Hmm. That's disconcerting. Rehabilitation doesn't seem to be a high priority in my department either. Scarsdale told me that my job is containment and management of the mentally ill." Victoria shook her head.

Francis dabbed at her face with a paper napkin. "Thank Goddess I'm leaving before things get worse!"

Victoria frowned. "Who's going to keep me sane and contained?"

Francis looked at her empathically. "Maybe you should consider leaving."

"What? And miss out on the fantastic early retirement plan and law enforcement pension. Not to mention that in another year my student loans will be forgiven." Victoria sat back in her chair and sighed. "No, I'm in it for the long haul."

"It's not worth the golden handcuffs. You don't want to end up like Scarsdale."

Victoria laughed, "I could never be like Scarsdale. He was born that way."

The smile disappeared from Francis's face. "Victoria, this place hardens you and if it doesn't harden you, it corrupts you, and it's not just the inmates that'll do it to you.

Later that night Victoria thought about what Francis said as she and Devin lay in bed reading.

"Devin, have you noticed any changes in me?" she asked him.

"No, you don't look like you've gained any weight," Devin said, still reading from one of his financial reports.

"That's not what I meant." Victoria lowered the report from his hands to get his attention. "I mean, do I seem different since I started working at the prison?"

"You seem the same to me," he said, and went back to his reading.

Chapter 19

VICTORIA WAS REVIEWING the ever-changing paperwork guidelines issued from the Central Psychology Office in D.C. when she heard a knock at her door. Bonnie Maldonado hovered in the doorway. Maldonado was the last person she expected to see.

"Can I talk to you?" Maldonado flinched as she said it, like the words cut her.

Victoria glanced at the paperwork and then at Maldonado. "Yes, come in."

Maldonado took a seat. "Still don't feel comfortable talking to no shrink," she said, a palpable agitation in her voice. "People are gonna think I'm fucking crazy. I'm not fucking crazy."

"What's going on, Ms. Maldonado?" Victoria asked, assessing Maldonado's affect and demeanor.

"Couldn't fucking sleep last night. Guess hearing that lady talk about what happened, how it fucked up her life." Maldonado picked at a stray hangnail. "It just…. It just…" Maldonado stammered. "It just made me think about what I did."

Victoria's voice softened. "What did you do?"

"You read my file," Maldonado barked. "You know what they busted me for."

"No, Ms. Maldonado, I haven't and I don't. Would you like to tell me?" Victoria leaned back in her chair and crossed her legs. She could see Maldonado considering her invitation.

"Who's gonna know about what I tell you?" Maldonado asked, her tone defensive.

Victoria, the consummate professional, ran through the prison's limits of confidentiality. "If you tell me you're going to harm yourself or someone else or if you tell me about an active case of child abuse or an inappropriate relationship with a staff member I have to report that. Other than that, what we discuss will be held in confidence."

Maldonado cracked her knuckles. "What's in this for you? You get off on crime?"

"My job is to help people break destructive patterns and heal old wounds so they can stop hurting themselves and others and be happy."

"I don't really know if you can help me." Maldonado stared at the ground.

"You said the lady from the Victim Witness Program reminded you of your past. What did you mean?"

Maldonado sat stiffly in the chair. "It has to do with how I caught my state case."

"Uh huh." Victoria intentionally chose not to seem overly interested which made some inmates more defensive.

"I'd been out of jail for six months. I needed money to buy something for my brother. Just a quick in and out. 'Open the safe.

Give me the money.' That's it, that's all. But the woman couldn't remember the stupid safe combination." Maldonado's left leg shook up and down. "I started to freak out you know, I was thinking, *shit, somebody's gonna come in and I'm gonna get fucking busted again.* I just got out of Rocky Butte and wanted some time in the free world and this damn lady… " She exhaled, slamming her hand down hard on her leg. "I just wonder, you know, if that lady, if she felt…" Maldonado stopped talking and started chewing on her thumbnail again, "if she felt like that lady who spoke yesterday did?"

"What do you think?"

"I don't want to talk about it anymore!" Maldonado got up from the chair.

"Please stay," Victoria held her hand out. "Tell me about your job. Where do you work?"

"The chapel."

Saccharine sweet ladies who spoke self-righteously of their special relationship with Jesus or Allah and gossiped about the evil-doings of other inmates worked in the chapel. Maldonado just didn't fit the bill.

"Why the chapel?"

Maldonado sat back down. "Used to work on the plumbing crew, but," she looked down at the floor, "I lost my job."

"Why did you lose your job?"

"I was fixing a sink and this bitch tried to tell me how to do my job and tried to grab the wrench out of my hand. I just grabbed it back and swung."

Victoria remained still.

"I got blamed for starting it and ended up in the SHU and then I lost my job. Most of the females that work in the tool room are down for murder, but *they don't trust me* with tools no more. Whatever, I ain't trippin'. They want to lose their best plumber, that's on them."

Victoria noted that most of Bonnie Maldonado's sense of worth and certainty seemed to come from working on the maintenance crew. She wondered how Maldonado managed working for the Religious Services Department.

"What do you do in the chapel?" she asked and took a sip of her coffee.

"Sort books in the library, like make sure the books are alphabetized by author."

"Do you like your job?"

"Do you like yours?" Maldonado grinned.

Victoria smiled but didn't answer.

"It's not bad," Maldonado said. "Never thought I'd end up working in a chapel though. I've been reading a few books…"

Victoria glanced at her watch. The time had flown by. Another inmate was pacing up and down the hallway to make sure that Victoria saw her. She wondered when she'd have time to get the paperwork done. "I'm terribly sorry, Ms. Maldonado, but we're going to have to stop for today."

Maldonado looked at the clock.

Victoria opened her date book. "Come back tomorrow and I'll schedule you for regular sessions twice a week and we can work on whatever's bothering you."

"I don't think so." Maldonado got up from the chair and began to walk out, but stopped and turned back to say something. "I'm sorry I woke you up that one time."

Victoria smiled. "I'm glad that you reached out that night. I'm going to put you on the call-out tomorrow, come if you want to."

Maldonado opened the door avoiding eye contact with Ms. Johnson, the other inmate waiting to see her.

"Ready for me?" Johnson asked.

"Yes, come in." Victoria ushered in inmate Johnson, a white woman in her late thirties. She was treating her for depression and anger management.

Johnson sat down and launched into how sad she was feeling about being separated from her children in El Paso and how frustrated she was with the "lazy prison staff" and all the "trifling bitches always gossiping about everybody and stealing everything that ain't nailed down."

Typically, it was hard for Victoria to listen to inmate Johnson's weekly rant and rave about her problems with everyone else, but today it was even harder. Victoria's mind kept wandering back to Bonnie Maldonado and how she seemed a strange combination of youthful innocence and rage.

"Um hmm," Victoria replied, pretending to be attentive to what Johnson was saying.

Chapter 20

For a moment Bonnie felt lighter, but a sick feeling in her stomach quickly replaced the good feelings. She started to wonder if she'd made a mistake telling Dr. Thomas so much. *I need to be careful*, she thought, *Bottom line, Dr. Thomas is a cop, like all the others*.

The next morning Bonnie grabbed her cigarettes and put them in her shirt pocket, then walked to the officer's station to check the call-out sheet before heading to the chapel. Officer Dark and Lovely sat tipped back in the chair with his feet up on the desk and his arms behind his head. He smiled at the young, bleached blonde inmate sitting on the edge of his desk flirting with him. Bonnie had to pull the call-out sheet from underneath her ass.

The blonde turned and sneered at Bonnie. "Watch it, bitch!"

"Ooh, cat fight!" Dark and Lovely made a snarling noise. His eyes met the blonde's. She giggled. Bonnie ignored their exchange of sexual innuendoes and searched for her name on the call out sheet. "Maldonado 24827-056 Unit A/B Chapel Orderly 1430 Dr. Thomas Psych Build."

She tossed the call out sheet back on to the desk and waited for Dark and Lovely to unlock the housing unit's front door for open movement. He deliberately took his time while more than two dozen women waited for him. Bonnie was pissed. She knew that they'd all have to rush to their next destination in less than seven minutes before doors everywhere at the prison were locked again and they found themselves out of bounds and shit out of luck.

Bonnie spent the morning sorting books in the library and then in the afternoon she started cleaning the chapel with Karen.

"Can you go get the vacuum out of the closet in the sanctuary?" Karen asked.

"Can you? I want to keep my distance from those bible-thumping Jesus freaks."

"It's just the Spanish ladies," Karen laughed and continued mopping the bathroom floor. "They're harmless."

"Are you serious?" Bonnie snickered. "They freak me out the worst, down on their hands and knees crying and praying so loud that if there was a God he'd tell them to 'shut the fuck up.'"

Karen shook her head. "You really are crazy, Maldonado."

"Speaking of that, what time is it?" Bonnie put down the scrub brush she was using to clean the toilets and wiped her hands on her pants.

"It's 2:25 PM."

"I gotta go."

"Fine, leave me to do all the dirty work. You're lucky you're so cute," Karen giggled, and pretended to swing the mop at her.

"Whatever! At least you'll smell pine-fresh at the end of the day. See ya!" Bonnie smiled, embarrassed, but at the same time flattered by Karen's flirtation. She walked out of the Chapel and headed towards the Psychology Building. What was she going to talk to Dr. Thomas about? She didn't feel like she had anything to say. *Maybe we'll just sit and stare at each other,* she thought.

Bonnie sauntered up the stairs of the Psychology Building and knocked on Dr. Thomas's door.

Dr. Thomas waved her in and continued writing notes. Bonnie watched Dr. Thomas's hands as she scribbled on the notepad; her well-manicured nails and gold wedding ring caught Bonnie's eyes. She looked closely at her for the first time and saw a confident, attractive woman in her mid-thirties with striking green eyes. Dr. Thomas had shoulder length brown hair with reddish highlights that looked perfect, like hair you would see in a shampoo commercial, silky and straight, with every strand in its' place.

"I'm glad you came back, Ms. Maldonado."

Bonnie glared at her through her black eyeliner ringed eyes. "I'd get a shot if I didn't show up for the call out."

She looked around Dr. Thomas's office at the many well-cared for plants on the windowsill, the psychology and self-help books on her real walnut bookshelf and the gold-framed plaque with "Victoria L. Rosenberg, Ph.D." that hung on the wall.

"Rosenberg. Is that German?" she asked, wanting to take the focus off of her.

"Yes, it is."

Bonnie glanced at the framed photographs on the wall, one of a mountain and another of a river that snaked its way through a wooded forest. "Where's that?"

"Central Oregon in the Three Sisters' Wilderness Area."

"Thought those mountains looked familiar. I'm from Oregon. Is that where you're from?"

"Let's focus on you. What would you like to say about those pictures?" Dr. Thomas took a sip of her water.

Bonnie rolled her eyes. "I know staff ain't supposed to talk about their personal lives with convicts. Whatever." Bonnie studied the clouds above the picture of the mountain. "They remind me of my old boyfriend, Tim. He died in a motorcycle accident near Mt. Hood."

"I'm sorry."

"I don't need your pity," Bonnie snapped at Dr. Thomas. She felt the blood rush to her face.

"That's good, Ms. Maldonado, because I wasn't giving you any. It's never easy to lose a loved one."

Bonnie stared at her hands. Her nails were chipped, and her fingers were full of paper cuts from filing library cards "Well, I'm over it now." He died a long time ago. It doesn't matter anymore."

"What was he like?"

Bonnie noticed that Dr. Thomas had lowered her voice a bit. She tried to ignore the feeling that she was being "shrinked" and kept talking.

"He didn't take no shit from no one. He knew what he wanted and never listened to anyone else. He protected me."

"Who did you need protection from?"

"I don't want to talk about it. Okay?" Bonnie pulled her arms even tighter around her body and looked out the window.

"Tell me more about your parents?"

"My dad was an asshole and my mom was always trying to make him happy."

"Do they visit?"

"They did once."

"Do they write?"

"My mom sends me a card at Christmas."

"How's that?"

"How's what?" Bonnie turned and faced Dr. Thomas.

"How does that feel?" Dr. Thomas's face was expressionless.

Bonnie balled up her fists. "I don't really fucking care."

Dr. Thomas looked at her intently. "Hmmm, is that true, Ms. Maldonado, that you really don't care?"

"I'm done here." Bonnie bolted for the door. "You're worse than that federal prosecutor with your fucking questions." She slammed the door behind her.

Bonnie didn't care that it wasn't open movement. She'd take her chances. She bolted out of the Psych Building and headed for the chapel. Once there she made a beeline for the bathroom. She walked into the stall farthest from the door. There was no toilet paper in it. Irritated, she kicked open the door to the next stall to find it without toilet paper too. *Bitches always stealing everything!* Bonnie sat down on the toilet to pee.

She missed Tim, and missing Tim made her miss dope. She had met Tim when she was fifteen standing outside a Plaid Pantry convenience store trying to get someone to buy her cigarettes. Tim drove up on a red Harley with orange and yellow flames.

"Buy me a pack of smokes?" She'd asked him casually as he got off his bike and strode towards the entrance.

"Sure, why not?" He grinned.

"How about a six pack while you're at it?" Bonnie smiled.

Tim laughed as he walked past her pushing open the glass door. Ten minutes later, he came out with a case of Bud and a pack of Camels. She rode with him back to his place.

Tim was much older than her, a solid 200-pound man with long dirty blond hair and a full beard. He smelled of body odor, cigarettes, and beer and was missing a few teeth from bar fights. His arms were covered in faded homemade, bluish-black prison tattoos, mostly naked women and serpents. He had a three-leaf clover on his left shoulder, Odin's Cross on his right forearm, a swastika on his back, and two lightning bolts on his chest. He'd gotten most of his tattoos in his early twenties during his seven-year prison sentence for aggravated manslaughter. She knew his original charge was second-degree murder, but he'd never discussed the details of his case, and she didn't want to know.

She started doing "small jobs" with Tim—shoplifting cigarettes and cases of beer, a few petty thefts here and there when people left valuables in their cars or left their garage doors open. Then the guys taught her how to hotwire cars. She practiced until she was able to do it in less than a minute. Bonnie loved the thrill of a successful car theft and the feel of the Colt Python 38 she kept tucked in her pants behind her back.

Tim loved riding his Harley on Highway 26, tree-lined with tall pines and Douglas Fir. It was his favorite ride. She'd taken it many times with him.

She was watching TV when she got the call.

"Ma'am, this is the Oregon Highway Patrol. We're calling to notify you that a Harley Davidson with plates belonging to Tim Reynolds was crushed by a log truck this afternoon and we have an unidentified body of a white male that we believe is Tim Reynolds, but we'd like you to come down to the hospital morgue and ID him for us."

"Stop fucking with me, Sketch!" she'd told the voice on the other end of the phone.

"I'm sorry, ma'am, I wish this were a joke. The brakes on a log truck coming down one of the passes went out and the truck struck Mr. Reynolds's bike. The driver was killed instantly. We'll need you to come down and ID his body."

She drove to the hospital in disbelief.

"Might've had a chance if he'd worn a helmet," the tech at the morgue told her. "I recommend you don't lift the sheet above the shoulders.

Bonnie grabbed the sheet from him and yanked it off. The sight of the mutilated body caused her legs to buckle. She struggled to steady herself.

Tim's face was mangled beyond recognition. She couldn't tell it was him until she saw the double lightning bolt on his chest and her name tattooed below the three leaf clover on what was left of his arm.

Bonnie broke into angry sobs. "Fuck you, mother fucker, you can't die on me."

The tech had tried to get her out of the room. She'd shoved him into a tray of silver tools and walked out in a daze, unable to erase the memory of Tim's disfigured body. She went into their bathroom and opened the first aid kit where Tim kept his dope. Tim had never let her shoot up.

"This shit will kill you," he told her once and grabbed her arm like he was going to break it. "I'll do it for ya, if I ever catch you messing around with it."

But with Tim dead, there was nothing stopping her. She took out one of his rigs and the baggie with the smack and sat on the bathroom floor. She had never cooked dope before, but had watched Tim. She put the dope in the spoon, squirted water into it, and held the lighter underneath. The spoon blackened as it cooked it. The metal on the lighter burned her thumb. Still, she pressed down, then found a vein and slammed the needle into her arm—an immediate warmth rushed through her shoulders and neck, down her spine. The real pain, the pain in her heart and mind, were gone. She and Tim were now one.

"Fuck this shit!" Bonnie got up from the toilet. She walked into the chapel library and found Karen sorting books. "Cover for me!"

"411?" Karen asked.

"Next open movement, me and Mrs. Jones."

Karen shook her head. "It's a lot keepin' up with the Jones's."

"Can't drink, can't fuck."

"You sure about that?" Karen winked at her and went to shelve another book.

Bonnie glanced at the book. It was the *Miracle of Mindfulness*, the book she'd read in the SHU. "Let me see that book." She took it from Karen, opened it and read a page.

"To master our breath is to be in control of our bodies and minds. Each time we find it difficult to gain control of ourselves, the method of watching the breath should be used. Breathing in a long breath. Breathing out a long breath. Calming the activity of the breath-body, I shall breathe in. Calming the activity of the breath-body, I shall breathe out."

She walked to an empty room in the chapel, sat down, closed her eyes, and began breathing. The breathing made her feel lighter.

She continued to take deep breaths. A wave of peace washed over her. She felt a sense of calm, instead of the pain and fog her mind experienced with the dope. An hour later she got up from the floor where she was sitting and instead of going to see Tennessee, she went back to shelve books.

Chapter 21

"WOULD YOU PREFER not to be here?" Victoria asked, taking another sip of her coffee. It was her fourth session with Bonnie Maldonado.

Maldonado looked at her with disdain. "I'd prefer to be back home."

Victoria realized it was a stupid question. "Where's home?" she asked, hoping to keep the conversation going.

"I told you, Oregon."

"Oh right, the pictures, we talked about that last week. What part?" *This isn't going well,* she thought.

"Just outside of Portland."

"Are your parents still together?"

"Unfortunately."

"What do they do?" she asked. Every question felt like pulling teeth.

"Is this twenty fucking questions? My dad worked as an electrician for Boeing. He's retired now. My mom worked at the dog track. She got fired cause she's always wasted on Valium."

"You seem to be rather cavalier about this?"

"You seem to have an expensive vocabulary?" Maldonado glared at her.

Victoria matched Maldonado's glare with her own sharp gaze. She wasn't going to let Maldonado off the hook. "Do you have any siblings?"

"Are you listening or pretending to listen?" Maldonado continued to test her. "I told you before, I have a brother and I had a sister."

"Had?"

"She drowned."

Victoria looked for a trace of sadness on Maldonado's face. She didn't see it. "I'm very sorry."

"Why? It's not your fault," Maldonado said sarcastically. "She drowned in the bathtub when I was a baby. I don't even remember her."

Victoria made a mental note to come back to the discussion about the sister who drowned at a later point.

"Are you close with your brother?"

Maldonado ran her fingers through her hair a couple of times before she spoke. "Used to be closer to him than anyone else in my family, but we grew apart."

Victoria sensed some sadness in Maldonado.

"Last week you said your father was a real jerk"

"No, I said he was an asshole!"

Victoria could see that she was hitting raw nerve after nerve with Maldonado. "Tell me."

Maldonado stared at her nails for a few moments. "My dad doesn't like to waste money. Almost everything, even clothes, is a 'wasteful luxury' in his mind. He made us earn money to pay for our clothes and we only got to shop at Goodwill. He said he wanted us to understand the value of money."

"So you had to use your allowance to pay for your school clothes?" Victoria asked, sipping her bottled water.

"Allowance? We didn't get any fucking allowance. On weekends he dropped us off at the strawberry fields to pick berries with the Mexicans. He'd dump us there in the early morning and pick us up at sunset."

"How old were you?"

"I was six and Danny was ten."

"He would drop you off by yourselves?"

"Yep, just me and Danny and a bag with peanut butter and jelly sandwiches." Maldonado's voice was devoid of emotion.

When Victoria first started working at the prison and inmates told her stories like this she'd thought they were lying or at least exaggerating, until she saw the cigarette burns on their arms and they told her about the beatings they'd given their own children. Now she knew parents were capable of unbelievable atrocities against their children. She counseled several women who had murdered their children and some who had co-participated in their children's sexual victimization with pedophiliac boyfriends and husbands. She'd written enough Children's Protective Services reports to know that what Bonnie was saying was likely true, perhaps even worse than she was describing it.

"And you made enough money picking berries to buy your clothes?"

"No, when we weren't berry picking we were walking along the trailheads of the Columbia River with black trash bags looking for empty pop cans, those were worth five cents, and beer bottles were ten. My dad would dump us off and we'd walk around for hours looking in the bushes and along the water's edge for them. It was gross; the cans were full of dead slugs and cigarette butts."

Victoria tried to imagine what would make a man be so miserly. "Was your father raised during the Depression?"

"No, but he was poor growing up. He started working at twelve to help support his family. My grandma only spoke Polish and my grandfather spoke mostly Italian, so they had a hard time communicating with one another. He always said his life hadn't been easy, so why should ours be?"

"That sounds hard. Also sounds like your father took his frustrations out on you and your brother."

"Yeah." Maldonado crossed her arms over her chest. "It was."

"What was your mom like?"

"A mean ass drunk."

Victoria nodded.

Bonnie suddenly looked wistful. "Well, sometimes when my dad was away on business trips she'd put on records and get in these sentimental moods. She'd sing to me and dance around the house." Maldonado brushed back the hair from her face. "I liked it. I could. I picture her in a beautiful dress waltzing across a high school gym floor with a handsome guy in a tux. She was nicest to me then." Maldonado paused, the light that was there for a moment faded. "But the next day, she was always a bitter bitch. Blamed me and Danny for being married to my father." Maldonado's head drooped.

"I'm not sure how that's your fault?"

"Makes two of us. She blamed me for my sister's death too. Said if I hadn't been crying she'd never have left Angela alone in the bathtub. I think she wished I'd died instead."

Victoria knew that what Maldonado sensed could be true. Some parents who lost a child took their anger out on their surviving children and bargained with God about why one child was taken over the other.

"So your mom was depressed and not there for you and your brother?"

"No, she was 'there for me,' Bonnie said in a mocking tone. "I skinned my knees up in a bike accident this one time and she came out of her bedroom refilled her glass with rum and coke, seen my skinned knees and made me take one of her pills. I didn't want to. Made me dizzy, but then my knees stopped hurting and then I just felt nothing."

Victoria had observed this pattern earlier and charted it in Maldonado's file. *Clt. feels safer and more in control expressing anger, rather than sadness.*

"That sounds awful, Ms. Maldonado. Clearly you were not nurtured as a child." Maldonado looked glassy-eyed and Victoria wondered if she had heard her. "Ms. Maldonado, what are you thinking about right now?"

Maldonado seemed startled to hear Victoria's voice. "Huh? Oh, nothing, just thinking."

Victoria glanced at the clock. She had gone ten minutes over time with Maldonado. "Our time is up for today," she said and got up to open the door.

"So you get me feeling all this shit and then you're just like 'times up.' Fuck that?" Maldonado grabbed her jacket off the chair and barely looked at her as she got up to leave.

Victoria regretted not ending the session on time and providing more of a container for Maldonado. "Ms. Maldonado, I'm sorry," Victoria began, but Maldonado was out the door.

Victoria charted notes of their session. She felt sorry for Maldonado. Her life had been one tragedy after the next. Still, she was frustrated that Maldonado pushed her away when she was reaching out to help her.

As soon as she finished charting the notes there was a knock on her door. It was Inmate Benally, a skinny Native American woman with long brown hair in her early thirties who Victoria had seen for depression when Benally first arrived.

"Come in, Ms. Benally."

Benally sat down. Victoria glanced at Benally's uniform. It had been altered; pegged at the legs and taken in around the waist, which was against prison policy. She also noticed Benally's boots were caked with mud.

"What brings you here today?" Victoria asked, trying not to reveal her irritation that Benally had tracked mud into her office.

"I need help with my family," she began. "They're fighting. They keep blaming each other for me being here. I don't know what to do."

"I'm not sure what you can do," Victoria said.

"You don't understand. They have my kids and they're getting tired of caring for them. My oldest keeps running away. I think they're being abused."

"Why do you think that?" Victoria asked, knowing that she was likely going to have to file a child abuse report.

"My little girl said my brother, her uncle, tries to touch her where she pees from. I believe her, cause when I was growing up he did that to me."

Victoria sighed as she pulled a Child Protective Service report from her desk drawer and grabbed a pen from the black wire-mesh penholder on her desk. "Okay, Ms. Benally, I'm going to need you to answer a few questions and then I'm going to call Child Protective Services."

Tears poured down Benally's face as she recounted the details of her own abuse. Victoria completed the form then picked up the phone and dialed only to be met with a recorded message. "All of our workers are busy right now. Please leave your name and number and a worker will get back to you."

Last month Victoria waited on hold for over an hour only to have an operator tell her that a worker would have to call her back. Three days had passed before someone returned her call. She wondered what had happened to the child in the meantime.

She left her name and number and hung up.

Victoria couldn't imagine how it would feel to know your child was being abused. She knew it was a difficult choice for Benally to tell her about the abuse, knowing that her children could be put in foster care. Many kids got abused in foster care and some kids were even put up for adoption if their parents were in prison. Victoria had heard of several instances where the mother had somehow been talked out of, or accidentally signed away, her parental rights, and her children were put up for adoption. Victoria found that counseling those women was almost unbearable.

"What now?" Ms. Benally asked, looking intently at Victoria and wiping her nose and the mascara that ran down her face.

Victoria exhaled and leaned back in her chair. "You can go. They'll call back."

Ms. Benally hesitated at the door. "Will everything be okay?"

Victoria looked at Benally for a moment before speaking. She wanted to choose her words carefully to keep the woman from panicking. "Most of the time, CPS doesn't call you back. They just do an investigation. Honestly, you'll probably know more just by calling home."

"My family won't know it was me, will they?" Tears fell from her brown eyes.

Victoria shrugged her shoulders. "It's supposed to be confidential."

"Nothing on the Rez is confidential!" Benally said and walked out.

Victoria picked up the phone again and dialed.

"JP Morgan Chase and Company, Devin Thomas speaking." His voice was comforting.

"Hi, honey, it's me."

"What's up?"

"Oh, just a hard couple of sessions."

"I know all about hard," he said, seductively.

Victoria wrapped the phone cord around her finger. She wanted to play back but when she looked out the window and glimpsed Benally waiting in line to go to the Dining Hall with the other inmates, she just couldn't.

"It's really stressful here!"

"Quit, come work downtown. You could work with a whole different kind of criminal," Devin laughed.

"I want you to see where I work," she told him.

He laughed. "I can imagine what a prison looks like?"

"They decorated for Christmas. They're so creative. The women made pastoral snow scenes and snowmen out of maxi-pads. You've got to come see it."

"You're not selling me on this. I've worked hard not to be in prison," he said.

Victoria huffed. "I'm not saying I want you to go to prison."

"That's exactly what you said. Baby, I've gotta get back to work now if you want me to be able to meet you for dinner."

Victoria hung up the phone feeling frustrated with her husband. He didn't seem to understand or respect her work. She decided to phone Captain Brown to get permission to bring Devin in for a tour after she finished charting notes.

Chapter 22

THE ALARM CLOCK buzzed her awake at 5:00 AM. She reached over and turned it off. "Get up, Devin, you promised."

"I didn't promise anything," he said, rolling over and pulling the covers over his head.

Victoria pulled them off of him. "I'll buy you a latte."

"You're crazy if you think that's going to work on me."

She straddled him. "Please, you said you'd come."

"Well, if that's what you have in mind, then yes, I'm sure I..."

"That's not what I meant," she said, playfully smacking his thigh.

He twisted his body until he was on top and pinned her hands. "This means you have to go with me to a Cardinals game."

"Deal," she said, "now get off of me, I can't be late."

"You look good in that suit," Victoria said, admiring her husband as they exited the sallyport. He was dressed in a brown suit with a rust-colored tie. "The inmates are going to love you."

He pursed his lips. "I'm glad you work in a women's prison."

They walked across the yard towards her office.

"This is the pen? Looks more like a college campus than a …." Before Devin could finish his sentence, they were greeted with whistles and catcalls.

"And that's for you, Devin."

"I think I may be scarred from this experience."

As they approached the housing unit Victoria noticed several inmates in a circle hovering around another inmate who was wheezing. She was turning blue.

"Wait here." Victoria sprinted towards the medical building leaving Devin with the half-dozen women hovering around an inmate making a high-pitched squeal as she tried to catch her breath.

Moments later, PA Maxwell barreled down the sidewalk in the motorized medical cart. "We've got to get her to the treatment room. Help me lift her."

PA Maxwell, with the help of Devin and Victoria, lifted the inmate on to the medical vehicle. PA Maxwell fastened a strap across the inmate's chest and buckled it in and then drove towards the medical building.

Devin wiped the sweat from his brow. "I see why you work here, you're an adrenaline junkie."

"Interesting diagnosis, Freud. Let me show you the magic of Christmas in prison and then I'll set you free."

He shook his head. "For someone who prides herself in being culturally sensitive."

Chapter 23

KAREN HANDED BONNIE a stack of holiday cards. "Chaplain Edwards wants us to sort these."

Bonnie made a pile of Christmas cards and another pile of New Years' cards. Then she came across some Hanukah cards.

"Why do Jews get so many fucking special cards? It's not like there's ten in the whole fucking joint. Always got some big shot lawyer. "

Karen laughed and shook her head. "Maldonado, you crack me up."

Bonnie had never known any Jews personally. Tim was the one who told her how Jews ran Hollywood and he taught her how to identify them.

"Billy Crystal, Barbara Streisand, Barry Manilow, Neil Diamond, Paul Simon, Bob Dylan-all Jewish scum!"

"How can you tell, Tim?"

"Look at their skin. They ain't white, they're like green or some shit. They have them big noses. Also their names; Goldblatt, Goldstein, Feinstein, Finklestein, anything with a gold or stein is a sign they're Jews."

"I thought Neil Diamond and Billy Crystal were Italian. They look Italian."

"They ain't Italian! They're Jews," Tim insisted.

"They don't have those names." Bonnie had argued with him.

"Look stupid, those are their stage names. You can tell they're Jews because they changed their names to something representing money. They're obsessed with money. Besides that, Wops don't look anything like Kikes. Look at Fonzi and then at Billy Crystal. Italians are better looking." Tim had shook his head at how stupid she was.

Bonnie had almost finished sorting the pile of holiday cards when she inadvertently bumped the rickety bookshelf she was using to sort the cards on. The cards cascaded to the floor.

"Shit!" Bonnie slammed the shelf with her hand. "I'm going outside for a smoke."

Karen got up from her desk. "Hey bitch, don't think you're leaving me here to clean up your miss." Karen moved her head side to side and pointed her finger at Bonnie. Then she busted out laughing. "Wait for me, I need a smoke too."

Bonnie and Karen walked outside to smoke.

"Why don't they get the Prison Industry Corp to make us some new book shelves? This one's a piece of junk." Bonnie took a toke off her cigarette.

"That slave labor ain't for our needs. All that furniture goes to other businesses." Karen replied bitterly. "Oh shit, someone's having a bad day," she said and pointed her finger.

Bonnie looked across the compound and saw what Karen was referring to. An inmate was being put on the medical cart. She looked closer. Dr. Thomas, P.A. Maxwell, and some black guy she didn't recognize were lifting an inmate onto the medical cart.

"Yeah, that is a bad day," Bonnie said. "Let's get back to work."

Karen gave her a funny look. "Okay, Boss."

Bonnie flicked her cigarette on the ground and got up from the bench.

Chapter 24

BONNIE SAT ACROSS from Dr. Thomas. She'd shown up for the call-out even though she felt unsure of where this was going. "Was that the new shrink?" She asked.

Dr. Thomas seemed confused by her question. "Who?"

"The black guy you were walking with."

Dr. Thomas laughed. "No, that was my husband."

"Your husband?" Bonnie stared at Dr. Thomas and shifted uncomfortably in her chair. "My boyfriend Tim, he …." She stopped herself from telling Dr. Thomas what Tim thought of white women with black dudes or white men with black women.

"Tim seems to be on your mind a lot."

"Yeah, he had a lot of opinions about things. He was older than me, so I listened to what he had to say."

"What about now?" Dr. Thomas leaned in towards her.

Bonnie looked down at her scuffed black boots. She felt uncomfortable when Dr. Thomas moved closer and uncomfortable about her new knowledge of Dr. Thomas's love life, but at the same time, she didn't want to leave. "I'm figuring things out for myself. It's just that I've never talked to anyone about what I feel. No one has really cared that much about me."

"No one at all?" Dr. Thomas was trying to make eye contact again. It was kind of annoying. She tried to look past her.

"Maybe my brother did, but... There was one person." Bonnie hesitated.

"Who was that?"

"Truthfully?" Bonnie lifted her gaze from the floor and met Dr. Thomas's eyes and took a deep breath. "I had this old lady back in State."

"You had a girlfriend?"

Bonnie sat up defensively. "Like you're in any position to judge me."

"I'm not judging you. Tell me about her?"

Bonnie bit on her thumbnail. "Cheryl and me were together most of my time in State. She'd done ten when I met her, but she was down for twenty for second degree murder."

"Who'd she kill?"

"Her old man. He was sneaking around with someone and she wanted to scare him, but when she saw him in bed with her sister she shot him."

Dr. Thomas's eyes widened. "Were you ever concerned that she might hurt you?"

"Cheryl hurt me?" Bonnie laughed. "She had a temper, might throw something at me, but she loved me too much to really hurt me."

"Were you with women on the outside?"

Bonnie tried to read Dr. Thomas's face, but couldn't. "No, the perks of being with Cheryl was easy dope. Her sister felt so guilty, she'd sneak it in for Cheryl."

Dr. Thomas took a sip of her coffee. "Do you keep in touch?"

"I never made her any promises and she didn't expect anything from me." Bonnie wiped her nose with the back of her hand. "Cheryl was more like a mother than a lover, always nagging me to 'make something of myself.' I even took the GED to get her off my ass. I scored in the top 90th percentile at the prison."

"That's fantastic." Dr. Thomas smiled. "It sounds like she was a really positive influence in your life."

"She's the one who made me get a job at the prison's carpentry and contstruction shop. Told me I needed to learn some skills. I told her I had 'mad skills. I can hotwire and shoplift, and I'm great at breaking and entering.'"

Dr. Thomas glanced at the clock. "We're going to have to stop for today, Ms. Maldonado."

Bonnie reluctantly got up from the chair. "Hard to believe that was an hour," she said.

"It wasn't. I have to go take care of some paperwork so I can't do a full session with you today. Sorry. I'd like to see you one more time this week and then I'll be on vacation for two weeks."

"Lucky you," Bonnie said and walked out.

That night as she lay in her bunk she thought about Cheryl. Even though she'd made it with Cheryl a few times, it wasn't really her thing.

Bonnie hadn't been hot on the idea of working for maintenance, but she imagined she might learn something to help her pull off her crimes even better. So for the last five years of her sentence at the Oregon Women's Correctional Center she worked for Mr. Stanislaus. He supervised the prison plumbing, construction, and electrical work. Stanislaus, or Mr. S as they called him, was in his fifties, with shaggy, graying brown hair, a mustache, a large protruding stomach, and callused hands.

Mr. S was serious about his job and teaching the inmates self-sufficiency. He taught her to solder, use the square, and create a smooth cut using a piece of tape on the board so that it didn't splinter around the cut. Skills none of the other women seemed interested in learning. Even when she made costly mistakes that he had to explain to his boss Mr. S never raised his voice to her.

One afternoon on a smoke break as she was fumbling with a match to light her cigarette, he sat down next to her and lit it for her with his lighter. "Maldonado, you're a real hard worker. You seem bright. What the hell are you doing in a place like this?"

His closeness made her uneasy and she scooted to the left of the bench. "Guess I'm not that bright. I got caught didn't I?"

"You're going home soon aren't ya?" he asked, taking a drag off of his cigarette.

"Yeah, in November," she said, exhaling and making smoke rings with each puff.

"You're well-versed in plumbing, electrical maintenance, construction, and drywall you could earn a really good living. Any contractor would be lucky to have you as an apprentice." He smiled at her.

"And my old man said I'd never amount to anything," she said, tossing her cigarette butt on the ground.

Mr. S shook his head and crushed out his cigarette on his work boot. "Best get back to work."

That was the last conversation she'd had with him.

"Didn't you hear?" One of the women on the crew asked her when she showed up for work call the next day.

"Hear what?" she asked, rolling her eyes at the prison romance drama she had expected to hear.

"Mr. S had a heart attack and is in critical. They don't know if he's gonna pull through."

"What?" she gasped, trying to steady herself. She hurried inside the shop building.

"What's your name, inmate?" Bill Kovach, a white guy in his forties with a military haircut and no facial hair, glared at her.

"Maldonado," she said.

"Maldonado, you're five minutes late. I'm docking your first hour of pay."

"But I was..." she defended.

"You wanna spend the next month in seg?" His lip curled as he spoke. "I'm taking over Mr. S's crew until he gets back. Hit the yard inmates you're going to do weed removal today."

The next morning they learned Mr. S had died. Kovach was pulled from head foreman at the men's pen and was now assigned to OWCC. He was pissed. She overheard him tell another staff member that there was only one use for women and that "these women weren't good for that either."

She went to check out some tools like always. He made a beeline in her direction.

"Don't think you're running anything here, Maldonado. You will set down those tools and wait until I tell you what to do. You understand me, inmate?"

"But I've always..."

"Times change. You're not Stanislaus's girl no more. Go over to the classrooms. There's some wall-patching that needs to be done."

"Wall-patching?"

"You being insolent with me, Maldonado? Are you refusing an order?" The veins in his forehead bulged.

She felt the adrenaline rise in her body. "No, sir," she said.

"Then go get a putty knife and some putty and go to the Education Building. Do not pass go. Do not stop to collect $200. Go. NOW!"

She was more than happy to put some distance between her and Kovach and was surprised when he'd shown up twenty minutes later.

"Come help me inspect the electrical wiring in the closet. I heard it was faulty," he said, and ushered her into the closet.

She examined the wiring. "I don't see anything wrong."

He gave her an angry stare. "You think you know shit about electrical?"

"Yeah, I do. Mr. S told me I would make a good apprentice. I think he said journeyman," she said proudly.

"Stanislaus told you that you could become a journeyman?" He laughed.

Bonnie glared at him. "We talked about me doing apprentice work under somebody else's license."

Kovach laughed harder. "No one's gonna hire a female as an apprentice, let alone a contractor. Even in 1988, no one's gonna hire a broad for a man's job. Stanislaus probably just had the hots for you."

"Fuck you," she said.

Kovack smiled. "You're a feisty one." He stepped closer to her. "You spend too much time with the wrong kinds of tools in your hand. I got a tool you haven't used yet. I bet you don't even know how to use it, but I can show you. It's a power tool!" Kovach grabbed his crotch.

Bonnie pushed him. He grabbed her. She broke free and ran to the fire alarm, yanking it down.

Kovach's face went white. "You stupid bitch! Why'd you do that?"

"You better think of a reason asshole or I'll tell them the truth."

Several officers and a sergeant burst into the Education Building.

"Where's the fire?" the muscular, blond, sergeant asked, trying to catch his breath.

A bearded officer wiped the sweat from his forehead. "You okay, Kovach?"

Kovach forced a chuckle and shook his head. "Sorry, boys. No fire. I'm fine. You know how these hysterical females are. Saw some sparks when I was rewiring this panel, freaked out and pulled the alarm. Wish I could get my crew from the Pen to come in and help me take care of business. This is bullshit."

They sympathized with him.

Bonnie walked away feeling victorious, yet Kovach's venomous words seeped deep into her thoughts. *Maybe Mr. S had just been saying those things to be nice to me. Maybe he did want something, but what? He never even told sexual jokes. Maybe Kovach's right! Mr. S worked in the prison system most of his life, how would he know if I could get a job on the outs?*

Chapter 25

VICTORIA MADE HER way towards the Psychology Building. Officer Hamilton waved her down. She stopped and waited for him.

"Dr. Thomas how you doin'?"

"I'm good Mr. Hamilton, how are you?"

Hamilton smiled, "Great. Hey, you comin' to the Christmas party?"

"No, not this time."

He shook his head. "That's too bad."

"It's the same night as my husband's holiday party," she lied.

He leaned in towards her. "Yeah, I heard you like chocolate."

Victoria was stunned. "Only the good kind," she quipped. "And now if you'll excuse me, I have a job to do."

Hamilton's comment distracted her as she sat in her women's transitions therapy group. She ran two therapy groups a week. The transitions group was for women dealing with depression and anxiety from being incarcerated and the other was the trauma group. She saw about thirty women in group sessions and another ten individually. It was only a drop in the bucket of the inmates who needed therapy.

There were 1,500 female inmates at the prison, all of whom could benefit from some self-reflection. Of the women who sought treatment, most shared three things in common: abuse, low self-esteem, and substance abuse. But, since it was only she and Scarsdale, there were long waiting lists and most of the inmates were released before getting services.

After the group ended she rushed back to her office. She wanted to call Francis before her next session, but inmate Red Hawk, a stocky, Lakota woman in her late twenties, stood in front of her door. The call to Francis would have to wait.

"Good morning, Ms. Red Hawk."

Red Hawk nodded. She had shorn her long black hair since their last session. Like Maldonado, Red Hawk was abused as a child, struggled with addiction and suffered from low self-esteem. Unlike Maldonado, she was covered in tattoos. She had an elaborate buffalo skull with eagle feathers tattooed on her arm and the names of two men and several women on her forearms and neck.

"My mother died," Red Hawk said, staring at the floor.

"I'm so sorry," Victoria said. "That explains why you cut your hair."

Red Hawk set a large manila envelope on Victoria's desk. "Can you take this to the Native American Health Center so that one of the elders can burn it for my mother?"

Victoria knew that Red Hawk's black locks were in the envelope. She had become familiar with the Lakota traditional way of grieving from working with several Indian inmates.

"Ms. Red Hawk, I'd like to help you, but I'm concerned that someone might not understand and may view this as a favor."

Victoria wanted to honor Red Hawk's request, but it would jeopardize her job. Favoritism was considered a 'slippery slope' in the prison system. Inmates often set up staff by playing on their sympathies and making requests to test them and see if they would break or bend the rules for them. Once they did, they would pressure the staff into doing something more serious by threatening to reveal what breeches of security they had already engaged in.

Victoria did not want to be on the other end of an FBI investigation and get walked off the job for doing inmates special favors. A handful of her co-workers, male and female, had already been fired for bringing inmates everything from perfume and makeup to alcohol and drugs, because they felt sorry for the inmates or wanted to make some "easy money."

A year ago, everyone was talking about the dirty dozen—twelve staff members at a federal prison in New York who were fired for bringing notorious Mafioso inmates pasta, wine, and cigars.

Victoria remembered that Red Hawk worked in Maintenance and suddenly wondered if Russell had put her up to this. *Anyone is vulnerable*, she thought. "I'm sorry, Ms. Red Hawk, that's not within my job description."

"You say you want to help us, but then you don't." Red Hawk crossed her arms.

"I'm sorry, Ms. Red Hawk, I've got to follow the rules."

"Whatever, I'm just going to burn it in the fire pit at the next sweat lodge ceremony. Creator knows how long it's going to take until we have another sweat around here!" Red Hawk picked the envelope up off of Victoria's desk.

"That sounds like a viable alternative," Victoria said, noting that Red Hawk looked more severe without her hair, which had softened her hardness.

Red Hawk stared at her shoes. "I can't believe she's gone. I want to stay on the Red Road, but this is the fifth relative I've lost this year and I'm sick of my nasty roommates and that god-damned Chaplain who could give a shit about us Indians. I want to beat the fuck out of some of these people."

Victoria listened as Red Hawk spoke of feeling like she had no control over her life or her anger. Red Hawk's grieving always started out appropriate in their sessions, but then dissolved into blaming others for her problems, specifically her parents, her girlfriend, the cops, and the *Waisicu-* white man. She was also extremely harsh on herself, calling herself names and saying how "fucking stupid" she was. Red Hawk's self-loathing made her dangerous; self-loathing plus alcohol equaled uncontrollable rage.

When Red Hawk drank the rage searched for a canvass to express itself on. This rage was the reason Red Hawk was in prison now for aggravated manslaughter. In their third session, Red Hawk told Victoria she was at a party and got in a fight with her girlfriend's cousin. What she left out, but what Victoria read in her pre-sentence investigation report, was that she had stabbed him sixteen times. Her charges were dropped from murder to manslaughter because the cousin was also drunk, had a history of assault, and had started the fight.

Victoria had mixed emotions about Red Hawk. On one hand she saw how much Red Hawk struggled with a desire to improve herself, to practice the traditional ways of her culture and embrace the spiritual path that could save her. She empathized with Red Hawk and the legacy of racism, poverty, violence, and alcohol abuse that she grew up with. But on the other, Red Hawk was consumed with hatred and rage, full of ego, terrified at letting her guard down, terrified of getting hurt again. Even behind bars, Red Hawk had struggled with trying to stay sober. She would drink hooch—a homemade alcohol made from rotten fruit and yeast—to numb the pain. Victoria wished she could do more to help her, but Red Hawk's hatred and frustration was easily directed at her and the kind of therapy she needed would take more years than her prison sentence. Despite the violent nature of her crime, she would be out before her 30th birthday, and likely back on the reservation.

Victoria looked up and saw Bonnie Maldonado standing outside the room.

She turned to Red Hawk. "We're gonna need to stop for today, Ms. Red Hawk. Please take care of yourself and again, I'm sorry about your mother's death."

Red Hawk got up from the chair and walked out with the envelope.

Victoria watched Maldonado size up Red Hawk as she left. Then she entered the office, took off her jacket and draped it on the back of the chair behind her and sat down.

"How are you?" Victoria asked, relieved that Maldonado had showed for her session. She still worried that Maldonado would change her mind and stop coming.

"I was thinking a lot about the time I did in State and about Cheryl, my ex I was telling you about last week."

"Yes, I remember." Victoria nodded, pleased that Maldonado was ready to jump back in without prompting.

"There was this work supervisor dude who kept telling I could make something of myself. I didn't believe him. My dad was always telling me how fucking stupid I was." Maldonado started to chew on her nails. "Told me I'd probably end up in prison. Well, fuck, here I am."

Victoria noted Maldonado's oral fixation.

"What was your first charge?" she asked, taking a sip from her coffee cup.

Maldonado's leg began to shake again. Victoria noted that Maldonado's leg shook any time she didn't want to answer a question.

"Armed robbery."

"How long?"

"Eight years. "

"Was that the 7-11?"

Maldonado nodded and wiped her nose with the back of her hand. "Don't really want to talk about it."

Victoria held Maldonado's eye contact without blinking—a strategy that made the inmates take her more seriously. "Sometimes what you don't want to do is what you need to do most. What's the story?"

Maldonado smacked her hand down hard on her leg apparently to stop the shaking. "I was fucked up over Tim's death and nursing a $100 day habit."

"Habit?"

"Heroin. I needed money and I needed to help Danny."

"Why did your brother need your help?"

"He was on disability from Vietnam. He fucked up big time—friendly fire thing. Came home a cripple with a dishonorable discharge. My father shunned him, wouldn't let him come home. He only went to prove something to that asshole."

Victoria shook her head. "That's very sad."

"If my dad hadn't been such a dick, my brother never would have gone to Vietnam in the first place, trying to prove something to him."

Victoria pictured Maldonado's father like the fathers of many of the other female inmates she'd worked with—authoritarian, rigid, hostile, perfectionists, many former military officers or preachers. "Your father sounds like a very brutal man."

Maldonado cocked an eyebrow. "You don't know the half of it! Anyways, Danny ended up in this assisted living joint. They took his SSD and vet checks, gave him a shitty little room and three meals a day. Sound familiar?"

Victoria nodded, acknowledging Maldonado's reference to prison life.

"My brother wanted a TV for his room."

"Why did you feel like you had to buy it for him?"

Victoria wondered if Maldonado's mother blaming her for her older sister's death led her to take on the blame of her brother's disability.

Maldonado's eyes watered. "He was my brother!" she said indignantly.

Victoria looked out the window and saw several officers running across the prison yard. *Oh great, not now!* "I'm sorry, Ms. Maldonado, there seems to be an emergency."

Maldonado turned and looked out the window.

"I'm going to have to ask you to wait outside." Victoria ushered Maldonado out of her office and raced across the hall to Brad's office.

"What's happening?" Victoria asked. She could feel the adrenaline rising in her body. "I just saw several staff running across the compound."

Shaw was listening to a radio transmission and bolted up from his desk. "They had a body alarm in the dining hall. Let's go." Brad locked his office door.

Victoria walked briskly down the hall to where Maldonado sat waiting for her. "Ms. Maldonado, come back in an hour and we can finish our session."

Maldonado got up and walked out.

"Ready to rock and roll?" Brad asked, coming up behind her.

Victoria locked the entrance to the Psychology building.

Inmates jeered as she and Counselor Shaw sprinted past them towards the Dining Hall. Her keys jingled loudly as they bounced against her hip. Lieutenant Williams was holding the door open to the Dining Hall as several staff bustled inside. Victoria followed the other staff into a back room in the Food Services area.

Napuna and Tracy were cuffing a tall white inmate with long strawberry blonde hair and a black homemade four-leaf clover tattoo on her arm.

"Stand down," Officer Jones commanded into her radio.

"What happened?" Victoria asked, out of breath.

In the corner of the room one of the Filipina physician's assistants hovered over a Mexican inmate doing something to her face. The Mexican inmate screamed, *"Dios mio, por favor Señor,"* as the PA examined her.

Jones shook her head. "Apparently this Spanish lady snitched on the other one who was sneaking food out of the kitchen and she decided to teach her a lesson by throwing boiling water on her. She probably would've gotten away with it too, but Foreman Enriquez was just coming out of the store room and saw it go down."

Victoria peered at the young woman, her face was blistering from the scalding water. Victoria felt sick to her stomach.

Chapter 26

BONNIE RETURNED TO the Psych Building, but the door was locked so she sat down on a bench outside to wait for Dr. Thomas. She remembered the night she'd come home from the bar and sat down on the tattered brown couch in her one bedroom apartment to count her tips. She still needed $150 more to buy her brother the TV. There was no way she could earn that kind of money before Christmas.

She turned on the radio and lit a cigarette. A Joni Mitchell song played. She new the words and sang along.

"*Up in the sterilized room where they let you be lazy. Knowing your attitude's all wrong you gotta change and that's not easy.*" She took another drag from her cigarette and went back to singing, "*Advice and religion you can't take it, you can't seem to believe it.*"

She burned holes in the coffee table. "Fuck, what am I going to do?" she yelled.

"*So why does it come as such a shock to know you really have no one, only a river of changing faces looking for an ocean...*"

She bolted up from the couch, went into the bedroom and pulled the black stainless steel Smith and Wesson 686P out of the top dresser drawer where she kept it hidden under her bras and underwear. Then she sat back down on the couch and fingered the trigger. It was Tim's favorite gun, a double action revolver with a .357 Magnum Cartridge.

Mike, the clerk at the 7-11 on Glisan, was always flirting with her. He gave her free Big Gulps and sold her Camels for the price of generics. The other day, he'd unknowingly tipped off the location of the safe. She wasn't even stalking the place. It was just second nature after being with Tim.

An hour later, she sat outside the 7-11 in Tim's bruised white Impala. This wasn't the store where Mike worked, but she figured they were all the same—Slurpee machines, stale hot dogs rotating on the rotisserie, and safes full of money.

As soon as the store was empty, she grabbed the loaded gun from underneath the seat. The cold air startled her awake to what she was doing. It was too late to turn around. Dressed in an over-sized wool, hunting jacket and a stocking cap with the eyes cut out, her hair tucked under the cap, she entered the store and pointed the gun at the clerk. It seemed to have magical powers, moving the woman backwards towards the office where they kept the safe. The cold steel in her hand was like a magic wand, she loved the power it gave her. The trembling woman begged, "Please don't hurt me."

"Hurry the fuck up!" Bonnie told her.

The woman fumbled nervously with the combination lock, going too far right then too far left. The woman was crying now. Her fear made Bonnie angry. She wanted to kill the woman to make her own fear go away.

She tried to tune out the woman's crying and focused on the sound of the twisting knobs of the safe. It clicked open. Relieved, she holstered her weapon in the back of her pants and began stuffing money into a bag.

She hadn't noticed the squad car pull up or the cop who entered silently and crept past the brightly colored packages of candy and bubble gum, past the churning Slurpee machine. She hadn't heard anything until he yelled out, "Freeze!"

Bonnie thought about going for her gun.

"Freeze!" the cop yelled again, "or, I'll blow you away."

Bonnie froze then slowly put her hands in the air. The officer yanked the ski mask from her head. Bonnie's long brown hair fell around her shoulders.

"What the hell?" He shook his head in disbelief as he walked her out to the squad car.

She didn't like being in the back of the squad car. The car smelled like body odor and the seats were greasy. Her hands were cuffed tight behind her, the metal cut into her skin. "These cuffs are too fucking tight," she yelled and kicked the back of the seat as they drove downtown. She knew she was fucked. She knew this time, she was gonna do hard time.

"Do you have anything to say to your victim or in your defense, Miss Maldonado?" the gray-haired, overweight judge, asked sternly. Bonnie could tell he wanted her to show remorse for her crime; most judges hated to sentence women.

"Yeah, your honor, I do." Bonnie knew if she told him a good sob story he'd get to play the hero and go light on her. The thought disgusted her. "I'm sorry," she said and gave him her most defiant look, "that I got caught."

The 7-11 clerk, a petite, red head dressed in a pink sweater and a pair of black pants, burst into tears. The woman's family tried to comfort her. They glared at Bonnie. Her public defender smacked his head with his hand.

The judge bellowed out her sentence, "Miss Bonnie Maldonado, I sentence you to ten years at the Oregon Women's Correctional Center. Next case!" He racked the gavel down so hard that the head of the mallet broke off the stick.

"Sorry for the interruption, Ms. Maldonado," Dr. Thomas apologized.

"Shit happens," Bonnie said and followed Dr. Thomas to her office. Dr. Thomas sat at her desk and Bonnie sat across from her.

"So you were saying you felt guilty you weren't able to keep your brother from enlisting. Did you really believe the TV would make things better?"

"Fuck, yeah."

"So you robbed a 7-11 to get the money?" Dr. Thomas looked at her and waited.

"I just wanted Danny to have a better life. My old man was always picking on him. One time my brother came home from school with a black eye. We were eating dinner and my dad started calling him a 'pussy.' My mom didn't say shit. She got up from the table, filled a glass of water from the tap, took a handful of pills, and went to the bedroom to watch TV. My dad picked up my plate and threw it against the wall. 'We're done eating,' he yelled. 'Get in the garage now!'"

Bonnie looked to see if Dr. Thomas was reacting to anything she said. She seemed to be listening, but didn't say anything, so Bonnie continued. "It was October. The garage was cold. He dug through a box of athletic equipment and pulled out two pairs of boxing gloves."

Dr. Thomas nodded. "Then what happened?"

"He yelled at us, told us to put on the gloves. He said 'since you like being beat up I'm gonna let your sister have some fun with you.'"

Bonnie suddenly felt the urge to crack her knuckles. She brought her hands together and popped the pinkie and ring finger of her right hand.

"I told him, 'I ain't fightin' Danny.' He said 'well then, you have two choices. You can fight your brother or I can beat the crap out of both of you. Decide.'"

Dr. Thomas ran her fingers through her hair, brushing a lock behind her ear. "How old were you?"

"Nine. Danny was thirteen, small for his age and sensitive. I was the tougher one. I thought I could fake fight my brother, because my dad's beating would be worse. Felt like he was trying to get us to do his dirty work for him."

She remembered how defeated her brother looked with that black eye. "I'll fight him," she'd yelled, but it was code for "Fuck you."

Dr. Thomas cleared her throat.

Bonnie looked at Dr. Thomas. She couldn't get a read. "He did this bullshit announcer thing. 'In this corner the biggest sissy boy north of San Francisco. And in the other corner, tonight's surefire win, Bonnie the bulldagger.'"

"He said that?" Dr. Thomas shook her head.

"Yeah, I told you he was an asshole."

"That's child abuse."

"That was his version of discipline and entertainment." Bonnie leaned back and crossed her arms tight around her chest remembering that night. The boxing had started slowly—right hook, left jab, block, more choreographed at first, but then it changed. Upper cut, stronger right hook, straight punch to the face. She had to do more to block. She had to dance faster. Her brother's blows were coming in harder. Her father had gotten to him. She didn't want to hit Danny. If she fought like she was capable of, her father would walk away the winner and her and Danny the losers. She wasn't having that.

Then she felt the sting of the glove on her right cheek. Her brother had a different look in his eye, like someone else had taken over his body. "Don't let him do that to you, Bonnie." Her dad had yelled out. "Pretend you're swinging at me. Come on tough girl."

Bonnie imagined punching and kicking the sheer fucking meanness out of her father, robbing him of his last mean-spirited breath. She imagined being at his funeral, holding her mother's arm, and standing next to Danny, relieved he was dead.

"Seemed like we were boxing forever. My brother's nose was bleeding and my right cheek was all scraped up. Man, it stung from the sweat." She didn't tell Dr. Thomas how the tears had stung too.

Dr. Thomas nodded again, but said nothing.

Bonnie continued. "My old man was yelling at us, 'If you want to give up, fall to the ground. Which one of you is the bigger baby?' Neither of us was willing to wimp out, so we kept on fighting. It went on for an hour and a half. I remember vomiting on the garage floor, but that didn't stop my brother. He just kept on punching me."

Dr. Thomas's eyes seemed to widen, but she sat there motionless.

Bonnie remembered crying. She never cried, but it was too much. She threw punches at her brother, more violently, but his punches came faster, making contact with her face—right hook, left jab, right jab left hook, uppercut, roundhouse. She tried to block, but missed. There was no way to win. Defeated, she fell to the ground, skinning her knee on the cement floor.

"One, two, three out!" her father yelled, as she lay there bewildered by her brother's betrayal.

"My dad opened a beer for my brother after he kicked my ass and he told me with a shit-eating grin on his face, 'the people you love the most will hurt you the most. Don't ever let your guard down.'"

"Good God." Dr. Thomas shook her head back and forth. "That's awful."

"That's how he was," Bonnie said matter-of-factly. "My brother wanted to make my dad proud of him so when he was sixteen, he lied about his age, and signed up for the Army. He must've thought after he came back my father would finally be proud of him and treat him with respect. If he got killed, my father would see him as a hero."

"And when he came back?"

"I didn't think it was possible, but he actually hated him more after that."

Dr. Thomas cupped her chin in her hand. "I can see how you wanted to make a difference in your brother's life, but I don't understand why you would put yourself or anyone else in harm's way to make his life better?"

"I don't expect you to understand! You've obviously had an easy fucking life!"

Bonnie noticed Dr. Thomas glancing up at the clock on her bookshelf. "I get it, our time's up!" Bonnie barked and headed for the door.

"Ms. Maldonado, I'm gone over the holiday. I hope you have a good Christmas."

"Yeah right. Merry fucking Christmas to you too!" she yelled, slamming the door behind her.

Bonnie's hands still trembled with rage as she stood for the 4:00 o'clock count. She was pissed at herself for thinking that some well-to-do shrink cop who was fucking a black dude would ever understand her. *Why am I wasting my time?* She thought.

Chapter 27

VICTORIA FELT FOR Maldonado. Physical abuse was one thing, but vicious ongoing mental cruelty was another. She could see that Maldonado didn't have much of a choice. It had molded her character.

She took a deep breath and tried to regain her composure. In five minutes she would be meeting a new inmate. She picked up the psychiatric consult sheet: *Ramona Vasquez 35 y.o. divorced Hispanic female with three children. Reports history of depression, suicide attempts, and violent outbursts. Please provide counseling to assist with adjustment to prison.*

Victoria got up and walked to the waiting area where an attractive, Latina with long black hair, sat at the edge of a beige plastic chair staring at the ground.

"Ms. Vasquez?"

Vasquez looked up. "*Si.*"

Three tattooed dots formed a triangle above her left eyebrow and she had a tear drop tattooed under her right eye. The teardrop meant one of three things—she had done jail time, someone she loved had, or a loved one had been killed in a gang fight. She had no idea what the three dots meant.

"I'm Dr. Thomas, one of the psychologists here. Please come on back with me." Vasquez followed her to her office. Victoria motioned to her to sit down. "I'd like to ask you a few questions."

Victoria imagined Vasquez was good looking in her youth, but now she looked weathered by hard living. She had a scar on her forehead and a half dozen scarred over razor cuts on her left wrist.

"Where are you from, Ms. Vasquez?"

"New Mexico," Vasquez said, picking at her cuticles. "I need to paint these."

"What part?" Victoria asked and jotted down observations of Vasquez's behavior.

"Bum fuuucck."

"Never been, but I hear it's beautiful there." Victoria smiled. "It says here you have three kids."

"I don't have them. My mother has them in Las Cruces."

"So, what brings you here?"

"The marshals."

Victoria tried not to roll her eyes. Vasquez was giving her a run for her money. "What is your sentence?"

Vasquez pulled her long black hair out of her face and into a ponytail that dissipated when she let it go and smiled. "PWID Heroin."

"How long is your sentence?"

"Seven years, but I already served two in county and I'm gonna get a year off for taking the drug program. So, with good time and a six-month halfway house I figure I'll be out in three."

Victoria tapped her pen on the arm of her office chair. "Sounds like you've been thinking about this a lot."

"I told my youngest boy I'd be home before he's ten." Vasquez sniffled and wiped her nose on her sleeve. "He was five when I left."

"Kleenex?" Victoria picked up box of tissues on her desk.

"I'm fine."

"Tell me about your tattoo."

"It's for my brother. He was killed by some wanna-be *Eme*."

"Actually," Victoria said, pointing her pen at the three bluish-black dots above Vasquez's left eye, "I was wondering about the dots."

Vasquez smiled. "*La Vida Loca!* It means my crazy life."

Victoria wondered what kinds of tattoos psychologists would have if they were the types to tattoo symbols on their bodies, which generally, they weren't. Freudians might have cigars or silhouettes of Sigmund Freud. Jungians yin-yang symbols or intricate mandalas, which she thought would be cool. Family therapists might have elaborate tattoos of genograms on their backs depicting their family trees and their family pathology, wavy lines for conflict, double lines for enmeshment. She got stumped when trying to imagine what kinds of tattoos cognitive-behavioral therapists might have.

"How was your life crazy?" she asked Vasquez who continued to look disapprovingly at her chipped fingernail polish.

"How wasn't it?" Vasquez countered wryly.

"I'm assuming you also used drugs."

Ms. Vasquez pulled up her shirtsleeves to show Victoria her track marks.

Victoria wanted to gasp when she looked at Vasquez's frail arms covered in bluish-black carbon marks, but she held in her reaction. "How long have you been shooting up?"

"Since I was fourteen." Vasquez played with her hair again.

"Your boyfriend?" Victoria guessed. She had found that when a girl started using a drug like heroin at a young age it was almost always given to her by someone very close to her like a parent, lover, or a best friend.

"Yeah, he shot me up on my birthday. Totally hooked me then turned me out to pay for his habit."

"When was the last time you used drugs?" Victoria asked.

"Back in county, but I'm done with that. I'm taking the drug program and getting back to my kids."

Victoria read over the psych consult. "It says here you're depressed. You don't seem depressed."

Ms. Vasquez pulled out a cheap lipstick sold on the Commissary and began applying a dark shade of red to her lips. "I'm okay right now, but when I first got here I was a mess. The psych put me on some meds." She pursed her lips and rubbed them together then returned the lipstick to the breast pocket of her khaki prison shirt. "That's a nice sweater you're wearing. Is that wool or cashmere?" Vasquez asked.

"I'm not sure." Victoria was amused that Vasquez was so concerned with appearances.

"It looks like this cashmere sweater I have."

"Huh." Victoria paused and looked at Ms. Vasquez. "I don't have any more questions for you. Do you have any questions for me?"

"Are there any groups for women who've been abused?"

"Do you have a history of abuse?"

Vasquez seemed annoyed by the question. "I had a couple of bad experiences when I was tricking and my ex-old man used to knock me around."

"We're starting a domestic violence group in March."

"I have to wait two months?"

"You're lucky, usually you'd have to wait at least three months for one to start."

Vasquez stood up and extended her hand to Victoria. "Thank you, Doctor."

Without thinking Victoria shook her hand. Vasquez's hands were cold and small and she noticed more carbon marks and half-sketched blue-black tattoos on her arms.

"I hope this doesn't offend you," Vasquez said, looking at Victoria's hair. "Have you ever thought about blonde highlights? They'd look a lot better than red."

Victoria didn't know how to respond. "Okay, take care, Ms. Vasquez."

"Think about it. You'd look great!"

Victoria barely shut her door before bursting out laughing. She walked back to her desk and was going to start charting a note in Vasquez's file when the phone rang.

She picked it up.

"Hi, honey, I've got some bad news."

"What now?" Victoria asked, dropping her pen on the desk.

"Mama's in the hospital. They think she had a minor stroke. She's okay, but they want to keep her for observation tonight and someone needs to stay with her."

"I'm so sorry, Devin. What about your sister?"

"She has the kids and besides when they release her, Mama needs quiet. The kids wouldn't give her any peace. I'm driving down there after I drop you off at the airport."

"So, you're not going." Victoria ran her fingers through her hair. "Of course, you need to stay. Should I cancel my plans and stay too?"

"No, go have fun with your family. There's no reason to stay here." He said.

"Our President's Day weekend getaway is only six weeks away. I hope she's better by then."

"Yeah," he said, "me too. I gotta go, Vic. I'll see you tonight." He hung up.

Chapter 28

*B*ONNIE *G*RABBED THE *money from the teller and ran toward the door. Out of nowhere the man appeared. He lunged at her. A gun went off. The sound was deafening. She felt an explosion of warm fluid on her skin.*

Bonnie woke in a panic and lunged towards the toilet puking violently.

"What's wrong with you bunkie?"

Harris hung her head over the bunk. Bonnie could see her gold tooth reflecting off the light in the hallway. She flushed the toilet and got up from the floor. "I'm fine." She turned on the sink, rinsed out her mouth, and wiped her face on a towel.

"I think you need to see the PA."

"I don't need to see the PA. I had a fucking nightmare."

"You're acting like a nightmare. You make more commotion than all four of my kids having a nightmare together."

"I'm fucking sorry."

"You ain't sorry for shit, Maldonado."

"You got a smoke?"

Harris threw a cigarette at her. It fell on the floor.

Bonnie snatched the cigarette up, dusted it off and put it in her mouth. "Thanks."

"I'm going back to sleep. Keep your shit down."

Bonnie walked to the cell door and peered out the window. She wanted to make sure the officer wasn't on their side of the unit making rounds. The coast was clear.

She grabbed the paperclip from the top of her locker and stuck it into the electrical outlet, her hands still shaking. The spark lit up the cell. She inhaled deeply trying to catch the cigarette paper on fire and puffed several times until the cherry burned bright. Then she walked over to the toilet and sat down to smoke.

She heard the sound of the officer coming down the corridor and quickly threw the cigarette into the toilet bowl, yanking down on the lever.

She got back into bed angry and still too terrified to shut her eyes. She lay awake on her bunk until 5:00 AM when she got up and went to find Tennessee.

"Hey Slick, I fucking told you straight up. You junkies always come crawling back." Tennessee gave Bonnie a hard look.

Bonnie rubbed her forehead and stared at the ground. "Yeah, you're fucking psychic."

"Don't get sassy with me, Maldonado. I'm doing your punk ass a favor and I don't have a lot of patience right now with Melanie in the Hole. Here's a list of shit you're going to bring me first. I'm not taking any more chances with you. You refused my kindness when I offered you a hand up." Tennessee gave her a commissary list with more than a dozen items checked.

Bonnie stuffed it in her back pocket. "I'll be back."

"That's what I said." Tennessee laughed.

Bonnie bit the inside of her mouth drawing blood. She wanted to fuck Tennessee up, but she needed the dope.

Throughout the day the images kept coming into her mind. She tried to distract herself with work, but she couldn't shake them, nothing worked. They kept coming back.

After count she went to commissary and bought the stuff that Tennessee wanted. Then she slung the mesh bag filled with soda, chips, and a dozen other commissary items over her shoulder and snuck into the unit.

"Here's your stuff." Bonnie handed her the bag. "Now, where's mine?"

"Manners Maldonado, didn't your mom teach you nothing? Come in and shut the door." Tennessee took Bonnie into her cell. "Now pin for me."

Bonnie stood at the cell door and peered through the window to make sure no guards were around while Tennessee pulled a dime-sized bag out of her vagina. She wiped it on her khaki pants and gave it to Bonnie. Bonnie grimaced.

"Must feel rotten that you can't control your urges." Tennessee laughed.

"Fuck you," Bonnie said, taking the tiny bag of dope from Tennessee's palm.

"I thought I wasn't your type, Maldonado? Might take you up on that if they don't let Melanie out soon." Tennessee ran her fingers through Bonnie's hair.

Bonnie pulled away. "This is my type. You got a needle?"

"Fresh out."

"Shit!" Bonnie tucked the bag in her bra under her left breast.

"See ya soon." Tennessee smiled.

Bonnie went back to the unit, grateful to find her cell empty. She snorted the dope. It burned her nose, but she felt the high quickly. She lay down on her bed. Just as she started nodding out a noise startled her. Officer Berger opened the cell door.

"You're supposed to be at work, Maldonado. What are you still doing here?"

"I couldn't sleep last night," she lied. "What time is it?"

"It's after ten. Didn't you hear the chaplain paging for you?"

"No, gimme a minute." Bonnie got up. Her mouth was dry. She stuck her head under the sink to get a drink of water. Then she made an attempt to fix her hair.

"You don't need to primp for where you're going."

"What do you mean?"

"You're out of bounds. I'm taking you to SHU."

"But I told you, I overslept."

"Save it for the DHO. Now turn around and cuff up." Berger grabbed her wrists and cuffed her. "Let's go."

Berger walked her to the Lieutenant's Office and called Chaplain Edwards. "I got her here now," she said into the telephone. "I'm going to strip her out and take her to SHU. Oh, okay, yeah, I'll keep her here until you come." Berger hung up the phone.

"It's your lucky day, Maldonado." Berger removed the cuffs from her wrists. "Take a seat on the bench out there."

Chaplain Edwards rounded the corner to the Lieutenant's Office and stopped briefly at the bench. "Ms. Maldonado, I don't know what's going on with you, but we need your help today cleaning the sanctuary. Let's go."

Bonnie got up and followed Chaplain Edwards to the Chapel.

"Please try to be on time in the future," he said, and walked into his office and shut the door.

Bonnie was shocked he'd gone to bat for her. She wondered if Dr. Thomas would have gone that far to help her. Even if she would have, she didn't give a shit right now. She was pissed at Dr. Thomas and hoped her Christmas vacation sucked.

Chapter 29

VICTORIA WAS NOT thrilled about going back to the prison after two weeks away from Devin and she felt like she needed a vacation after her vacation with her family. She decided to take the morning off and only do a half-day on her first day back.

She greeted the clerk as she walked to her office. "Good afternoon, Ms. Garcia."

"Good afternoon, Dr. Thomas. Did you have a nice Christmas?"

Victoria didn't want to explain that she didn't celebrate Christmas. "Yes. How about you?"

"I got to call home and talk to my girls. It was really nice. They sent me these pictures." Ms. Garcia held out photos of her daughters.

"They're adorable," Victoria said, leafing through the photos of the children.

Ms. Garcia spoke quietly, "Dr. Thomas, did you hear about Officer Hamilton, you know the one they call Dark and Lovely."

"No, I didn't even know they called Hamilton Dark and Lovely."

"They walked him off the compound the day after Christmas. They say he was bringing in drugs."

Victoria shook her head and unlocked her office. Once inside, she dialed Francis. Her answering machine picked up. "Call me when you get in," she said, and hung up.

Ms. Garcia knocked on her door. "Ms. Maldonado's here for her session."

Maldonado looked more disheveled than usual—her hair hadn't been brushed, her bangs hung in her face almost hiding her eyes, and her face was full of pimples.

Maldonado sat down and cracked her knuckles. "Did you have a nice fucking Christmas?"

Victoria took a deep breath and exhaled before responding. "Would you like to talk about our last session when you got up and walked out?"

"No!"

"I can't help you if you're not honest with me."

"Maybe I don't need your help." Maldonado leaned back and crossed her arms.

"If you don't care to go any deeper, you're welcome to quit."

"I was thinking about quitting." Maldonado looked out the window. Her voice quivered as she spoke, "because talking to you makes me have nightmares."

Victoria saw her opening. She leaned in towards Maldonado and spoke softly. "Do you want to tell me what they're about?"

"So you can think I'm crazy?" Maldonado shifted in her chair.

"No, so I can help you," she said in a matter-of-fact tone.

Maldonado swallowed hard. "A man gets shot, there's blood and body parts everywhere."

Victoria nodded. "How does he get shot?"

"With a gun," she said, annoyed.

Victoria ignored the taunt and asked again, "I mean, who shoots him? Are you being shot at too?"

"No, I'm shooting him. Look, that's all I want to say. Can I go smoke? I'm done."

Victoria had a hunch that there was more here, but she wanted to take it slow. She asked Maldonado about how she spent the last two weeks and she gradually eased into a discussion on coping skills.

"What did you do when you got upset on the outside," Victoria asked, "when things upset you, what did you do to handle it?"

"I'd go for a drive or get drunk. Sometimes I'd get high and watch TV."

"Did you get high a lot?"

"Yeah, I stayed fucked up pretty much most of the time."

Victoria looked directly at Bonnie Maldonado noting her disheveled appearance and the blemishes on her face. "Are you high now?"

Maldonado laughed and raised an eyebrow. "Do you really think that I'd tell you if I was and risk having the officers tear up my room and then have to go piss in a cup?"

"If you don't tell me who you bought the drugs from then I have nothing to report. If you tell me you're high, that's confidential in this session. It doesn't fall into those cases when I have to break confidentiality."

"No worries there. I'm not telling you shit."

"When did the nightmares start?"

"After our last session." Maldonado wiped her nose with the back of her hand.

"What took you back to using?"

"I thought we settled this, the goddamned nightmares!" Maldonado yelled.

Victoria tried to hide her satisfaction that Maldonado had actually answered her honestly. "Yes, but it's more than that, I'm sure you've had nightmares before. What do these nightmares mean?" Victoria wasn't going to let Maldonado push her away.

Maldonado looked at the clock on Victoria's bookshelf. "Aren't we out of time?"

Victoria glanced up. Maldonado was right, the clock showed ten minutes to the top of the hour, but if she could just keep her there for another hour she could get somewhere, break down some of Maldonado's walls. Going over the scheduled session was a sign of poor boundaries, but right now she didn't care. "I've got an open hour. This is important. Let's stay focused."

"Are you serious, Dr. Thomas?" Maldonado said, making Victoria's eye contact.

"Yes, I am, Bonnie."

Maldonado looked surprised. Victoria had broken a rule by addressing her by her first name.

"This is confidential right?" Maldonado asked, looking straight at her.

"Yes, Bonnie, we've been over that."

She looked at the door to make sure no one was standing outside. Her leg began shaking. "I'm here for driving the get-away car in a bank robbery."

"Okay."

"That's only part of it."

"There's more," Victoria said. A question disguised as a statement. A confident façade, designed to draw Maldonado in.

"I wasn't always just the driver," She said, her voice cracking.

Victoria held her poker face and monitored Maldonado's anxiety level.

"Sometimes I went in..." Maldonado hesitated for a moment and then lowered her voice before speaking, "to get the money. They didn't expect a woman."

Victoria thought she detected a gleam of pride in Maldonado's eyes, but she didn't respond. She sat still with her legs crossed and her hands in her lap, hoping that the more still she held her pose, the deeper Maldonado would go.

"This one time things didn't turn out like I expected." Maldonado started picking at a hangnail and her leg shook faster. "There was this bald guy and..." Her eyes darted around like she was re-living the experience. "I was leaving and, uh, he got in my way."

Victoria held her eye contact without blinking. "What did you do, Bonnie?"

Maldonado looked out the window. "I, um, I... I... shot him. I was almost out. He got in my way." She clenched her jaw like she was trying to keep from crying.

"What happened after you shot him?"

"I don't want to know. I don't want to think about it."

Victoria leaned in towards Bonnie Maldonado and spoke with a sense of urgency. "Stay with it Bonnie, try and tell me what happened."

"I could hear people screaming." Maldonado's hands trembled. She rested them on her lap to steady them. "There was blood everywhere."

Victoria looked into her eyes showing her that she wasn't going away, wasn't rejecting her, or judging her. "Then what happened?"

"I ran out… got into the car." Maldonado shifted in her chair.

Victoria noted Maldonado trying to distance herself from her actions. "What do you think happened to the man?"

"Uh," her voice quivered, "uh, well, I guess he died."

Victoria locked eyes with Bonnie Maldonado. "Is it just a guess?"

Maldonado bit her lip. The tears began streaming down her face. "No," she said, clutching her face in her hands.

Victoria took a tissue from the box on her desk and held it out to Maldonado. "What happened to him?"

Maldonado took the tissue and wiped her eyes. "He died."

Victoria felt a bit queasy. "How do you know that?"

Maldonado wadded up the tissue. "I heard about it on the news." She began crying again. "Are you gonna tell somebody about this?" Snot dripped from her nose.

Victoria handed her another tissue. "No, what you tell me about the past is confidential."

Maldonado took the tissue and wiped her hands and face with it.

"How did you feel after you killed him?"

"Sick. When I got home, my clothes were dirty. I took a shower." Maldonado stared at the floor.

Victoria thought it was interesting that she chose the word "dirty" instead of "bloody." *Clearly another way to distance herself,* she thought, imagining in her own mind's eye Maldonado killing the man. It was apparent now that their conversation last week had triggered flashbacks of the murder. It seemed odd to her that the perpetrator of a crime would have PTSD responses. She always thought of PTSD as a diagnosis for a victim of a crime, and not the reverse. She tried to recall the signs of PTSD—disturbing dreams associated with the traumatic event, avoidance of thoughts, feelings, or conversation about the traumatic event, irritability, intense distress associated with reminders of the event, drug use to escape. Bonnie Maldonado had them all.

"So this is what your nightmares are about?"

"Yeah." Maldonado looked up, wiped her eyes again and blew her nose on the tissue.

She seemed to be waiting for some sort of reassurance. She could normalize what Maldonado was going through and offer assistance in processing her crime, but she couldn't offer reassurance. Bonnie Maldonado had taken someone's life.

"How do I make it go away?" she pleaded.

Victoria sighed. "Talking about it is a good start. Your mind is processing what happened. Even if you use drugs to escape, the memory is still there and will continue to come back until you deal with it."

"Why is it coming up now?" Maldonado demanded an answer. "I never had nightmares before."

Victoria felt guilty that their sessions had triggered Maldonado's PTSD and led to her using drugs to cope.

"Maybe it's time to take a look at what you've done."

Maldonado nodded.

"Thank you for being honest with me, Bonnie. I can help more if you're honest."

"But remembering this shit is fucking me up! I want to forget my past and now you want me to talk about things?"

"Taking responsibility for your actions, rather than running from them, will bring you peace. To take responsibility, you must be honest with yourself and own up to what you've done. Talking to me about your past will allow you to do just that," Victoria said, hoping to reassure her and in some ways herself. Thoughts of Joanne started to fill her mind.

Maldonado was suddenly angry. "Why are you so willing to listen to my stories?"

Victoria lowered her voice feeling sure she could earn Bonnie Maldonado's trust. "Honestly, Bonnie, I hate to see people suffer. You've been suffering for a long time. I became a psychologist to help people experience the love and joy they've missed out on because they're doing things to harm themselves or others. If I can help you, then I feel I've made the world a better place. That's what's 'in it' for me. Your nightmares aren't going to go away overnight. You're going to need to explore your feelings and the realities surrounding this event. We're out of time, though. So we can talk more about it next week."

"That's it, huh?" Maldonado shook her head.

"No, that's not it, Bonnie. You've shared a lot with me today, more than you likely intended to share. You've been brave and honest. We'll talk more next week, pace yourself." Victoria got up from her chair and opened the door. "I'll see you next week."

Maldonado walked out without a word.

Victoria closed the door and walked over to the filing cabinet. She pulled out Maldonado's file, tossed it on her desk, and then sunk into her chair and exhaled loudly. She couldn't believe Maldonado had trusted her with her secret—she'd gotten away with murder

Victoria felt exhilarated. By not responding to Bonnie Maldonado's rejection she'd cracked through some serious armor taking Maldonado to a place she'd never gone with anyone else. It was like earning the trust of a feral cat. She'd never gone so deep with a client either. This new trust was unspeakably precious and delicate. She couldn't wait until their next session, which would determine the direction the therapy would take.

She picked up her pen and charted the notes from the session.

Client feels upset with poor choices and criminal behavior in past. She is haunted by past criminal actions and desires to change. There appears to be a link between her father's harsh discipline and her anti-social beliefs and behaviors. Client needs to learn to self-soothe and manage her emotions in a productive way. Her response to stress, anger, disappointment, etc. has been to use drugs or alcohol, engage in self-destructive behaviors (e.g. punching walls) or other forms of self-injurious behavior, and to isolate. Will continue to meet with client on a weekly basis and discuss childhood issues and past criminal behavior, teach coping skills, and work on improving self-esteem. Update to Provisional Diagnosis: Axis I: Post-Traumatic Stress Disorder, Poly-substance Abuse. Axis II: Personality Disorder with Borderline and Antisocial Features.

She didn't write anything about the murder.

Chapter 30

BONNIE SLAMMED OUT of the Psychology Building and back on to the compound. Her mind raced. She'd just told a cop, a fucking cop that she'd killed someone. She'd felt safe with Dr. Thomas, but now she wondered if Dr. Thomas was just a fancy cop who was probably reporting the crime to the FBI right now.

Her face flushed hot with rage and self-loathing. Adrenaline flooded her body as she thought about the possibility of getting the death penalty for killing the bald guy. She could go back to Dr. Thomas's office and choke her out, but then for sure she'd get a murder conviction.

"You're such a fucking idiot! What the fuck were you thinking? You just handed her the rope to hang you with!" She heard her father's voice in her head.

She hadn't even wanted to talk about the crime, let alone think about it, and Dr. Thomas still hadn't given her any real ways to make the nightmares stop.

Bonnie approached a group of Mexican women standing outside the housing unit smoking. "Can I bum a smoke off of someone?"

They pretended not to understand, but one, a boyish looking one, with short brown hair and a crisp, well-ironed uniform with pleats down the side, walked over.

"*Aqui*," she said smiling and handed Bonnie a cigarette. "I'm Chico."

"Got a light?" Bonnie just wanted a cigarette. She wasn't interested in making friends with any stud broads, let alone a Mexican one.

"*Por supuesto*," Chico said and handed Bonnie the cigarette she was smoking. Bonnie lit her cigarette off of it and handed it back. She immediately began coughing.

Chico went to touch her. "Are you okay, *Mija*?"

"I'm fine." Bonnie pulled away and walked towards the rec yard, trying to stifle her cough. The minute she turned the corner and was out of the woman's sight, she dropped the cigarette. *God damn it—I can't even smoke!*

The sensation of raindrops on her arm brought her back to the moment. It had started to rain and she realized that she'd left her jacket at the chapel and rushed to get it before she was soaked.

She could see her jacket on the floor in the corner of the room, but the room was now full of inmates sitting cross-legged on the floor with their eyes closed. They were facing a religious service volunteer, a gray haired woman she'd never seen before. The woman wore a bright purple shirt with matching baggy pants and a round silver pendant necklace. She looked to be in her fifties.

Bonnie went inside to retrieve her jacket. The gray-haired woman held a copper bowl in her hand and struck it with a wooden mallet.

The sound resonated loudly throughout the room and then softened into a faint echo. She found it soothing. The woman struck the bowl a second time and began speaking, "begin to imagine a warm, white light. Let the warm white light encircle you. Let it enfold you."

Bonnie picked up her jacket and turned to leave. Instead, she sat down on the floor and closed her eyes like the other women in the room.

"Feel the protection of the warm white light and let your mind wander deeper into the quiet stillness," the gray-haired woman said.

Bonnie took a deep breath and exhaled. The image of a lake appeared in her mind's eye, followed by the image of a white bird and then another. White birds just kept appearing. Her breathing slowed and she could no longer feel her body, just a warm vibration. It felt euphoric, like nodding out, but better somehow. She felt clearer, at peace. She wanted to wrap herself more deeply in the sensation, feel its weight against her. She felt like she could stay in it forever, perfectly content, losing herself in the silence.

The mallet struck the bowl again, but this time it felt jarring.

"Take another deep breath in, and as I count backward from three, I want you to come back to the room."

Bonnie didn't want to come back to the room. She wanted to stay in the silence.

"Three, becoming more and more aware of your body."

She tried to tune the woman out.

"Two, feeling your breathing. Feel your chest rise and fall with every breath. Beginning to notice the sounds around you, the people around you."

Bonnie didn't want to notice the people around her. She wanted to be free of them.

"And one, opening your eyes and coming back to the room."

Bonnie sighed loudly, reluctantly opening her eyes to the reality of the prison.

The woman bowed and then got up. "Namaste. I'll see you next week."

Several inmates circled her like sharks. Bonnie grabbed her jacket and walked out.

Chaplain Edwards bee-lined in her direction. She tensed up. *Did he know her secret?*

"Could you wash the windows in the sanctuary tomorrow?" he asked.

Disarmed, Bonnie saluted. "Aye Aye, Chaplain."

"That's a new one," he said and walked off laughing.

She hurried back to the unit as quickly as she could before the rain gave her a good soaking. The unit officer unlocked the door, but instead of letting her inside he demanded that she come with him.

"Where are we going?" she asked trying to hide her panic.

"The Lieutenants' Office," he said.

Bonnie eyed the double fences with the razor wire and considered her options. She saw the mobile patrol vehicle making its rounds. She could just run for the fence now, they'd shoot her and it would all be over.

"Keep moving," the officer ordered.

When they reached the Lieutenants' Office he told her to take a seat.

"She's all yours," he said to Officer Berger who was walking out of the bathroom with a young black inmate.

"You can go now while it's still open movement," she told the inmate.

Berger opened up a locker, pulled out a plastic cup and handed it Bonnie. "All right Maldonado, get in there. Mandatory UA."

Bonnie stood there dumbfounded.

"We don't have all day, Maldonado. If you're dirty we're gonna find out."

Bonnie exhaled and walked into the bathroom with Berger.

Chapter 31

THAT NIGHT BONNIE had the dream again where she shot the guy, but instead of him bleeding, she touched her stomach and felt her own blood oozing from her body. The dream jarred her awake and she'd been unable to fall back asleep.

She'd drank several cups of coffee trying to stay awake at work and now as she walked to the Psych Building for her appointment with Dr. Thomas it felt like her stomach was eating itself.

When she arrived, Dr. Thomas was on the phone. She hesitated then knocked. Dr. Thomas hung up the phone and opened the door. "Come on in, Ms. Maldonado."

Bonnie sat down. She wondered what Dr. Thomas was going to ask her and if she'd already reported her. She remembered that the news had identified the bank robber as a white male. She could always say she was just fucking with the prison shrink.

Dr. Thomas cleared the papers on her desk into a pile before putting them on the floor to the side of her chair. "So what's been going on for you? Anything coming up? Anything you want to talk about?" Dr. Thomas seemed flustered.

"Did you tell anyone?"

"I told you I wouldn't. Is there something you'd like to discuss?"

Bonnie thought for a moment. "There is one thing," she said feeling a bit embarrassed. "Why are people always talking about God and having faith?"

Dr. Thomas looked surprised. She crossed her legs and put her hands on her lap. "Why do you ask?"

Bonnie leaned back in her chair. "The other night I went to some sort of meditation thing. It was pretty corny."

"How so?" Dr. Thomas's face was expressionless.

"I don't know." Bonnie chewed at her fingernail. "This lady in this crazy purple outfit told us to imagine a white light around us. I couldn't visualize the light, but I saw something else." Bonnie hesitated shifting in the chair. "This is going to sound stupid, but I saw a lake and a bunch of white birds. I think they're called, cranes. First I saw just one on the water, but then I started to see 'em in the trees and bushes, floating on the water."

"That sounds very interesting and beautiful, Ms. Maldonado." Dr. Thomas took a sip of her bottled water.

"Very interesting, what the hell does that mean? Am I crazy?"

"What do the birds represent?"

"You're the shrink." Bonnie crossed her arms tight around her chest.

Dr. Thomas took another sip of her water, accidentally spilling it on her blouse. "What might it mean in terms of trying to find faith?

Bonnie looked confused. "I don't understand what you're getting at?"

Dr. Thomas dabbed at the drops of water on her blouse with a tissue. "Maybe the bird appearing was a symbol of God, or Spirit. The fact you looked around and saw the birds everywhere could mean the more you look, or have faith, the more you will find God. It could be a demonstration of faith." Dr. Thomas took a more cautious sip from her bottle of water.

"Okay, Doc, what have you been smoking?"

"Can you think about what I just said?"

Bonnie sat up. "Maybe, but that sounds kind of far-fetched."

"It's your vision."

"The bird becoming more birds was a symbol of God, of faith? Is that what you're saying?" Bonnie asked, her brow furrowed, but she already knew the answer to her question.

Dr. Thomas leaned back in her chair. "Try it on. Does it feel right?"

"Yeah, I think so."

"The vision is telling you that when you look you'll see God everywhere."

Bonnie looked directly at Dr. Thomas. "Do you believe in God, Dr. T?"

"It doesn't matter what I believe. Figure out what makes sense to you and what you believe."

"It would help to know how somebody like you believes cause all I see around here is a bunch of fucking hypocrites. Overnight religious wonders, busting heads one minute and praying to Jesus and judging everyone the next. I was wondering something else, if you're like a Christian and all that, how do you make sense of your situation?"

"My situation, what do you mean by that?" Dr. Thomas looked perplexed.

"You know, how do you understand your," Bonnie hesitated, "relationship?"

"I'm sorry I still don't understand what you're asking."

"The black guy? Doesn't the Bible say you can't intermarry with other species?"

Dr. Thomas looked at her confused. "Do you mean other races, Ms. Maldonado?"

"Yeah, whatever—isn't that against the bible and nature?" Bonnie stared at Dr. Thomas and s saw Dr. Thomas's face redden.

"Is that what you believe, that God would want to punish people who love one another, punish those people for that love?"

"I don't know."

"Do you believe God is a punishing God or a loving God?"

Bonnie felt her adrenaline rise. Her hands began to tremble. "If there was a loving God why did all this fucking shit happen to me? Why didn't God stop it? Why didn't God stop me? What's gonna happen to me because of what I did?" She felt hot tears in her eyes.

She quickly caught herself when she saw Dr. Thomas's eyes light up. She could feel Dr. Thomas hone in on the question like an interrogator who sees his chance to expose the culprit. *There's no way out. Here she comes!*

"You're thinking about how you'll be judged?" Dr. Thomas asked, sitting up straight in her chair.

"I guess," Bonnie said nonchalantly and tried to crack her knuckles again, but they were all cracked out. She cracked her neck to the side instead. It popped loudly.

"What are you afraid of? What are you afraid of happening?" Dr. Thomas fumbled over the words.

"I don't know. I just don't want to feel this way anymore."

"Feel what way, Bonnie?"

She knew Dr. Thomas was hoping that she would be real with her.

"You know."

"No, I don't." Dr. Thomas looked at her. "Try to tell me."

Bonnie could feel a lump in her throat. She bit down hard on her lip. "I don't want to feel bad anymore." The tears began streaming down her face. "Fuck! All my life I've been trying to put this shit behind me, just forget about it. Now I'm supposed to come in here and fucking talk about it! Fuck that!" She wiped the tears away with the back of her hand and bit her lip hard until she could taste blood. *I have to get it together!*

"Bonnie, you're getting real." Dr. Thomas's voice softened.

Bonnie looked up at her. She wanted to dart for the door, but at the same time it felt like Dr. Thomas could tell exactly what she felt and something about that held her in the chair. Then the memory of her father smacking her in the head for crying after she slammed her finger in the door flashed in her mind. She darted towards the door.

"I'm out of here!" she said and rushed out.

Chapter 32

VICTORIA LAY IN her bed wrapped in her down comforter spooning Devin's body, which rose and fell in a steady relaxed rhythm with each breath. She nestled closer, inhaling his sweet, familiar smell. She felt at peace, closed her eyes, and fell asleep again.

Moments later, the bedroom door burst open and light flooded the room. She was paralyzed with fear when she saw a man wearing a nylon stocking pulled tightly over his face, his features contorted. She tried to scream, but nothing happened. Her body filled with adrenaline. There was a rapid succession of gunshots; then everything went dark. Victoria began screaming and thrashed wildly trying to get out of the tangle of sheets.

Devin jolted up and fumbled for the light. "Victoria, are you okay?"

Victoria was panting, sweat dripped from her brow. Panicked, she touched his body looking for bullet holes. She found none. She scanned her body.

"Oh my God. I just had the worst nightmare."

"It's okay, Baby." He tried to reassure her.

She thought about what she'd read in Maldonado's file yesterday afternoon.

"What did you dream?" he asked.

Her hands trembled as she ran her fingers through her hair trying to calm herself. "Nothing, I'm okay now," she lied. "If it's okay with you I want to turn the TV on for awhile to calm my nerves?"

"Sure, go ahead." Devin touched her face softly.

"Thanks, Devin." She kissed his hand, then opened the nightstand drawer and pulled out the remote.

He turned off the light and went back to sleep.

Victoria found a marathon of Happy Days episodes on Nickelodeon, set the sleeper feature on the remote and dozed off mid-episode.

The next morning, Devin and Victoria, both dressed in blue jeans and sweaters, sipped their lattes as Devin exited the 101 and his gray SAAB leaned into the curves of Highway 116.

The yellow sign they passed on the way to wine country read *Rough Road Ahead*. Victoria hoped it was only a simple fact about the pavement and not something more ominous. She fought to quiet her superstitious mind she'd inherited from her mother. They were finally getting away for the weekend and to celebrate Valentine's Day.

Victoria loved to get out of the city and drive through the vineyards, the apple and olive orchards, and to stop along the way at the antique stores.

Devin briefly looked away from the road, trying to make eye contact with her. "What's on your mind, Baby?"

"Nothing." Victoria turned and looked out the window at the vineyards.

"I may not be a psychologist, but I know something's bothering you. You worried they're going to treat us like separate customers like that hotel in Tahoe or suddenly find that they're overbooked?" He turned down the volume on the radio.

She knew he hated leaving the Bay Area because those things had happened before. "This is Sonoma County, they're more progressive. I can't imagine anyone doing that here in 1997," she said.

Devin laughed. "Right, tons of black folk living up here in wine country. Come clean, what's bothering you?"

"I'm just thinking about this client."

"And you accuse me of bringing my work home all the time."

"You do bring your work home all the time and you asked me what was wrong. I wouldn't have brought it up otherwise." She turned the radio up and sang slightly off key to an old Temptations song. "Just my imagination, running away with me," she crooned.

Devin switched off the music.

"Hey, I was listening to that, turn it back on," she said annoyed.

"So, what's going on with this client?" he asked, looking tenderly at her with his soft brown eyes.

She couldn't be mad at him when he gave her those eyes. She wanted to tell him, but it just seemed too complicated.

"It's a tough case and she's starting to open up."

"That's good." Devin nodded approvingly.

"She's finally starting to trust me. She was horribly abused as a child."

"Sounds like a lot of your patients at the prison. What's so different about her?"

Victoria ran her fingers through her hair. "It's complicated."

"What do you mean *complicated*?" Devin gave her a funny look.

"To be honest, it's a little harder to work with her because she's got a history of serious violence and she used to be involved with some pretty horrible people."

"What kind of horrible people?"

Victoria hesitated. "White supremacists."

"White supremacists? Isn't that redundant? Aren't all white supremacists horrible people?" Devin shook his head and gripped the steering wheel a little tighter.

Victoria rolled down her window taking in the fresh air. "Do you remember the beating of the Nigerian professor in Portland, Oregon back in the eighties?"

Devin turned to look at Victoria. He was pissed. "She was one of those punks that beat him to death with a baseball bat?"

"No, thank God, she wasn't, but her file says she was affiliated with that group."

"Don't you think that makes her just as guilty?" Devin swerved to avoid a car that was edging into the roadway.

"She saw us together at the prison and she's got some opinions about that."

"Oh, does she?" Devin shook his head again. "I don't know how you put up with that shit, Vic."

"Clients have a difficult time knowing anything about their therapists because of their projections. They create a reality for their therapist that fits into their worldview."

Devin took his eyes off the road and stared at her. "Thanks for the lecture, Dr. Thomas, but I'm not a first year psych major and that's not what I'm talking about!"

"Devin, it's my job. I got training on managing counter-transference in graduate school. However, I never imagined, me, of all people," she laughed uncomfortably, "working so intimately with a white supremacist."

"I'm not sure how the irony of that is funny to you? Does she know you're Jewish and that your grandparents are holocaust survivors?"

"I guess I forgot to mention that in *her* therapy session." Victoria looked out the window. "These orchards are so beautiful."

"How can you even waste your time on her? Never hear you getting this involved with any of the *sistahs*." Devin adjusted the visor to block the sun from his eyes.

"That's because they don't come for therapy."

"Yeah, because your whole department's white for one thing. Plus we black folk don't typically do head shrinkers. Well, I do, but that's another story." He laughed.

"Very funny, "she said and smacked his leg.

Victoria wanted to tell Devin that she didn't think it was Bonnie's fault, that in some ways, she didn't blame her for the way she'd acted, or the things she'd done because of what had happened to her. She decided against it.

"We should go for more drives. We really shouldn't take our freedom for granted. You know some of those women I work with have never even been to the ocean."

"Yeah, if we had more time," he said.

Victoria shook her head. "I just don't understand why she hates blacks? She..."

Devin interrupted. "She hates blacks because she can, because it's easier than hating the real people in her life. Come on, Victoria, you're a psychologist. Isn't that called displacement? I learned that in Psych 101. How you can be so naïve?"

Devin signaled and pulled into a restaurant's parking lot. "Let's get something to eat. I'm starving," he said and reached into the back seat for his brown suede jacket.

Chapter 33

"GOOD MORNING, Ms. Maldonado." Dr. Thomas seemed excited to see her.

Bonnie hesitated at the door, she felt pulled by Dr. Thomas's warmth, but it made her cringe at the same time. She walked in and reluctantly sat down.

Dr. Thomas settled into her therapist pose. "How are you?"

"Mostly okay, but just had some trouble with a CO."

Dr. Thomas's eyes narrowed. "What happened?"

"He gave me some shit about my uniform. Almost wrote me up for insolence cause he said I was too slow in tucking my shirt in." Bonnie shook her head. "These damn cops hassle us about every little fucking thing."

"But you didn't get a shot?"

"No, he was just power tripping." Bonnie grabbed a tissue from the box on Dr. Thomas's desk and blew her nose.

Dr. Thomas leaned in closer. Bonnie noticed there were dark circles under Dr. Thomas's eyes. She seemed more intense than usual. "Last week when you said something about if there was a God, why would he let certain things happen?"

Bonnie felt her heart beat quicken. "I don't really want to talk about that."

"Can you try?"

Bonnie looked at Dr. Thomas's well-manicured nails and the reddish highlights in her hair. She leaned back in her chair and cracked her knuckles. "I bet you were popular in high school? Probably come from money too. The only place I fit was with bikers."

Bonnie looked at the ground. "At school people fucked with me, made fun of me, shit like that. They called me Goodwill Girl because of my clothes and treated me like I was one of the retarded kids."She took a deep breath trying to swallow the lump. "There was this god damn Mexican who lived a couple of houses down from me and... um.. I..."

Dr. Thomas looked at her expectantly. "It's okay, try to stay with it."

She swallowed again and tried to speak, "I was...um... walking past the bleachers on my way home from school and these seniors, football players, four of them underneath the bleachers. They had the Mexican kid in a headlock. They were punching him. Then they saw me." Her leg began to shake and she started speaking faster. "I tried to get out of there, but they ran up on me. Two of them grabbed me. I kicked them as hard as I could and tried to get loose. Then they dragged me under the bleachers. They started telling the Mexican kid he needed to prove he was a man. So they unbuttoned his pants and then unbuttoned mine." Bonnie stopped. She saw sadness in Dr. Thomas's eyes.

"Then what happened?"

"This guy and his kids were playing frisbee in the football field and it landed close to the bleachers, so he came over to get it and he seen what was happening and the football players took off running."

Dr. Thomas nodded. She looked relieved.

"There were too many of them for the guy to catch, but he grabbed the Mexican kid then started going off on me." Bonnie's eyes watered. *Fuck, I don't want to cry!*

"What do you mean?"

Bonnie bit down hard on her lip trying to stop the tears. When she regained her composure, she began again. "He called me a 'slut' and said, 'you ought to be ashamed of yourself out here with all these boys.'"

"What?" Dr. Thomas looked like she was going to jump out of her seat. "That's horrible! Didn't he know that they were going to assault you?"

"No." Bonnie wiped the tears from her eyes. "He just thought I was a slut. That I wanted it." She picked at her lip, pulling off pieces of chapped skin and wiping them on her pants.

"What happened after that?"

"I didn't want to be around any more fucking wetbacks after that."

Dr. Thomas reached over and picked up a bottle of water that was sitting on her desk, opened it, and took a sip. "Have you ever considered his being Mexican didn't have anything to do with it?"

"What do you mean?" Bonnie asked.

"Never mind, what happened after that?"

Bonnie continued picking at her lip. "I dropped out, started doing my own thing."

"How old were you?"

"Fifteen. I met Tim right after that. We spent a lot of time down at the river drinking and just hanging out smoking pot."

"Tim was your boyfriend who died in the motorcycle accident, right?" Dr. Thomas leaned back in her chair and crossed her legs.

Bonnie nodded. "After Tim died I started shooting up and had a habit to support. So, for a while, I was running with the guys. We had a nice little business going on, but then I caught my first case."

"What was that?"

"Burglary."

"What did you steal?" Dr. Thomas tried hard to sound casual.

"Jewelry, stereo equipment from my neighbor' house. I seen him put a key under a rock for another neighbor to feed his cats. Unfortunately that dude seen me go in through the back door and called the cops."

"How long was your sentence?"

"I plea-bargained down to six months with one year probation. Did my time at Rocky Butte and then..." her voice cracked. She glimpsed the concern in Dr. Thomas's eyes. It was too intense. She looked away.

"What happened then?" Dr. Thomas asked.

Bonnie took a deep breath and exhaled through her nose. She didn't want to think about it, but the memory came roaring back.

Tony had picked her up the day she got out of Rocky Butte and took her back to his place where a few of the Lighting Brothers, Sketch, B.J., Mike, and Randy, were sitting at the table playing poker. Lynyrd Skynyrd's "Sweet Home Alabama" was on the stereo.

Sketch was smoking a cigarette and singing through his teeth. He set his cards down and walked over to Bonnie, took the cigarette out of his mouth, and kissed her. His breath smelt like whiskey and cigarettes.

"Hey, baby girl, how'd they treat ya up at the Butte? I guess the food can't be as bad as it was when I was there, cause you look like you've gained about twenty pounds."

"No, it's still crap." She laughed.

Tony sat down on the duct-taped black leather couch in the living room. "Bet you want some of these." Tony tossed her a pack of Camels. "I remember when I was down all they'd sell us were those fucking generic smokes. If I never smoke another GPC, it'll be too soon."

Bonnie laughed and lit a cigarette.

"Bet you've been missing this too." Sketch shook a dime bag of heroin.

She took a deep drag off the cigarette. It had been hard to go without it for six months but she didn't want it to own her again.

"Gotta beer? Haven't had a chance to celebrate the fact I can drink legally and don't need you jokers to buy for me anymore."

Sketch tapped some powder into a spoon and held the lighter underneath. "You're not thinking you're too good for us now are ya, baby girl?"

Sketch had always competed with Tim for Bonnie's attention. She never paid him much mind. She wasn't interested in Sketch. He was too wild, unpredictable. Tim was steady, even when he was doing a job he was level headed. She'd admired that.

"No, I don't think I'm too good for you." She laughed.

Sketch pulled back the plunger on the needle and sucked up the dope. "You lick a lot of pussy behind bars, Bonnie? Lose your taste for men too?"

"What?" Bonnie asked, cracking open the beer. "No, I ain't been with no one since Tim died, and I never thought about sleeping with no female. Nobody turned me out if that's what you're asking."

Sketch grabbed Bonnie, pulled her onto his lap, and into a half nelson twisting her neck under his arm. She struggled to get free, but he held her down and injected the needle into her left arm.

"There, bitch," Sketch said, "now you won't be thinking you're too good for us."

Bonnie remembered feeling dizzy, unable to breathe. Later, she woke up naked on a mattress in Tony's house. Her body ached. She searched the room for her clothes but couldn't find them. She grabbed a plaid flannel shirt and a pair of jeans that belonged to one of the guys and went to the bathroom to pee. Her vagina stung as the urine streamed out. She looked in the mirror. Her right eye was almost swollen shut. She washed the blood from her face.

She was numb. She would have done anything they'd asked of her, any crime, any favor, anything but this. She felt betrayed and ashamed. She couldn't find her shoes, but had to go.

She walked barefooted until she was picked up by the police and taken to the hospital. The police wanted to press charges, but she refused to cooperate. She knew that the LBs would come after her again if she snitched on them.

After she was treated, one of the cops offered to drive her home. She told him she didn't have a home so he dropped her off at a homeless shelter. Bonnie had spent the night on a cot curled tight in the fetal position. Her father's words echoed through her ears. *The ones you love will hurt you the most!*

"Ms. Maldonado?" Dr. Thomas was staring at her. "Are you okay?"

"Sorry, where was I?"

"I'm not sure where you were just now, you seemed to have dissociated for a minute. You were talking about how you'd been sentenced to six months in jail and then your friend Tony picked you up."

Bonnie shifted in her chair, unable to get comfortable and continued to pull at the string on her uniform. She wasn't sure what Dr. Thomas meant, but she seemed to have forgotten where she was. "Yeah, Tony picked me up after I got out and about five or six months later I caught my next case."

"That was the 7-11 Robbery?"

Bonnie nodded. Dr. Thomas's questioning seemed unrelenting. *Maybe Dr. Thomas missed her calling, maybe she should have been a fucking prosecutor.*

"Did eight years of a ten year sentence at the Oregon Women's Correctional Center—that was a real prison. This is like day care. Gun towers at every corner."

"What happened after that?"

"They set me free!"

Dr. Thomas glanced at the clock on the edge of her bookshelf.

"Time's up, eh?" she asked, conflicted. A part of her wanted to bolt from the chair, but another part of her wanted to stay. It was hard to talk about this stuff with Dr. Thomas, but once she finally started talking it was hard to stop.

"Yes, we're going to have to stop for the day, but I want to hear more about what happened after you got out of state prison when we meet next week."

Bonnie got up from the chair.

"Ms. Maldonado?"

"Yes." Bonnie turned around.

"Don't forget your jacket." Dr. Thomas pointed to the chair.

She blushed. "Oh yeah, thanks." She grabbed her jacket up off the chair and walked out the door.

Chapter 34

VICTORIA WALKED TO her filing cabinet and unlocked it. She took out Maldonado's file, then sat down to chart some notes. It was easy for her now to see the origin and progression of Bonnie's rage and need for control. She understood why Bonnie would be drawn to take back the control stripped from her by men, her father in particular.

Victoria found herself consumed by thoughts of Bonnie Maldonado; her problems, her past, how Victoria could help her. All week she anticipated their session, feeling as though the week was dragging on, and then, the fifty minutes had flown by.

She picked up the phone and dialed. It rang three times. She was just about to hang up when he answered.

"Dr. Peter Murphy."

She immediately felt comforted by the sound of his voice. "Hi, Peter."

"Victoria, how are you?" She heard the surprise in his tone.

"I'm good. How are you? How's the practice?"

"I have a long waiting list, so things couldn't be better as far as work is concerned."

"That's terrific!" Victoria fidgeted with the phone cord, wrapping her finger in it.

"How's the prison?" he asked.

"We're getting a new warden in a few weeks, so things could get better or worse. Do you have a few minutes?"

"Sure, Victoria, what's up?"

"There's a case I'd like to consult with you on. Do you have time?"

"Sure, I have twenty minutes right now."

"Actually, I was wondering if we could get together in person."

"Absolutely, I'd love to see you."

"How about tomorrow night at Pasand in Berkeley?" She asked, aware that she was smiling.

"Sounds great!"

She hung up pleased that he agreed to meet with her, but a little concerned about the can of worms she was opening.

Chapter 35

BONNIE DUSTED THE bookshelves in the chapel library. It felt good to open up to Dr. Thomas. She was the only person she could imagine telling this stuff to, but she wasn't ready to talk about Sketch and the guys.

Dr. Thomas was different from the other psychs she'd seen before. She seemed more real, more caring than the others. She hadn't pushed her away or seemed different after she told her about the robbery. Quite the opposite, Dr. Thomas had seemed almost pleased with her, more interested. She'd searched for clues of judgment or fear in Dr. Thomas's face, in her voice, but she found none.

Chaplain Edwards poked his head into the library. "Ms. Maldonado, when you're done in there, can you vacuum my office and take out the trash?"

"Sure, Chaplain." Bonnie threw the paper towel in the garbage and walked to the broom closet for the vacuum. She opened the door and was startled to find two of the Christian women making out. They looked mortified and took off towards the bathroom.

"Damn hypocrites." Bonnie shook her head and wheeled out the vacuum cleaner. She knocked on Chaplain Edwards's door. He waved her in. Bonnie took the bag of trash out of the can, knotted it, and set it in the hallway, then began lining the can with a fresh bag.

"Still going to therapy?" Chaplain Edwards asked.

Bonnie didn't feel like it was any of his business if she was, but out of respect she answered him. "Yeah, still going."

"Do you find it useful?"

"I thought Dr. Thomas was uptight at first, but she's grown on me."

Chaplain Edwards smiled. "She takes her job very seriously."

"Yeah, she does."

"And she has the most beautiful green eyes."

"I guess." Bonnie nodded and turned on the vacuum.

Chapter 36

VICTORIA WAS GRATEFUL to find a parking spot close to the restaurant. As she walked to the entrance, she glimpsed Peter sitting at a table by the window. She'd forgotten how handsome he was. His wavy brown hair nicely framed his clean-shaven face.

Peter got up from his chair to greet her when she walked through the door. He wore a suit jacket and slacks, a more business-casual look than Devin's banker's suits.

"Victoria, it's so good to see you."

"Hi Peter. Thanks for meeting me." Victoria took off her coat and hung it on the back of the chair.

"Hey, any excuse," he said smiling, a glint in his brown eyes.

She sat down and a young man came and filled their water glasses.

"So, how are things with Devin?"

"Good, and you? Are you seeing anyone?" She sipped her water trying to be nonchalant with the question.

"I've been on a few dates here and there, but I'm still looking."

The waitress, an Indian woman in her late twenties with long brown hair and a pierced nose, smiled at Peter before looking at Victoria. "Are you ready to order?"

Victoria handed her the menu. "I'll have the *veggie korma*."

"And you, sir?"

"*Chicken masala* and an order of *pakora*." Peter handed her the menu. "And can you bring us some *nan* too."

After the woman left, Victoria looked seriously at Peter. She wanted to get to the real reason for her call, or at least the one she gave for calling. "Peter, sorry to talk shop, but I was curious about something."

"What's that?" Peter lifted his water glass and took a sip.

"Have you ever been so focused on a case that you can't stop thinking about the course treatment should take?"

"I get really involved in all my cases. What do you mean?"

"Do you," she hesitated, "spend a lot of time thinking about a particular client and how you can fix them—like replay the session over and over and think about what you could have done better? Or wish you had more time with a particular client so you could break through their defenses and resolve their problems?"

"You mean like you wish you could cure a particular client and you find yourself more invested in their treatment than your other clients, is that what you mean?"

"Exactly." Victoria nodded.

"No, that's never happened to me before."

Victoria felt sick to her stomach. "Really?"

"Of course that's happened, Victoria." Peter laughed out loud. "I can't believe I was able to keep a straight face."

"Tricks of the trade." Victoria grinned. She leaned in closer to him, setting her elbow on the table. "How do you manage that kind of counter-transference?"

"First, I figure out why my save-the-world mentality is coming up. Then I try to figure out what need I'm meeting or trying to meet by trying to save them. In other words, what do I think it'll give me if I can fix them?" Peter smiled.

She loved his smile. "You've obviously spent a lot of time analyzing your own counter-transference. I appreciate your candor, Peter. I've never experienced this before, and I'm feeling totally overwhelmed."

Peter took another sip of his water and nodded. "Yeah, it can be very intense."

"So it's not crazy that I'm going through this?"

"No, Victoria." Peter reached forward and squeezed her hand.

She felt her stomach flutter. "What does it mean then?"

"It just means that something is going on. This client is symbolizing something else for you and you need to figure out what it is."

Victoria looked out the window. "I think I know."

"What do you think it is?"

"It's…"

"*Veggie pakora*," the waitress interrupted. She put the appetizers on the table.

Victoria picked up a *pakora* and dipped it into the tamarind sauce and took a bite.

"This woman I'm working with," she said, her mouth full, "truly intrigues me. She was like a white supremacist on the outside."

"That must be challenging for you?" Peter looked concerned.

"The prison is full of them, Peter, but I'm not sure how serious she was about it. Her boyfriend was a white supremacist biker."

"So what's the pull with this one?" he asked.

"Well, her crimes are antisocial, but she feels remorse and seems to be on a search for something more meaningful than the life she led. I want to understand her more, to help her reach the other side of her potential. Maybe if I can help her to love and accept herself and others I can somehow impact the racist and anti-Semitic beliefs of people like her, people who don't accept couples like Devin and me. Does that make any sense at all?" Victoria waited for Peter to respond, fearful that she had revealed too much.

Peter wiped his mouth with a napkin. "That's deep. No wonder you feel hooked!"

"Oh God, you think I'm out of my mind don't you?" The sick feeling returned.

"No, no at all. I had a client once who was in an abusive relationship and didn't want to leave her husband. I wanted her to leave him so badly. I realized I'd wished my mom had done that. I felt like her leaving would help me feel more resolved about my parent's relationship. I'd finally make up for not being able to protect my mother from my father. Counter transference is never logical. It's always something emotional, something deeply felt. Don't try to judge it, just work on observing it, analyzing it, and managing it. That's enough right there."

"Thank you for your honesty, Peter. That's really helpful." She pushed away the last of the *pakora* and sat back, relieved.

Peter's face lit up and he smiled at her. "You're tough, Victoria. I can only imagine how hard it is to work there. My neurotic patients bring up enough stuff for me. I can't imagine what prisoners are like to work with."

Victoria felt herself blushing and hoped he didn't notice the effect his words still had on her. "Never a dull moment, that's for sure." She brought her napkin to her face and pretended to wipe her mouth just to be safe.

After dinner, Peter walked her to her car. She hugged him good-bye. He kissed her on the cheek and opened her car door for her. She remembered the time they'd gone to coffee to study for their final exams. Instead they talked existentialism and whether human change was really possible or if they had embarked on futile careers.

Peter had walked her to her car and kissed her then too, though not on the cheek. She was attracted to him, but felt conflicted about getting involved with someone as focused on human behavior as she was—would every conversation involve processing or be about some esoteric philosophy? The following weekend she'd gone to a poetry slam at the Java House in Oakland with some school friends. One of her classmates was at a table with her boyfriend and a couple of his friends. Devin was one of them.

Victoria and Devin hit if off from the moment they were intro-duced. They spent the night talking and laughing. She immediately fell in love with his smile and gorgeous brown eyes. She hadn't for-gotten Peter, but Devin was so easy-going and in the moment.

"It's refreshing to talk about something other than the angst and struggle of the human spirit," she'd told Devin. But now as she stood here with Peter, she wondered what she was missing.

Chapter 37

IT WAS THE second session of the Domestic Violence group. There were ten women in the group. All reported histories of being battered by their husbands, boyfriends, or a female companion. Some of them reported beatings so severe that they required hospitalization. A few bore visible scars from the beatings; all had emotional ones.

It was Ramona Vasquez's turn to share. Victoria turned in her chair to face Vasquez as she spoke.

"My husband tied me down raped me in my ass. My kids were in the other room. My oldest son walked in crying, asked him what he was doing. He told him to get out or he was next." Vasquez spoke about her abuse like she was a newscaster reading the news.

A few women gasped, another shook her head and mumbled something under her breath. Victoria noticed that some of the members seemed to be put off by Vasquez's lack of emotion. Victoria reminded herself that one of the symptoms of Post-Traumatic Stress Disorder was emotional numbing.

"When I get out of prison, I want to help other abused Chicanas." Vasquez smiled a perfect smile.

Victoria nodded. "That's a very noble endeavor, Ms. Vasquez."

"Thank you." She smiled again.

"Well, ladies," Victoria said, looking around the room at the women sitting in a semi-circle, "that's all the time we have for today. I'll see you all next week."

The women got up and stacked their chairs on the side of the room. Victoria left the group room and went back to her office.

Victoria was still thinking about Vasquez's behavior in the group when she heard a knock on her door. She looked up from her notes and saw Bonnie Maldonado. She seemed agitated. Victoria checked the clock on the bookshelf. Bonnie was early.

"Is everything all right, Ms. Maldonado?"

"I just really need to talk to you about some stuff and the hour goes by so quick. Do you have some extra time?" Maldonado lightly punched the doorframe with her right hand.

Victoria looked at the pile of paperwork on her desk. She had a release report due at the end of the day she'd barely started. She still hadn't finished the notes from group.

"Come on in," Victoria said, hoping not to sound overly pleased. "What do you want to talk about?"

Bonnie sat down. "The robberies."

Chapter 38

BONNIE REMEMBERED THE day she met with the Receiving and Discharge Officer at the Oregon Women's Correctional Center. He handed her a cardboard box with her name written on it. The clothes she was wearing when she'd robbed the 7-11 were inside— a pair of jeans, a forest green sweater, and a red wool jacket. The mask was gone; used as evidence to convict her. The clothes smelled musty and the jeans were tight. "I'm surprised you didn't steal this?" She pulled out two five-dollar bills from the front pocket. "I sure as hell would have if I were you."

The R&D Officer was slightly amused. "I hope I never see you again, Maldonado, and I mean that in a good way." He handed her a white envelope with fifty dollars and a bus ticket.

It was a cold November morning when she got off the bus at Third and Burnside in downtown Portland. She wasn't about to ask Sketch and the guys for anything or her parents. She came across a short woman who couldn't have been more than four and half feet tall with long gray hair smoking a cigarette and talking through an open window to a dog in the front seat of a yellow Nova. The backseat was filled with clothes and other random bags of stuff. She was clearly living in her car.

"You know where I can score a quarter bag of heroin?" Bonnie asked.

The woman grinned a toothless smile and got into her car and shut the door. A few minutes later, she emerged. Bonnie handed her twenty-five dollars in exchange for a small bag of white powder. Bonnie fingered it impatiently. "You got a rig?"

"Always be prepared. That's the Boy Scout's motto." The toothless woman rummaged through a bag and presented Bonnie with a syringe and a metal spoon. "On the house."

Bonnie sat down in an empty doorway and cooked the dope. When it liquefied, she rolled up her sleeve and shot-up. It felt good, like coming home.

Around sunset she came to and realized she had to find a place to stay fast. She walked across the Burnside Bridge to the east side of town. Eight years ago, before she caught her case, there was a cheap motel where the hookers went. It was still there and still cheap —$29 a night, which left her six dollars. She'd figure something else out tomorrow. Now she needed sleep. She collapsed on the bed her with shoes and the lights still on.

In the morning, she was startled by the sound of pounding on the door.

"Ma'am, check out time was 10:00 AM."

"I know. I'm not checking out until tomorrow," she had lied.

When she looked out the window to see if he was gone, she noticed a shopping cart in the bushes of the motel's parking lot. It gave her an idea. She hung the *Do Not Disturb* sign on the door handle and then stripped the bedspread from the bed and wrapped the TV in it. There was a pawnshop down on Union Avenue. She'd been there once or twice when she'd needed money.

She grabbed the TV and raced down the stairs to the shopping cart. She plopped it in. The weight of the TV made the wheels of the cart sink into the dirt. "Mother fucker," she cursed, realizing her mistake too late. She pulled and pulled at it until she finally freed it from the dirt and pushed it on to the concrete. The rusted wheels squeaked as she headed south towards the pawnshop.

She came upon a frail old lady fumbling with the keys to a sky-blue Buick, her arms weighed down with bags of groceries. Bonnie edged the shopping cart into an alley and watched as the old woman struggled to get her key in the lock. One of her grocery bags slipped from her arms and the contents were spilling on the ground.

Bonnie walked over and picked up the three oranges that had tumbled out of the brown bag. "Can I help you?" she asked.

"Yes, dear." The old woman smiled and handed Bonnie the keys.

Bonnie put the oranges back in the bag, then unlocked the door and put the bag in the backseat. She took the other bag from the old woman's arms and put it in the car.

"Oh, thank you for helping me, dear. Let me give you some money." The old woman opened the clasp on her pocketbook and reached in. A twenty-dollar bill fell out. The old woman didn't notice. Bonnie reached down and picked it up. The old woman fished out a dollar and handed it to her.

"Thanks," Bonnie said accepting the dollar. "Here, you dropped this." Bonnie handed her back the twenty.

"You're such a dear. It's so hard to find honest people these days. Thank you, young lady." The old woman patted her on the shoulder, then shuffled over to the driver's side of the car and took her seat. "Oh heavens, where did I put my keys?" The old woman unlatched her pocketbook.

Bonnie looked down. The keys were still in her hand. She walked over the driver's side of the car. "Here they are," she said and handed them to the old woman.

The old woman patted her on the hand. "Thank you, dear." She smiled and put the keys in the ignition. "You are my guardian angel today." She turned the key engaging the engine and waved goodbye.

Bonnie waited until the old lady was out of sight then hustled back to the shopping cart with the TV. She walked the last block with the TV cradled in her arms.

She was relieved to see the shop still there and open. She strode inside and set the TV down on the counter. She didn't recognize the young man behind the counter. *What was the name of the guy I used to sell to? Mike? Mark? Max!*

"How's Max?" she asked the guy at the counter.

The guy sighed. "Dad's been dead for three years now."

Bonnie thought it was strange that someone could have died and been dead for three years while she was locked up.

"I'm sorry for your loss."

"Thanks, you selling this TV?"

"Nah, just takin' it for a walk." She laughed. "How much for this beauty?" She pretended to polish the screen with the edge of her sweater.

"It's kind of old." He plugged it in and changed the channels. "Reception seems good. I'll give you twenty-five dollars for it and that's mostly because you asked about my dad. You must be a nice lady if you knew my dad on a first name basis."

"I've been out of town for a few years, but your dad, Max, was a great guy. Real fair." She tried to make something up that would make him feel good about his father. "Thanks, Max's son." She waved goodbye.

Bonnie knew they'd be looking for her on the eastside, so she walked across the Morrison Bridge and up to Pioneer Square. She stood outside the Nordstrom's store.

"Can you help me out? I'm trying to get a room for me and my babies," she told a woman walking out of the store with her arms full of shopping bags. The lie came easily and so did the money. The woman opened her purse and handed Bonnie a five-dollar bill. She continued asking for money outside the store, darting inside whenever she saw a cop car drive past. By the end of the day she had eighteen dollars.

She found a hotel that rented rooms for forty dollars a week. The place was nasty. It stunk like Pine-Sol and pee, but it was better than a prison cell or staying with her parents. The guy at the desk rented her a room on the second floor. It was clean enough. It had a twin bed with an off white bedspread and a little wooden table. There was a sink with a mirror above it, a tiny closet with a couple of wire hangers, and a bathroom with a toilet and a shower. A couple of days ago she was sharing a room this size with two other women.

"Life styles of the rich and fucking famous," she laughed aloud.

After she paid for her room, she went to the liquor store for cigarettes. Being in the store triggered memories of the botched 7-11 job. She grabbed a green bottle of Thunderbird and made a beeline to the counter. "A pack of Camels and a book of matches," she said to the clerk, wondering if he could tell she was the enemy.

He smiled at her, bagged her items, and told her to have a nice day. She guessed not.

She lit up a cigarette and walked the three blocks to Waterfront Park where she sat down on a bench facing the dark river and unscrewed the top on the Thunderbird and took a sip. *So much better than prison hooch*, she thought.

A guy with long brown-hair wearing a Pink Floyd T-shirt skate boarded up to her. He looked close to her age, maybe a little younger. "Hey, can I bum a smoke?" he asked, pushing his hair out of his face.

"I suppose. What's your name?"

"Gary."

Gary was cute, especially after only having cops and shitheads like Kovach to look at. "Gary, sit down and join me for a drink. I'm celebrating my freedom."

Gary took a seat on the bench next to her. She handed him the bottle of Thunderbird. He took a swig. "Freedom, huh? You just get out of jail or something?" He slid the skateboard back and forth with his feet as they talked.

"More like prison."

"Damn girl, you're big time." He grinned a smile that sent shivers up her spine.

She took a drag off her cigarette. "You look like you might know something about the big time."

Gary laughed. "Nah, I'm small time, except for maybe one grand theft auto. Of course, there's always the ones they ain't caught me for."

"I got a place just a couple of blocks from here." She smiled.

Gary kicked up his skateboard into his hand. "Lead the way."

Chapter 39

BONNIE SAT ACROSS from Dr. Thomas and fiddled with a loose string on her khaki shirt. "I guess I should start by telling you about my boyfriend Gary."

"The one who went back to his ex-girlfriend?"

"Yep, that one. Met him after I got out of state. He let me stay with him. He had kids. I don't like kids but I liked them okay. His ex was a stripper. They're always changing their schedules or calling them in at the last minute, so the kids would stay with us when she worked nights. It was like *insta-family*. I'd read his daughter stories and play video games with son."

"Sounds nice," Dr. Thomas said.

Bonnie nodded. "It was for awhile. I worked as a waitress at this diner called Velji's and Gary was making decent money at the Les Schwab Tire Store." Bonnie hadn't even tried to look for a job in carpentry, believing that "no one would hire a woman" like Kovach told her.

"So what went wrong?"

"My habit was getting too expensive and I got Gary hooked too." She grabbed a tissue and wiped her nose. "This one night, I remember I was sitting on the couch watching TV with the kids and Gary said he needed to talk to me. I followed him into the hallway. He told me he had to go to work.' I was like, 'At this hour?' He gave me this look, Dr. T, that I'd never seen on his face. 'Ain't no better time to rob a liquor store,' he said."

Dr. Thomas leaned back in her chair. "So Gary started to feel the desperation you talked about before you went to the 7-11."

"Yeah, I didn't think we needed the money that bad. I tried to talk him out of it, but he wasn't listening to me."

Bonnie remembered how he pushed her out of his way and walked out. She'd crushed out her cigarette in the yellow ashtray on the dining room table, then went to the refrigerator grabbed a beer and sat back down on the couch to watch TV with the kids wondering what she would do if Gary didn't come back.

"What happened?" Dr. Thomas asked. Bonnie could see the suspense was killing her.

"He came back alright, stinking like a freaking brewery. He and his buddies robbed two liquor stores that night. They took booze and money. Said I'd inspired him, some shit like that, and handed me a roll of twenties. 'This is for your brother. Buy him some new clothes or a video or something.' He said."

Dr. Thomas lifted her hand to her chin. "That must have played on your soft spot for your brother."

Bonnie nodded. "Yeah, but I told him 'don't push your luck, Gary. That's how you get caught.' He just laughed and pushed another one of my soft spots."

"What did he do?"

"Waved a bag of dope in my face. That was the strongest relationship in my life."

"How did you get back involved with the …?" Dr. Thomas hesitated.

Bonnie jumped in. "Couldn't resist the challenge. Hell, I don't like being kept out of the action. He said some of the guys were coming over to play cards and tried to get me out of the house. I knew he was up to something."

She remembered how Gary had pulled her off her feet and onto his lap. "Look Bon, you've already had a load of trouble. The less you know the better. Now get off me and clean up the table." She had gotten up and grabbed the dishes from the table and threw them at the sink, breaking the plates. "I have more experience than you do, asshole." She had yelled at him.

"What was he planning?" Dr. Thomas asked.

Bonnie squinted. "Armed bank robbery."

"Were you nervous since things had gone bad before?"

"I felt nervous about using a gun again, at first anyway. I told him about this broad I met in the joint who said it's just as easy to rob a bank with a note telling them you have a gun as it is to bring one. He said the gun was an insurance policy in case anything went wrong, but I didn't want to get caught with a gun if we got busted, so I offered to drive. But then they decided that I would hand the teller the note."

That night was etched in her mind.

"You got any more Cheetos in there, Bonnie?"

"Sure, Lyle, hang on." Bonnie got up and grabbed a half-eaten bag of Cheetos and poured them into a bowl.

"The service is great at this joint." Lyle joked, his front teeth stained orange.

Joe shook his empty beer can. "How about some more beer too?"

Bonnie went to the refrigerator and overheard Joe mumble something to Gary.

"She's cool." She heard Gary tell him. "She'll drive."

"I thought that was my job?" Lyle asked. "How about if she hands them the note instead? They'll never expect a woman."

"Bonnie, come on over here." Gary lit a cigarette.

She grabbed a six-pack and put it on the counter top next to the dining room table where they were playing poker, then opened a can of Budweiser and handed it to Joe.

Joe wiped crumbs from his mustache. "Lyle will drive. I'll cover the door. Gary, you'll back Bonnie. Bonnie, you'll write the note. Can you manage that?" Joe scanned her face like he was looking for fear.

She pulled a can from the six-pack, opened it and took a sip. "Yeah, I can handle that," she said and noticed her eye twitched when she said it. She hoped he didn't see it. She didn't want to hand the teller the note. She wanted to drive, but she didn't want to miss out on the action.

"Okay, here's what you're gonna do," Joe said. "You're gonna go up to the teller and hand her a note that reads- *This is a hold up. Put all the money in this purse. Any sudden movements and someone will get hurt.* You're gonna write it on the back of a deposit slip. You got it?" Joe gave her a stern look.

"Got it," she said, wondering what she was getting herself into, but it was too late. Joe was already planning her disguise.

Dr. Thomas took a sip from her water bottle. "So you agreed to hold up the teller?"

"Yeah, but with a note, not a gun, that felt a little better, like maybe I wouldn't get as much time if we got busted."

"Were you scared of getting hurt, like getting shot at by the bank security or the police?"

Bonnie shook her head. "It seems weird to think about it now, but the thought of getting hurt never even crossed my mind. I didn't think like that. I was more concerned with getting caught and wanted to make sure I had a good disguise."

"How did you disguise yourself?"

She hesitated. *Dr. Thomas seems trustworthy, but it could come back to haunt me. Still they don't have any solid proof and I can still say I made it all up 'cause I was bored and had time to kill.* She decided it was okay to tell her.

"I bought a long red wig and styled it, trying to make it look convincing. Gary told me he'd always had a thing for redheads. Gary was crazy." Bonnie smiled, but she felt herself wanting to cry.

Dr. Thomas seemed to look through her. "Sounds like you really miss him?"

"Yeah, I do," she said and wiped away a tear. She remembered how sexy he looked before the robbery. He'd looked a little like Steve Perry with a beard. He'd gone to the first robbery undisguised, but then shaved his beard and cut his hair short when he got home later that night. It was like Gary was gone after that, replaced by someone else.

"If it wasn't for me getting caught…"

Dr. Tomas handed her a tissue. "Tell me about the first robbery, Bonnie."

Bonnie wiped her eyes. "One of the other waitresses I worked with had stomach flu, so I called in and told them I was sick. Since Friday and Saturday were my days off, I figured it would be easy to say I was fine by Sunday. I drove Gary's car and met the guys down by the Columbia River where they were pretending to be fishing. That was their alibi. They went to the bait shop, bought worms and a couple of six-packs, and lodged their fishing poles in the rocks along the riverbank."

"Sounds like a pretty elaborate plan."

"It was," Bonnie said. "Worked real well. One of the guys dropped Gary and the other guy off outside of the Skippers a block from the bank and he was going to wait across the street with the motor running. I walked into the bank. My heart was beating so loud. I walked up to where you get the withdrawal and deposit slips and I wrote out a note. It said, 'this is a hold up. Put all the money in this purse. Any sudden movements and someone will get hurt.' My hand was shaking so bad from all the adrenaline. The teller was Chinese, I don't even know if she could read English."

Dr. Thomas looked like she rolled her eyes at her, but she wasn't sure.

"She told me, 'you fill other side of slip with number for withdrawal.'" Bonnie said mocking the woman's broken English. "I told her, 'this is a hold up, chink lady. Keep your fucking mouth closed. Open up the till and give everything to me slowly so I can put it in my purse. Do anything crazy and you, or someone else, is gonna to die.'"

Bonnie remembered fake smiling at the teller and pretending she was a customer closing her account. "It's been lovely banking with you and I would prefer that in twenties and hundreds," she'd told the woman.

Joe had pretended to write a deposit slip while Gary waited in line for the next teller. The line was getting shorter. The teller was still taking the money out of the till and handing it to her as she stuffed it in her purse. "

Next in line," she heard another teller say to Gary. Gary patted himself down like he was looking for something.

"Ah, shoot," he said. "I left my wallet in the car." She watched him walk out. "That's all," the teller said, her voice quivered.

Bonnie spoke quietly. "Unless you want to die you better keep quiet. We'll be watching you. You understand?"

The woman nodded. She looked like she was going to cry.

"Nice banking with you." Bonnie said. She walked out briskly and headed for the car.

Once inside the car she ducked down. Gary was in the back seat hiding. Lyle started to pull out of the parking lot and Joe ran over to the car and jumped in. They tore off heading west to Highway 84. Lyle took the 82nd Ave Exit and dropped Bonnie off on Stark Street.

"You done good, Bonnie." Gary smiled. "Take the bus home. Joe and I will go back to the river and then stop by the Acropolis on the way back. That way, if anything happens, we can say that we were out fishing most of the day, but our luck was bad, so we went to the strip bar to improve our moods. Carolyn will cover me if I need her to. Guard that money, girl."

"Did you feel bad about robbing the bank?" Dr. Thomas asked.

Bonnie wanted to laugh. She wondered what Dr. Thomas would think of her if she told her the truth.

Elated was the word she thought described what she felt after robbing that bank. She pulled it off without a hitch. No one got hurt and she walked off with almost nine thousand dollars.

"No, I didn't feel bad. I just made close to nine thousand dollars. Not bad for an hour's worth of work."

Bonnie could see that Dr. Thomas didn't agree with her on that. She remembered how proud Gary was of her. He'd scooped her up in arms and kissed her.

Dr. Thomas brought her hand to her chin. Bonnie could see she was trying hard to understand her. "Why did you continue? Why didn't you stop while you were ahead?"

Bonnie leaned back in the chair. "Because they weren't going to give me any money of my own. They wanted me to split it three ways, have Gary and me share. I had to do another job."

Dr. Thomas looked at her clock. Bonnie followed her gaze. Two hours had already gone by. "It goes by so fast," Bonnie said. There was still so much she wanted to get off her chest.

"We're going to need to pick this up in our next session," Dr. Thomas said. "It takes great courage to face your past. I think you're doing a really good job."

"Thanks, Dr. Thomas. It feels good to talk to someone about this."

When Bonnie got back to her room, she immediately put on her headphones so she wouldn't have to talk to Harris. She lay down on her bunk thinking about how she had agreed to rob another bank just to get her cut on the first one. She felt a rage boiling up inside her. *Why hadn't she demanded they pay her an equal share of the first job?*

Gary promised to talk to the guys about her getting a fair cut. Instead Joe brought up the idea of robbing another bank. She remembered how eager she was to strike again. It made her feel powerful in a way she wasn't ready to share with Dr. Thomas and when Joe included her in the plan she couldn't say no.

"I was thinking we could hit a First Interstate next in Eugene or Tacoma. They have less security procedures than the other banks. Bonnie you take the note again, Lyle you drive. Gary and I will provide cover."

"You got it Joe, but I want a fair cut." Bonnie crushed out her cigarette.

Gary shot her a look. "Bonnie should get a fourth of the action."

Bonnie stared back at him.

"And," he stammered. "And her fair share for the work she's already done."

Joe coughed. "That wasn't the deal, Gary." He pulled at his mustache and glanced over at Lyle.

Lyle shrugged his shoulders.

"What kind of fucked up deal is that Joe? I put my ass on the line and don't get a fair cut? Shit, I put myself way more out there than Lyle." She tried to reason with him.

Lyle fell back in his chair and clutched his chest like he was mortally wounded.

Joe got up and put his arms on Bonnie's shoulders. "Deal, but only if you keep your cool like you did that last go-round. You might be our lucky charm."

Bonnie had never felt lucky in her life and couldn't imagine being anybody's lucky charm, but maybe Joe was right, the robbery had gone perfectly, except for the teller not reading the note, everything had gone as planned.

Chapter 40

VICTORIA SAT ON the mauve couch in Peter's private practice office and admired the beautiful masks and objects from his travels. His walls were decorated with colorful framed pieces of modern art. She imagined having an office like this, above a café, filled with comfortable furniture—a stark contrast to her prison office filled with the clunky inmate made furniture.

Peter sat down next to her on the couch, took a sip of his latte and then turned to face her. "Where's Devin, tonight?"

"He's in Seattle for business."

"How are things going?" he asked.

She could sense him trying to read her, it made her uncomfortable. *Tricks of the trade*, she thought. "Good. He's been pretty busy lately."

He took a sip of his latte. "How are things with that client?"

"She's opening up a lot more."

Peter set his latte on the side table and turned toward her, looking more deeply into her eyes. "What happened?"

"Well, we were talking about how she went back to…"

He interrupted her. "Come on, Victoria, I'm talking about us. What happened with us?"

Victoria was caught in his gaze. She felt herself wanting him. She quickly averted his eyes and glanced at the paintings on his wall. "I don't know. You're so intense. Maybe I have a fear of intimacy," she joked, half-wondering if it was true.

Peter moved closer to her on the couch. She could feel her stomach flip flop. "He's so worried about his job, about rising up the corporate ladder that he takes you for granted. What kind of marriage is that? What kind of partnership? Devin doesn't get you like I do. I get you, Victoria."

Her face flushed. "I've gotta go," she said and stood up from the couch. "I can't do this."

"You say that, but I don't believe you. You're here for a reason and it's not just for a consultation."

"Yes, I'm still attracted to you, but I can't do this." Victoria grabbed her purse and headed for the door. She stopped before opening it and turned to face him. He'd followed her to the entry-way. "I really have to go." She said, turning her face away just in case he tried to kiss her.

"I'll walk you to your car."

"No, you don't have to do that."

"I know. I want to. I didn't mean to chase you out."

They descended the stairs in silence and walked to a side street where she was parked. She clicked the automatic lock open.

"Can I give you a hug goodbye?" he asked.

Victoria knew she should say no, but she wanted to feel his arms around her.

"Okay," she said, surrendering to the embrace. It felt good, comfortable, familiar, but wrong. She broke the circle of their bodies. "I need to be home when Devin calls." She opened the door and tossed her purse into the passenger's seat.

"Goodnight, Victoria," he said and closed the door.

Chapter 41

BONNIE SWALLOWED HARD. She realized that without thinking, she'd blurted out the guys' names. She looked at Dr. Thomas for a sign that she might be making a mental note, but she saw none. She had said Gary's name before when talking to Dr. Thomas, but she didn't care, he had nothing coming as far she was concerned.

"So I was in the backseat. I'd pulled the wig off and the car just kept stalling out."

"That must have been tense," Dr. Thomas commented.

"Yeah, I was just like 'oh shit, come the fuck on.' I kept yelling at him to keep trying. I even prayed to God. I ain't never prayed for anything. And it worked. He turned the key and the motor started."

"Then what happened?" Dr. Thomas asked. She looked like she was on the edge of her seat.

"He revved that fucking engine hard, floored the accelerator and took off to the Denny's where Gary's car was parked. We ditched the Pontiac and piled into Gary's car, but then the guys started fighting. Lyle told Joe he didn't need a fucking sermon about his drinking and he opened the car door to get out. Right as he did we saw the cop car. I had a sick feeling in my stomach. I wasn't ready to do time again. Gary yelled at Lyle to get in, but it wasn't until Joe cocked his gun that he stopped fucking around and got back in. The lights flashed on the patrol car and I thought we're totally fucked, but then the cop car made a quick U-turn and headed toward the highway in the opposite direction. Made out with two and half grand that day."

"What did you do with the money?" Dr. Thomas asked.

"Shit, I didn't even get a chance to spend it all."

"You were really lucky the first couples of times."

"That's what Gary said. He kept saying we were lucky and we should take a break. But everybody else wanted to keep going."

"Did you?"

"I got caught up, you know? It was something I was good at and the guys kept telling me what a kick-ass job I'd done. It felt good. But Gary was pissed. He said they were going to notice a pattern. So, I told him I'd change things up a bit?"

"What did you do?"

"I ditched the red wig and wore a baseball cap and sunglasses. Then they couldn't tell I was female."

"You did that with your state case."

"Yeah. "Bonnie smiled. "I'd done it before."

Bonnie remembered Lyle cracking himself up, "I'm going to wear the red wig next time." He joked. But Gary didn't think any of it was funny. She remembered the serious look on his face.

"That morning Gary said he had 'a bad feeling' but I didn't listen. I should've listened." Bonnie shook her head. "I think there were even signs, but I was stubborn."

Dr. Thomas took another sip of her coffee. Bonnie thought she saw a hint of a smile visible on her face. "Signs?"

Bonnie nodded. "I know it sounds crazy, but as we were driving up to Vancouver I turned on the radio and this crazy song came on. It went something like, *'lay your pistol down babe, lay your pistol down, pistol packing mama lay your pistol down.'* It freaked me out. I remember Lyle joking with Gary, telling him he hoped he wasn't psychic."

"Wow, that does sound like a sign," Dr. Thomas said. "What were the others?"

"I went into the bank and I was totally unrecognizable. My hair was pulled up inside a ball cap and I wore sunglasses. My look was tight. But my stomach felt funny. I told myself I was just excited. I'm not sure why we decided I'd carry the 9mm. I can't remember exactly, except that we felt I should have it just in case, beef up our insurance policy. I walked up to the counter and wrote the note on the deposit slip. Only this time I forgot to write the command *no sudden movements or someone will get hurt.* That's why things went bad. I fucked up."

"Bad how?" Dr. Thomas asked.

"The teller gasped when I handed it to her and the other tellers immediately recognized what was going on. Gary saw my cover was blown. He yelled for everybody to get down and pulled out his gun. I remember there was this Indian lady with glasses and she started screaming and fell to the floor."

Bonnie remembered the teller was shaking and crying too. The lady kept dropping bills on the floor missing the bag. "Focus," Bonnie has hissed through clenched teeth, unaware that, in the commotion, she'd pulled out the gun and was pointing it at the teller's head.

"Bonnie are you still with me?"

Bonnie looked at Dr. Thomas. "Yeah, what happened?"

"You were telling me about the Indian woman and then you blanked out again."

"Oh, so I was getting the money and Gary yelled that we had to go, but there were still piles of bills in the drawer. It made me angry. Can't really explain it. I reached across the counter and grabbed the clerk. I was pissed at her for fucking everything up. Gary and Joe ran out."

"What did you do?"

"I came to my senses. Let go of the woman and ran for the door. I was almost out when this bald guy grabbed me and tried to take the bag..." Bonnie stopped suddenly.

"The bald guy grabbed you and tried to take the bag?" Dr. Thomas repeated.

"Yeah," Bonnie said, staring into space.

"Then what happened?"

"I...I turned toward him. I, um," her voice quivered, "I shot..."

"Where did you shoot?" Dr. Thomas asked.

"Into his stomach." Bonnie swallowed hard. It was like she could see the bald guy in front of her.

"And then?" Dr. Thomas asked.

"I shot him two more times." Bonnie clutched her forehead holding her hand over her eyes. "I remember running to the car and Lyle was angry, he kept asking 'what took us so long' and saying he was about to drive off without us. Joe told him to 'shut up and drive.' When he pressed his foot to the accelerator I slammed into the back seat of the car and I noticed my clothes felt wet. I remember thinking that I'd been so nervous I'd soaked my clothes with sweat."

Dr. Thomas nodded.

"I remember looking out the window at the trees as we sped down the freeway back to Portland and Lyle telling Gary that he couldn't let anybody see me. I wasn't sure what he was talking about and then I looked down and saw I was bleeding, but I hadn't felt any pain. I figured the adrenaline had kept me from feeling the pain. When I got home I went straight to the bathroom and took off my clothes. I looked around for the wound, but couldn't find it. That's when it hit me. I'm not sure why it didn't hit me sooner. I locked the door. Got into the shower. I must have stayed in there for a long time because I heard this loud thud and then Gary ripped open the shower curtain. He scared the shit out of me. He told me I scared him. He thought maybe I was gonna slit my wrists or something."

"What were you thinking about it in that moment?" Dr. Thomas asked.

"I was thinking, 'Why the fuck would I do that?' You know, I wasn't suicidal."

"What made you stay in the shower so long?"

She looked at the floor. "I was just trying to get clean. Get rid of that copper smell, you know?"

Dr. Thomas shook her head. "No, I don't."

She exhaled. "Blood has this nasty copper smell to it. I got all the blood off of me, but I couldn't get the smell out of my nostrils."

Dr. Thomas looked like she was going to gag. "So you were soaked with blood?"

Bonnie nodded. "I got out of the shower and sat on the toilet. Gary picked up my dirty clothes and came back with a needle, he didn't want to talk."

Bonnie remembered grabbing a leather belt off the door hook and tying it around her upper arm and edging the needle in, then getting in bed to lie down. She heard the washer going and thought it was a strange time to do laundry.

"I asked him how much money we got when he came back into the bedroom. He just sat there staring at me with this weird look on his face and told me it'd been a long day and we could count the money in the morning."

"Did you ever talk about it?"

"No, this is the first time I've talked about it, except what I told you about before."

"How do you feel about what you did?"

"I don't like to talk about it."

"Do you feel bad that you killed someone?"

"It just doesn't feel real most of the time. It's hard to believe that I did."

"But you did," Dr. Thomas said.

"Sometimes it feels like I just dreamt it all up, sometimes I feel like it's his own damn fault for getting in my way." Bonnie wondered what Dr. Thomas was thinking.

"So you feel he deserved it because he was in your way?"

"When I think about that woman who came and talked about being robbed, that made me feel bad. I could tell she was a really nice lady. When I think about what she went through I feel bad, because I know that must be what it was like for the people in the bank. It's weird you know, the thing that sticks out the most is that I felt good when I was robbing the banks."

"Good?" Dr. Thomas raised her eyebrows.

"Well, you can judge me if you want, but I'm just telling you the truth. That was when I felt like I had my shit together."

"So you felt like you were in control?"

"Fuck yeah, people did what I told them to. I said fucking drop and they did. Despite what my old man said I made shit happen."

"Your dad?"

"Yeah, that fucking bastard. I felt like I was showing him I could be more fearless and tougher than he could ever be." She suddenly felt a lump in her throat. Tears streaked her face. She wiped a tear from her eye with the back of her hand.

Dr. Thomas handed her a tissue. "I see why that was so important to you and I really appreciate your honesty with me, Bonnie. It takes more courage to get honest with yourself and face your emotions than it does to rob a bank."

"Fuck!" She took the tissue and wiped her face with it. "I didn't want to hurt anybody. But it proved that I was strong."

"Did it? You had a gun. You killed someone, a man who was trying to keep other people from getting hurt by trying to stop you. Rather than trying to prove your worth you could realize that you are inherently worthy."

"What do you mean?"

The phone on Dr. Thomas's desk rang. She ignored it.

"Don't you need to get that?" Bonnie asked.

"No, they can leave a message," Dr. Thomas said, looking somewhat annoyed by the interruption. "I mean that you are worthy and lovable as you are."

She was confused by what Dr. Thomas was saying and surprised that Dr. Thomas wasn't answering her phone. Staff always answered their phones even if they were talking to inmates.

"I don't feel worthy. I don't want to be lovable. I want to keep people away from me so they don't fuck with me. Every time I let someone get close, look what happens. My parents didn't love me. Tim died. And Gary, I never loved anyone like Gary. He fucking dumped me and went back to his ex."

"Maybe it was the kind of people you were letting close to you. Maybe you trusted the wrong people."

Bonnie noticed a warm look in Dr. Thomas's eyes, one she had never seen in her mother's eyes. "Do you think I'm lovable, Dr. Thomas?"

"Yes, I think you're lovable."

"Do you love me, Dr. Thomas?" she asked.

Dr. Thomas seemed startled by her question. Her eyes blinked several times before she answered. "Yes, Ms. Maldonado, I do love you."

Bonnie was stunned. "Really?"

"Really," Dr. Thomas said and glanced at the clock. "We're going to have to stop for today. I'll see you next week."

Bonnie got up from her chair and headed to the door, surprised by the abrupt ending of their session. Lately, Dr. Thomas would allow their sessions to go past the 50 minutes.

"I love you too, Dr. Thomas." Bonnie said and walked out.

Chapter 42

VICTORIA FELT A bit unsure if she had handled the situation with Bonnie appropriately, telling her that she loved her. On the one hand she felt like it would be helpful for Bonnie's issues with internalizing a positive object relation and what was unconditional positive regard if not love. Surely Carl Rogers would have approved. On the other, telling a client, let alone a client who was an inmate at a federal prison, that she had feelings of unconditional positive regard by using the word "love" was practically an invitation to be fired for staff misconduct. She questioned herself, becoming increasingly paranoid that this episode could get seriously misunderstood and lead to an investigation. *Was it really that out of line to say it? Did the positive therapeutic impact of answering Maldonado's question outweigh the concern of a potential misunderstanding in a correctional environment?*

Brad suddenly opened her door without knocking and walked in. "Victoria, didn't you hear your phone ringing?"

"Yes," Victoria said defensively, annoyed that Brad had barged into her office, "but I was in a session and didn't want to lose my train of thought."

"They need us at the front entrance immediately."

"For what?"

"Mike Russell somehow got into the armory and is threatening to shoot himself or anyone who tries to get near him."

"Oh my God. Why?" she asked, but then it dawned on her and Brad confirmed it.

"He got a tip they were going to walk him out for sexual misconduct and he somehow managed to get inside the armory. Victoria, we need to go," he said impatiently. "Bob is out today. They're trying to reach him to help the hostage negotiation team, but you're the back up mental health consultant and they need you now."

"Shit!" Victoria grabbed her purse, a notebook, and a pen.

The paranoia increased. *What if they really do think my answering Bonnie's question about loving her is the same thing? No,* she tried to reassure herself, *this is different. Russell is having a sexual relationship with an inmate, otherwise why would he go to such extremes.* Victoria reasoned that she was only showing unconditional positive regard, part of her professional expectations. She was merely answering Bonnie's question that she cared for her. She was talking about *agape love,* love for one's fellow, not a sexual love like Mike Russell was being accused of.

She locked her door. Brad had already cleared the building of inmates.

"They've locked down all of the units," he said. "We need to hurry."

They walked briskly to the front entrance.

"I can't believe he locked himself in the armory."

Brad shook his head. "You know what that means, don't you?"

Victoria looked confused. "What?"

"The front entrance is compromised. There's bulletproof glass in the control room, but the officer can't get out and he can't let anyone in or out of the front entrance. We can't go out the front entrance without potentially getting shot."

"Oh my God," she gasped. She tried to imagine what she was going to do. No doubt the new warden would be looking to her expertise.

"The only way in or out now is the rear gate."

"I need to call my husband," she said.

Brad gave her a serious look. "There's no time for that."

As they approached the top of the yard, Victoria saw the SORT team members outside the fence line surrounding the front entrance and the Disturbance Control Team in a semicircle formation on the inside of the prison. Only then did the seriousness of what was going on hit her.

"Okay, good, Dr. Thomas is finally here." Lt. Lopez put his hand on her shoulder. "Here's the deal, Doc. Mike Russell is locked in the armory. He has access to all the guns and scores of ammo. We've contacted the FBI and they're on their way. We're going tactical just as soon as we can. In the meantime, you're going to help us with negotiations. Officer Landers and Berger have both been to negotiation training. They're gonna be your negotiators. Usually Scarsdale is our mental health consultant, but today's your lucky day. The Warden and the other executive staff have set up the Command Center at the SORT building outside the prison compound. Captain Brown has the TOC set up in the Warden's Conference Room. You're going to be at the NOC."

"What's the NOC?" Victoria asked.

"Sleeping in class, Doc?" Lopez shook his head.

"What do you mean? I've never been trained in hostage negotiations."

"Everyone gets basic hostage negotiation training in FLETC. Some of this should sound vaguely familiar to you."

Victoria's face flushed red. "I'm sorry, lieutenant. I just don't remember."

"Negotiations Operations Center and Tactical Operations Center. Knock and talk. But in this case you're doing the knocking and the boys will do the talking." Lt. Lopez explained. "The SORT team will introduce the throw phone into the front entrance as close as they can get to the armory without risking getting shot. The NOC is located at the Warden's secretary's office where there is a direct line of site to the armory and front entrance. Once SORT introduces the phone you can begin negotiations with Russell. Better get over there now."

Victoria walked briskly to the Warden's secretary's office where she found Ms. Fernando tapping up large white pieces of paper on the walls. Officers Berger and Tracy were nervously plugging in cords to what looked like some sort of electronic device in a suitcase.

"This is the hostage phone," Berger said, noticing the curious look on Victoria's face.

"Okay, we're in," Tracy said. He put on a pair of headphones and pressed a button on the phone. She could hear the sound of the phone ringing on a set of small speakers attached to the phone.

"Hello?" a voice answered.

"Mike, is that you?"

"Who is this?" the voice demanded.

"This is Officer Paul Tracy, Mike. How are you doing?"

"How the fuck do you think I'm doing, Tracy?" Russell slammed the phone down.

Tracy took off the headphones. He looked around. "Scarsdale not coming?"

"No, they've asked me to fill in for him." She said.

"Have you ever been a mental health consultant to a hostage negotiation team before?"

"No, but I'm sure I can help. The most important thing is rapport, getting him talking, getting him comfortable with you."

Berger grabbed a black felt tip marker and wrote the word "barbs" on one sheet of paper and the word "hooks" on another.

"Why don't you give it a few minutes, Officer Tracy, and then try him again. Asking him how he is was more of a barb, let's see if we can find any hooks," she said.

"Maybe you can start by asking him to tell you what he's upset about?" Victoria offered. Berger nodded.

Officer Tracy put on the headset again and pushed the dial button. Russell picked up.

"What?" he asked.

"It sounds like you're pretty upset. Can you tell me what's going on?"

Victoria scribbled the word "good" on a piece of paper and showed it to Officer Tracy.

"Haven't you heard?"

"Heard what, Mike?" Officer Tracy asked, nonchalantly.

"They're going to walk me out. They say I've been fucking the inmates. Can you believe that shit?"

"Well, Mike, I don't know anything about that. I do know that people are really concerned about your safety right now and I know that this is really out of character for you. Whatever the other situation might be, this is taking things a little too far."

"You don't think firing me from my job when they have no evidence is taking things too far?"

Officer Tracy looked at her and Berger. Victoria gave him a thumbs up and whispered, "Good job. Nice and easy."

"I can't speak for the executive staff, but I do know that this is really unlike you, and I'm sure your family is worried about you, Mike." Berger patted Tracy on the back.

"My family should be worried. How the hell can I take care of them without a job? I want to speak with the Warden. Why did they put a punk ass kid on the phone to talk to me?" The agitation in Russell's voice rose.

Victoria saw Tracy's face redden. "Mike, you know as well as I do that wardens don't negotiate. That's why they put my GS-9 ass on the phone."

Mike laughed. "You're funny, Tracy."

"Well, sir, it's good to hear you laugh, but this is serious. We need to get you out of there so we can get this thing resolved and people can go home to their families. I'm sure your wife is waiting for you." Officer Tracy mock wiped the sweat from his brow.

"You think she's going to be waiting for me after this, after the shit they're accusing me of? You married, Tracy?"

"Yes, sir," Officer Tracy said.

"You think your wife would want you after you were accused of dipping your dick in inmate pussy?"

Victoria bristled at his comment, but Officer Tracy was solid.

"Well sir, innocent until proven guilty. That's my approach, and I hope it would be hers too. Now how about coming out and we can get this whole thing settled. The longer you're in there, the more people are going to think you have something to hide."

"Is the chaplain around?"

"You want to speak to Chaplain Edwards?" Tracy asked.

Victoria scribbled a note on a piece of paper and gave it to Ms. Fernando. "Can you take this to the TOC for Captain Brown's approval?"

Ms. Fernando nodded and disappeared with the note.

"Yes, I want to speak to the Rev."

"Okay, Mike, we'll see if we can find him for you."

"Call me back when you do." Russell slammed down the phone.

"Are you sure this is a good idea?" Tracy asked Victoria. "In training they tell us that shrinks and clergy should never be the negotiators."

Victoria answered diplomatically, "there's a good reason for that policy, but we're not going to use the chaplain as a negotiator. You're doing a great job of negotiating with him and establishing rapport, but Russell has personally asked to speak to Chaplain Edwards. Besides, I'm sure they're only going to give us so much time before they go tactical, especially because the front entrance is compromised, and when the FBI gets here, which is imminently, they're not going to be concerned with Mike's life. If Chaplain Edwards can talk him down then maybe we can save the BOP some ammo and bloodshed."

Officer Tracy nodded his head. "Okay, I see your point."

Victoria exhaled and leaned back in her chair wondering where she'd mustered the chutzpah for that speech.

The phone rang. Berger got up and answered it. "It's the Warden for you," she said and handed Victoria the phone.

"Hello, sir," she said.

"I hear Mike wants to talk with Chaplain Edwards, and you feel that's okay?"

"With your approval, sir, he won't be negotiating, because I know there's a policy against that."

"Yes, there is. We'll send Chaplain Edwards over. He's at the Training Center right now calming down several staff member's families, but we'll get him there."

"Thank you, Warden."

"We're counting on you, Doc."

"Yes, sir." Victoria hung up the phone. She hoped that she had made the right suggestion.

"What did he say?" Officer Tracy asked.

"They're going to send Chaplain Edwards, but it's going to be a minute because he's at the Training Center trying to keep staff's family members calm."

Victoria sat in a chair and stared out the window. She'd been right about Mike Russell. He had called her to get more information from her and to keep her from making more reports. *An innocent man would never go this far,* she thought. She wondered who else knew and why it had taken this long for them to consider firing him.

Ten minutes later Chaplain Edwards appeared in the doorway, sweat beading on his brow. "I heard Mike Russell would like to talk to me," he said, his jaw slack and that solemn look on his face that somehow unnerved her, though she didn't really understand why.

Tracy got up from his chair and handed Chaplain Edwards the headset. Chaplain Edwards wiped the sweat from his brow and put the headset on.

"When you're ready, we'll push this button and it will ring the throw phone. You got that?" Tracy asked.

Chaplain Edwards nodded. "Go ahead," he said.

Officer Tracy pushed the button. They heard the phone ring over the speaker.

Russell answered.

"Hello, Mike, this is Chaplain Edwards."

The line was silent for a few moments then they could hear the sound of his breathing.

"They're accusing me of sleeping with inmates, Chaplain. Do you believe them?" Russell said.

"That's between you and God, Mike."

"Yeah."

Victoria could hear the emotion in Mike's voice and then the sound of weeping. Chaplain Edwards looked up at her and around the room. She could tell he was not sure what to say.

He put his hand on his chin and then rolled it up his face until it was covering his eyes and began speaking again. "God will forgive you, Mike. I'm not sure about your wife and you may not have your job, but God will forgive you, you are his son."

There was a loud noise, like a gunshot.

Victoria gasped.

"Dear God," Chaplain Edwards exclaimed. He jerked the head set off and sat up.

Victoria went to him and put her hand on his shoulder. "It's not your fault, Chaplain."

Chaplain Edwards hung his head.

Berger and Tracy rushed to the window. "They got him," Berger yelled.

"Oh my God, they killed him!" Chaplain Edwards exclaimed.

"No, Chap." Officer Tracy shook his head excitedly. "SORT has him. Looks like they let off a flash bang while you were talking to him. Must've been able to get into the armory and take him down. They're escorting him into an FBI vehicle."

"Oh, thank God," Victoria said and got up from where she was sitting.

"Really," Chaplain Edwards said, agreeing with her.

They exchanged relieved looks.

"Just another day in paradise," Officer Tracy said and reached for the ringing phone. "Thank you. Yes, sir, we're going now." He hung up. "Captain Brown wants us to report to the visiting room for a debriefing."

Chapter 43

BONNIE WALKED INTO her room and slammed the door. "Why the hell are they making us stay in the god damned unit?"

"You didn't hear?" Harris asked.

"Hear what?" Bonnie said agitated.

"We're on lockdown."

"Why are we on lockdown? Another broad get her man to hijack a helicopter?"

"Nope, Mr. Russell from Maintenance took another staff member hostage at the front entrance and is threatening to kill them."

"What the fuck? Why?"

"They say he was having an affair with a female staff and she broke it off."

For a moment Bonnie wondered if it was Dr. Thomas, she felt sick to her stomach with worry. *No, Dr. Thomas is into black dudes and looks happy with her husband, even if he is black. Russell isn't her type at all.* She reassured herself.

She was glad she'd told Dr. Thomas how much she meant to her.

"Who do you think it is?" Bonnie asked Harris.

Harris pursed her lips like she'd eaten something sour. "I have a hard time imaginin' who would be into Mr. Russell."

Bonnie nodded. "Me too, but whoever it is, I hope she's okay."

"I feel you," Harris confided. "I mean some of these officers can be bitches, but no woman belongs to a man like that, and if she says it's over, than it's over, and he should be man enough to let her go in peace."

"True that, Bunkie," Bonnie said, realizing that this was the most she and Harris had ever talked.

Bonnie sat back down on her bunk and leaned against the wall. She closed her eyes. *God, if you do exist, make sure that crazy Mr. Russell doesn't gun nobody down, especially Dr. T.*

Chapter 44

"Dr. T, it's so good to see you!" Bonnie practically burst through Victoria's door.

"It's good to see you too, Ms. Maldonado," Victoria said, trying to be more conscious of following the prison rules of calling Bonnie by her surname.

"I was so glad to hear it wasn't you that Mr. Russell had taken hostage. I mean I didn't think it was you, cause he's not your type, you know. I'm so glad you're okay."

Victoria was confused, but nodded and agreed that she too was glad that she was safe, and thanked Bonnie for her concern. "I'd like to get back to where we left off. Why didn't you stop after the murder?"

Bonnie took a sip of instant coffee from her plastic khaki colored coffee cup. "I thought you'd at least ask me how I was before you went there. You probably don't have much need for foreplay either."

Victoria blushed. "Sorry, Ms. Maldonado, I'm just cognizant of how quickly our time goes by and this is important. How are you?" *Shit, I'm totally blowing this!* She thought.

"Hmm." Bonnie bit her lip. "I don't really know. Good I guess. Glad to be off lockdown and out of my cell."

Victoria took a sip of her water. "I bet."

"So you want to know why I didn't stop? I keep asking myself. I guess because we'd only made a few hundred from the last robbery and I felt guilty because I'd fucked it up. I wanted to make up for that."

Victoria nodded. She was amazed by the depth of emotional distancing Bonnie had from the facts and reality of her crimes, including the murder. She was particularly struck by the word "made" when referring to the money they robbed from the bank, like it was a day's work.

"Why was making up for that so important?" Victoria asked.

"Because I wanted to get back in control," Bonnie snarled when she said it.

Victoria studied the cold snarl. It sent shivers down her spine. She held her face neutral. "I see, so what happened?"

"We waited a month for things to cool down and then we planned another job. Joe decided I would drive and Lyle would give the note."

"And you felt comfortable with that? You could be in control?"

"I figured I could do my part."

"I see, please continue."

"I waited in the car with the engine running and when they were all inside the car I headed toward the freeway. I was so careful. Stopped at every red light. I didn't want to draw attention to us, but it seemed like every streetlight was against us. We were two lights from the freeway on-ramp and I wanted to run the light, but Joe told me to 'cool it.' So I waited. As soon as the light turned green I slammed my foot down on the pedal. There was a loud cracking noise. The car jolted and spun. I slammed my head into the windshield."

"Oh my God!"

Next thing I remember I'm waking up chained to a hospital bed. My head hurt like hell and these two cops are standing at the edge of the bed reading me my rights."

Victoria raised an eyebrow. "So you have no memory of the accident."

Bonnie shook her head. "Not really, just that I was waiting for the light to change to get on the freeway and then it all went black."

"And you never saw Gary again."

"No, he took off and left me there. I mean he kept in touch with me through this waitress I worked with at Velji's diner. He would tell her how he was and she would send cryptic messages, at least until I got sentenced and then he wrote me a couple of letters before he went back to his ex."

Victoria could hear the sadness in Bonnie's voice.

"Several months ago we talked about how you felt compelled to rob the 7-11, not only to support your drug habit, but to provide for your brother because you felt responsible for his well-being, which is tied into the guilt you have over your sister's drowning death. You also said that there was something that made you feel powerful when you were robbing banks. Do you want to say more about that?"

"Wow, way to sum that up, Dr. T." Bonnie looked at her hands and was quiet for a long time. She seemed deep in thought.

Victoria couldn't tell what she was thinking and wondered if she'd gone too far, gotten too clinical with her questions. She was getting ready to ask another question when Bonnie broke the silence and answered.

"Like I said, it was something I was good at. When I was robbing banks I felt alive in a way that I've never felt before. It made me feel in control and like all those things my dad said couldn't touch me. I was calling the shots."

Victoria took a sip of her coffee. "Sounds very powerful."

"It was. It was like when I was high, all the hurt just disappeared."

"But it came right back after, didn't it?"

Bonnie looked away. "Yeah, only worse though, cause then I had more reasons to feel like a fuck up. The money didn't make the sick feeling go away and it took more and more dope to escape. Had to shove that shit even further back in my mind, block it out like it wasn't real, like it was someone else, especially what happened at that one bank."

"The murder." Victoria folded her hands into her lap.

Bonnie nodded again.

"Have you had any more nightmares?"

"No, and I'm trying not to think about the bald guy. I mean, if I could change that I would. I wonder sometimes, you know, did he have a family? I mean, he must have had a family. Everyone has a family. But was he close to them? Was he married? Did he have any kids? I think about that kind of stuff." Bonnie's eyes got misty.

Victoria motioned to the tissue box on her desk. "Knowing you killed someone is a hard reality to live with."

Bonnie grabbed a tissue and wiped her eyes. "Yeah, but I have to face what I did."

"How will facing it change you?" Victoria finished the last of her coffee and threw the cup in the garbage can under her desk.

"Facing it means knowing what I'm capable of." Bonnie shifted in her chair. "I have enough anger and rage inside of me to kill again and I know that if I'm not careful and keep doing certain things I will."

"Um hmm." Victoria nodded. She was glad that she hadn't met Bonnie in any other circumstance. The thought was frightening. "How do you feel knowing that about yourself?"

Bonnie tore at the edges of the wadded tissue in her hand. "Scared."

Victoria nodded. Many of her inmate clients had that kind of rage. Only a rare few were willing to take a deep look at their anger and what fed it.

"What are you going to do with that knowledge? How will you be careful?"

"I have to deal with my feelings. I have a lot of pain inside of me and when I feel it, when I let those feelings take over instead of talking about 'em or doing that meditation stuff, when I just let them feelings build I want to fuck somebody up big time. The shit that my dad did to me, and some stuff that happened with Sketch, and those guys at school, even some of the things Tim did to me, that shit all adds up." She wiped her eyes with the frayed tissue.

"Here." Victoria offered her another tissue. "Has talking with me helped?"

"Yeah, but it still hurts." Bonnie blew her nose.

"And the meditation, it seems like that's been helping you a lot?"

"Yeah, I never thought sitting still would be so good for you." Bonnie laughed.

"Why do you think that is?"

"I don't know. At first when I sit down I feel weird, there's all these thoughts in my head, memories from my past. Sometimes I think about getting out and using or not being able to get a job. Other times I sit there and my stomach starts growling and I want to leave, because I feel like everyone can hear my stomach and I feel embarrassed. Or it's like everyone else in the group can sit still but I can't. If I just sit there long enough though my mind slows down and my stomach stops growling. Then it's almost like I can't feel my body anymore. It's real quiet and I just have this sense that every- thing is okay. Kind of like with heroin."

Victoria marveled at Bonnie. She could not believe that this was the same woman she'd first met with nearly two years ago. "I can't tell you how inspired I am by you."

"Inspired by me?" Bonnie looked confused.

"Yes." Victoria smiled. "You've made some significant changes in your life. You've taken a lot of risks, learned to trust me and opened up even though I know it's really hard for you. You've found real ways to cope with your emotions that don't involve using, hurt- ing others, or hurting yourself."

Bonnie grinned. "Thanks, Dr. T, I couldn't have done any of it without you."

"No, Bonnie, don't thank me, you did the heavy lifting."

Tears welled up in Bonnie's eyes. "I never thought that life could be like this."

"Like what?" Victoria leaned back in her chair and crossed her legs.

"I don't know, like I could feel good about myself and not want to use." Bonnie hesitated and looked at her. "But I still worry I'll go back to how I was on the outs."

Victoria nodded. "That's a healthy fear. You know that side of yourself, the old side. But there's another side of you that you're just beginning to learn about. Victoria smiled. "You've shown me a side of you that wants to heal, that wants to grow, to understand, and better yourself."

"Jeez, Dr. Thomas, you're making me blush." Bonnie covered her face.

Victoria noticed Bonnie's cheeks had turned crimson.

"I'm just speaking what's true. I'm not giving you unwarranted compliments."

"Thank you, Dr. T."

"You're welcome."

Bonnie looked at the clock. "Is our time up?"

Victoria nodded.

"Okay, Dr. T, I'll see you next week. Be careful driving home, there are a lot of crazy drivers out there."

"Thank you, Bonnie, I will."

Victoria shut the door behind her and sat down in her chair. A smile crept across her face. *Wow*, she thought, *that was amazing!*

Chapter 45

BONNIE OPENED THE October issue of *Free at Last*, a Christian prison ministry paper that came bi-monthly in bulk for the inmates. She sat at the clerk's desk in the chapel and unfolded it. She paged through it reading letters to the editor from inmates who had given themselves to God. Some of the letters were corny, but one guy wrote about how prison saved his life. She could relate. If she hadn't come to prison when she did, she probably would have overdosed or been shot in one of the robberies.

Just as she finished reading an article about *Keeping Your Cool in Prison*, full of tips on "not letting the system crack you," another article—*Sister Helen Offers Peace and Salvation on Death Row*, caught her attention.

The article talked about Sister Helen Prejean, a nun in New Orleans who visited the men on death row. Sister Helen worked to end the death penalty and a movie called *Dead Man Walking* was made about her life. Bonnie heard of the movie but had never seen it. Inmates weren't allowed to watch R-rated movies. In the article, Sister Helen asked, "Is God vengeful demanding a death for a death? Or, is God compassionate, luring souls into love so great that no one can be considered the 'enemy?'"

Bonnie stared at the page. Had she been caught for the murder and the robberies she probably would've gotten a death sentence, life for sure. She was lucky. Something tugged at her that she couldn't explain when she read Sister Helen's words. She was reminded of the woman who'd spoken at the prison a year ago. She pulled out a piece of paper and pencil from the desk and wrote to Sister Helen.

"Dr. Thomas, look at this," Bonnie said, showing Dr. Thomas the letter as she walked through her office door for their weekly session.

"What is it?"

"I got a letter from Sister Helen. She wrote me back." Bonnie was out of breath and grinning.

"Sister Helen Prejean?" Dr. Thomas looked confused. "The nun from New Orleans?"

"I wrote to her a few weeks ago and she wrote me back. Can you believe that?"

"What does it say?" Dr. Thomas leaned forward in her chair.

"She's impressed that I want to help the guys on Death Row. She said it might take a little more work to get my correspondence approved, but that they could use a little cheering up from someone like me."

Even though she didn't believe in Jesus or follow the ways of the church, to have Sister Helen, a nun, believing in her, despite the fact that she was locked up, made her feel like she wasn't all bad.

"That's terrific, Bonnie. You aren't even out of prison and you're making a positive impact on the world. Nice work!"

Bonnie looked around and spoke in a hushed voice, "I can't bring back the guy I killed, but if I can help someone that's giving back to society, right?"

"Yes." Dr. Thomas smiled at her. "I'm so proud of you."

"Yeah, I'm using my powers for good, not evil."

"You got a new boyfriend or something?" Harris asked when she walked into the room and saw Bonnie sprawled out on her bunk with a bunch of envelopes and paper.

"No," she said annoyed.

"Who you writing then?"

"Not that it's any of your business, Bunkie, but I'm writing these dudes on death row at Angola State Prison."

"You lookin' for tips on how to get rid of a dead body?" Harris grinned.

"That ain't funny, Harris."

"You won't admit it, but you gonna miss me when I'm gone in two weeks and finally home with my kids for Thanksgiving. But don't worry, I'll say a prayer for your sorry ass."

Bonnie put on the headphones to her walkman and ignored Harris and went back to writing. She still felt uncomfortable getting close to people, especially black people. It was easier to write the guys on death row—the miles and bars between them kept her safe. They thanked her and told her how much her letters meant, so she knew she was making a difference and she finally felt good at something that didn't hurt anybody.

She did write one guy who was black, a young guy sentenced to die for the rape and murder of a teenage girl. At first she didn't want to write Kevin because of his crime, and because she thought they wouldn't have anything in common. Still, he was one of the names of pen pals she was given, so she wrote him. After she told him to stop asking her for a picture of her they'd started writing in earnest about their lives. Kevin told her he'd been molested by his mother's boyfriend when he was a boy. Just knowing that Kevin had been abused helped her forgive him a little for what he'd done. She also discovered that he liked animals.

The other day we saw a mother deer and two fawns outside the fence line, she wrote him, *and sometimes we see burrowing owls and prairie squirrels. The guards hate them because they tear up the yard. There are even geese and ducks that come every winter because there used to be a pond in the center of the prison yard, but they had it filled in years ago.*

Sometimes I can see birds flying outside my window, Kevin wrote back, *but I can't hear them. I miss listening to them birds sing. They got me locked down most the day with one hour of cage time. Ain't nobody in my family written or been to see me since my sentencing. I hope that they don't forget me again at Christmas.*

Bonnie felt for Kevin. Even though her mother had only visited her once the entire time she'd been down, she knew that she could always count on her mom sending a Christmas card. Writing Kevin and the other guys on death row kept her mind off of her own time and made her grateful that she had an "out date." Someday she would be free from the seven-by-eleven foot room that she shared with Harris. She would be going home, or at least be on the outside again.

Chapter 46

VICTORIA HEARD A knock on her door.

The new clerk, Ms. Barrios, stood in the doorway. *"Perdone, Doctora Thomas. Hay una persona aquí que quiere hablar con usted. Ella está muy triste."* Victoria had been trying to learn Spanish and the clerk was helping her practice it.

"There's someone who wants to talk to me and she's sad?" Victoria hoped that she understood what the clerk had just said.

"Sí."

"Quién es?" Victoria asked self-consciously. Ms. Barrios had joked that she sounded like an American tourist in Tijuana stumbling over her Spanish.

"Señora Vásquez." The clerk smiled.

Victoria looked at her schedule. She had an hour before the Prison Christmas Program started. "Okay, send her in."

Vasquez came in and sat down. She looked different. She wasn't wearing any make up. She stared at the floor and picked absently at a hangnail.

"What's wrong?" Victoria asked after an awkward silence.

"Merry fucking Christmas, I've got Hep C!" Ms. Vasquez's lips trembled for a moment and then she burst into tears.

"Hep C?"

"Yes, they just told me."

"I'm so sorry, Ms. Vasquez." Victoria pulled a tissue from the box on her desk. She handed the tissue toVasquez who took it and continued sobbing.

Victoria breathed in deeply and searched for the right words. "A lot of people are living with Hepatitis C. You just need to keep your immune system healthy. So all those good things you've been doing like exercising and eating I'm sure will make a difference. Keep doing those things."

"They said my liver is shot. All that dope." Vasquez dabbed at her eyes—the cheap tissue stuck to her face. Victoria wanted to point it out to her, but having bits of tissue stuck to her face was benign and ridiculous compared to what Vasquez was dealing with.

Victoria shifted in her seat, still trying to think of something comforting to say, "Did they tell you what you can do to take care of yourself?"

Vazquez nodded and continued crying.

"What did they say?" Victoria asked. An image of Joanne flashed in her mind. She tried to stay focused on Vasquez.

"They talked about some…some medicine…"

"Interferon," Victoria interrupted.

"Yeah, and they told me to take some Vitamin B and eat more green vegetables."

"Okay good."

Vasquez exploded. "Fuck that bullshit! They don't even sell no Vitamin B here. They only have a fucking multi-vitamin. If I want Vitamin B I gotta pay some bitch to swallow it in visiting and shit it out in the shower. I'm not going through that for some fucking Vitamin B."

Victoria leaned back in her chair unsure how to respond. "It sounds like you're angry about this?"

"Fuck yeah, I'm angry. It's not fucking fair. I've been clean for months, working on myself, going to group, talking 'bout shit that happened to me. Why this? Why now?"

Victoria sat quietly looking at Vasquez's tear stained face. "It's hard to make sense of it, to understand the challenges that are given to us."

Vasquez wiped the string of snot that fell from her nose. "What the fuck am I going to tell my mom? I'm sure she's going to say 'I told you so!'"

"I know this isn't easy."

"No, it's not! And my kids, how am I going to explain this to them? They're gonna freak out. They already feel like I chose drugs over them. I finally get off the dope and I'm ready to clean up my mess and start being there for them and now I find out my time is up. I can't get a fucking break!" Vasquez wiped the tears from her eyes.

Victoria suddenly felt totally inept. Nothing she could say would make the situation better. She felt like she did with Joanne. Nothing worked. Victoria searched for something positive to say to Vasquez, something that would give her a shred of hope.

"I know it's hard when you want to change and an obstacle this big comes in to your path. You can live with this diagnosis and have a good life. Remember you wanted to help people. There are a lot of Chicanas that need your help. You can share your story and maybe that will help them get out of abusive relationships. If you take good care of yourself, manage your stress, and keep your immune system up I'm sure you can live with this for a long time. We're all eventually going to die some day."

Victoria remembered how she'd begged Joanne the night before she died to go to rehab. Joanne said she'd think about it.

"Yeah, but now I know how I'm going to die." Vasquez dabbed at her eyes again and wiped off the bit of tissue that stuck to her face.

"You don't know you're going to die of Hepatitis C. I told you many people live with it for years. You could choke on a chicken bone tonight at dinner and die."

"That's not funny. You better not jinx me, Dr. Thomas. I hope you guys get CPR training because the medical staff here are horrible. I almost asked them to do another test, thinking that maybe they accidentally switched my blood with someone else's. They're that incompetent you know?"

Victoria knew what Vasquez was talking about, just last month she had evaluated an inmate for suicide over at the men's jail and determined that he needed to be on suicide watch. He was threatening to kill himself. He'd cut his leg with a toothbrush that he'd sharpened into a shank. She told the physician's assistant bandaging the inmate's leg to call the lieutenant as soon as he finished so they could put him in the suicide watch room. The minute she got home that night her phone rang. She answered it.

"Doc, this is PA Meyer. Got some bad news. Inmate Franklin took an overdose of pills."

"How the hell did that happen?" she asked, as she set down her briefcase. "He was supposed to go on suicide watch?"

"Well, ma'am, I took his medications into the cell to give him his pills and then someone called me out. When I got back..." there was a long pause, "well, the bottle of Vistaril was empty. He took about twenty pills. We're waiting for an ambulance to take him to the outside hospital and have his stomach pumped. He's pretty drowsy. Lieutenant Williams is with him now trying to keep him awake."

Victoria was incredulous the PA had been so careless.

"Yes, I know what you mean." Victoria nodded in agreement. "You could ask for another test, but considering your history of drug use it's unlikely it's a mistake."

Vasquez burst into tears again.

Victoria sat still in her chair, feeling small, part of her wanted to get angry with Ms. Vasquez. *What do you expect? You think you can do drugs and not have any physical consequences?* But she knew those feelings were just her own feelings of helplessness. She saw it in the other staff too when they were dealing with some heartbreaking situations. One of the worst was dealing with pregnant inmates who went into labor. The women would be taken to the outside hospital to deliver and twenty-four hours after they'd given birth they would return to prison. Their newborns would stay behind with family members or caseworkers. The feelings of rage and helplessness at the situation were overwhelming— a horrible situation the inmate had created with her choices and one that the system was ill equipped to deal with.

"Are you feeling like harming yourself, Ms. Vasquez?"

"Why the hell would I want to kill myself?" Vasquez lashed out. "I'm upset because I have this crap."

Victoria was surprised by Vasquez's vehemence. "I'm sorry, Ms. Vasquez, I just need to ask these things. So you don't have any plan to hurt yourself?"

"I said 'no.' I need to go." Vasquez got up from her chair with such force that it bumped Victoria's desk knocking over Victoria's paperclip holder.

Victoria ignored the mess and got up to open the door for Vasquez. "Ms. Vasquez, if anything changes and you feel like hurting yourself, please come and let me know, okay?"

Vasquez gave her a blank stare and walked out without a word.

Victoria looked at her watch. It was almost time for the Christmas Program to begin. During last year's Christmas Program, the inmates dressed up like angels in white paper gowns and wore little red paper flowers, dyed their tennis shoes black and glued them with glitter. Some wore green and red construction paper to look like poinsettia plants. They sang Christmas songs in English and Spanish and looked like nervous kindergartners at their first school Christmas concert. They were starved for attentions and recognition and it made her want to look away from their hungry eyes. It was terribly awkward and heart wrenching. She had smiled at them trying to give them what she felt they were denied by their parents, but the whole thing felt sad and tragic.

Victoria walked to the front entrance, turned in her keys to the Control Room, and drove to the Peet's Coffee about two miles from the prison. She ordered a non-fat latte and sat outside on a wooden bench. The fresh air felt good. She wrapped her hands around the warm paper cup and took a sip. The coffee was thick and smoky. *Just what the doctor ordered!*

She went to take another sip but was distracted by a gray cat running across the parking lot into a hedge that butted up against the main thoroughfare with four lanes of traffic. As she took another sip of her coffee she heard a kitten mew. She listened carefully and heard it again. She got up and walked through the parking lot to the decorative hedge adjacent to the road. She bent down to peak through the bushes. Just as she did, she saw five kittens nursing on the gray cat.

She made eye contact with the cat. Victoria didn't want to startle her, but the situation was not good. She looked at the kittens ambling through the underbrush only two feet from a four-lane intersection. Nothing was good about this. She rushed to the pet store in the strip mall.

"There are five kittens in a bush by the intersection. Their mother appears to be feral, any idea how we can get them before they wander into the street and get run over." She said out of breath to the twenty-something store clerk.

The store clerk gave her an apathetic look. "You could call Animal Control."

"Do you have their number?"

The store clerk dialed the number and handed her the cordless phone.

"Animal Control, please hold."

She looked at her watch. She'd been gone for thirty minutes. She was already late.

Several minutes passed until a voice came on the line again. "Animal Control."

"Yes, hi, I'm on the corner of Santa Rosa and Davis and there are five kittens in a flowerbed right next to the road and their mother appears to be feral. Can someone come help me get them before they wander into the street and get hit by the cars."

"Sure, we'll pick them up once you get 'em in a box."

"I was wondering if someone could come and help me. I'm not dressed for this. I don't have any gloves or anything. I was just getting coffee when I heard them. Can someone help me catch the mom so we can keep them together."

"Sorry lady, we won't take the mother if she's feral. We can pick 'em up once you get 'em in a box. We only have so many workers and this ain't an emergency."

"Are you serious?" Victoria asked, incensed.

"Yep," he said and hung up the phone.

"What an asshole!" She turned to the clerk. "Do you have a box?"

The clerk went to the backroom and returned with a very large cardboard box.

She took the box and crossed the parking lot careful not to get hit herself and set the box on the curb. She kneeled down to peek at the kittens under the shrubbery. This time she startled the mother who abruptly got up, disrupting the nursing kittens, and raced through the parking lot. Victoria moved in trying to catch the babies. The kittens scattered in every direction. She reached down and tried to grab a tabby, but he darted out into traffic. She heard a loud squeal from a car's tire. She stood up and looked into the street. The gray kitten was crushed under the weight of the car tire. It's lifeless head severed from its tiny body.

"Oh, my God," she yelled and pulled at her hair. Another kitten ran across the parking lot. "No," she screamed and quickly backed away from the shrubbery, dropping the box on the ground, convinced now that anything she did would only make things worse. She ran to her car and sobbed. She had to get back to the prison, but the tears blurred her vision. She wiped them and tried hard to study the road, lest she run over one of the kittens.

Chapter 47

Bonnie sat alone in an uncomfortable plastic chair attached to a fake wood paneled table at the far end of the chow hall eating dinner. The chairs were attached to the table to prevent inmates from hitting one another with them. The chow hall was the most dangerous place in a prison because it was where the largest number of inmates gathered at one time. This was the reason the majority of staff in the prison would come to the chow hall during meal times to make sure nothing went down. They called it "mainline" but she wasn't quite sure why.

Not much had happened in any of the prisons she'd been in, but Tim told her stories of stabbings and riots the chow hall at the Oregon State Penitentiary. The most interesting thing she ever saw was when a jealous femme caught her stud-broad eating with another woman and used a plastic fork to cut the woman's face. "You can have her, but you get her fucked up!" the jealous inmate yelled.

Bonnie looked up from her salad and this stocky Mexican inmate with short spiked hair was standing in front of her. She was cut like a body builder and her arms were covered in tattoos. She looked familiar.

"Hey, mind if I sit down?"

Bonnie was chewing on a piece of iceberg lettuce. She swallowed. "Go ahead."

The inmate set her blue plastic tray down on the table and swiveled the attached chair to the side so she could sit down. "My name's Chico." She held out her hand.

Bonnie reluctantly shook it. "Yeah, I think we met before. Bonnie."

"You remember me from last time?" Chico took a bite of the hamburger and mashed the over-cooked carrots with her fork. "Was the food always this bad?"

"Sometimes it's worse. What do you mean from last time?" Bonnie asked.

Chico winked. "I just back this afternoon. Caught another case."

Bonnie stabbed at her food trying to pick out her favorite vegetables from the salad and leaving the onions. She hated onions.

"What unit are you in?" Bonnie asked, trying to be friendly, but not too friendly.

"Bravo Unit, Lower Tier."

"Me too, what room?"

Chico fished in her front pocket and pulled out a strip of paper. "B109."

"Shut the fuck up? That's my room number."

Chico looked at the number again. "No, for real, that's what it says."

"That's wrong!"

"What the hell you mean by that?" Chico gave her a hard look.

"Means were triple bunked. I hope you don't snore." Bonnie wanted to say *I hope you don't plan on bringing any of your girlfriends back to our room.*

"Me snore?" Chico took another bite of her hamburger. "Cause I'm Mexican?"

"How long you down for?" Bonnie said, changing the subject. She didn't like talking to people she didn't know. She pushed her tray away and rested her elbow on the table, watching Chico as she struggled to keep the watery grape Jell-o on her spoon long enough to get it to her mouth. Chico gave up on the Jell-o and wiped her face with her hand. "Fourteen years."

"Damn!" Bonnie leaned back in the chair.

"They're getting serious about their war on drugs."

"By the time I leave, I'll have done about twelve between here and state, so it's doable. Take the drug program and you can get a year off your sentence."

Chico nodded. "That's cool. I've got an appeal in. I don't think I'm going to do more than six."

Bonnie thought Chico was optimistic. She'd seen a lot of chicks appeal their cases and give their families false hope. They wasted their time and money only to get a "Denied" letter back from the judge.

"When are you out?" Chico asked

"Eight months, seven days and a wake up, but who's counting?" Bonnie grinned.

"Right on." Chico bit into her hamburger again, spilling ketch-up down the front of her clean uniform.

Bonnie picked her tray up from the table. "I guess I'll see you back at the room."

"See ya." Chico waved.

Bonnie dropped off her tray at the dishwashing area and headed to the rec yard to walk the track and digest her food. The sun was setting. She loved walking the track at night, it felt freer, most of the staff had gone home and the majority of inmates were inside watching TV. It was easier to be invisible.

She thought about her future and the letter Sister Helen had recently sent her thanking her for being a great pen pal. The letter was now tacked to the bulletin board by her bed. She wondered if she could go to New Orleans and work with Sister Helen when she got released. She could get a fresh start in Louisiana, live at the monastery with Sister Helen and help with the guys on death row. She wondered if the parole board would approve her relocation. She knew that most jurisdictions didn't want to take on a serious felon if they didn't have to. They wanted people to go back to the areas where their families lived. Bonnie knew that even if her parents did let her use their address for release going back "home" would be the worst thing she could do.

She walked twelve times around the track, the equivalent of three miles, and then went back to the unit.

She opened the cell door and found Chico sitting on her bed talking to her other roommate, a new girl named McKenzie. McKenzie had moved into the room about a week before Harris released when they made the room a "three-man room" as they called it. Bonnie didn't like having to share the room with two other females. There was only eighteen inches between her bunk and McKenzie's. Chico was assigned to Harris's old bunk. Harris had been sleeping above her for two years. She'd finally gotten used to her and now she had to deal with two people in her space. She wasn't sure how she was going to keep her cool.

The prison was getting more and more crowded, and she'd overheard the evening watch officer complaining that the rate of women coming to prison was growing faster than that of men, but that the feds didn't have any plans to build a new prison for the women. She dreaded the thought that someday the "three-man rooms" would become "four-man rooms" and hoped that she would be out before that happened.

"I hope you don't mind me sitting here," Chico asked, looking a little guilty. "I just didn't want to climb up on the upper bunk yet."

"That's cool," Bonnie lied. She brushed her teeth and then sat down on the bed next to Chico.

"We were just talking about how bad the food was tonight."

"It's still better than Maricopa County food," McKenzie argued. "That shit was nasty. So, Chico, you never said what you were down for."

"I was dealing meth- over $25 G's a month." Chico's face lit up.

The three of them stayed up until 2:00 AM. Chico recounted all her close calls with the cops and all the times she "got over," on them before she "caught her second case." It reminded Bonnie of the good old days with Tim.

Bonnie didn't know what to make of Chico. She was so masculine for a woman. Her voice was deeper than most women's were and she had the mannerisms of a man.

Chapter 48

VICTORIA WALKED INTO the kitchen and set her purse down on the gray slate counter next to the fruit bowl and kissed Devin who was stirring a pot on the stove. "Umm, what are you making?" she asked.

"My mother's gumbo. Figured we could use a little comfort food." He glanced at her. "By the way you look, I guessed right. Dare I ask how your day was?"

"So awful, I don't even want to talk about it," Victoria sighed as she washed her hands in the sink.

"That white supremacist chick figure out you don't celebrate Christmas or something?" He smirked.

"You know, Devin, she just happens to be my most successful patient to date." Victoria dried her hands on a paper towel.

Devin took down two bowls from the cupboard and heaped them full of Gumbo. "Don't worry, I left out the pork, just don't tell my mother."

"Thanks," she said and sat down at the table. "I'm considering writing a vignette about my work with her for Forensic Psychology."

He sat down next to her. "That'll be interesting."

Her pager made a loud beeping noise.

"God damn it, not again!" She looked at her pager. She got up from the table without a word to Devin and went to the bedroom and picked up the phone.

"Is this call in reference to an inmate?" the control room officer asked.

"This is Dr. Thomas, you just paged me." The irritation in her voice was plain.

"Stand by," the control officer advised. "L.T. I've got the psych on the phone."

"Patch her through," she heard Lt. Lopez on the other end of the phone.

"One moment ma'am, I'll transfer you."

"Thank you." She hated it when they called her ma'am.

"Sorry to interrupt your evening, but I've got some bad news for you. An inmate tried to kill herself in the shower. She cut herself up pretty damn good, lost a lot of blood. The ambulance just took her to the outside hospital."

"That's awful, Lieutenant."

"What's awful is that there's blood everywhere and one of my staff had a cut on her hand and didn't even think to put on gloves before she started trying to help this knucklehead. Anyway we're going to need you to come in and do some paperwork."

Victoria rubbed her temples. She could feel a migraine coming on. "What's the inmate's name?"

"Vasquez, Ramona Vasquez."

Victoria gasped.

"You all right, Doc?"

"I'll be right in." She hung up the phone. She felt light-headed and sat down on the bed.

Devin stood in the bedroom doorway with a kitchen towel draped over his right shoulder. "What's up?"

"One of my clients attempted suicide."

He took the towel from his shoulder and wiped his hands. "Is she okay?"

"No, they had to take her to the outside hospital." Victoria stared at the wall. "I just saw her yesterday," Victoria's head throbbed. "Why didn't I see it coming? I should have put her on suicide watch." She continued to rub her forehead. "Oh my God, I can't believe I missed it. I should have known better."

"Come on, Vic, you're not a mind reader," Devin reassured. "In my line of work we can see trends, but we can't tell what the stock market is going to do. There are too many different factors involved."

Victoria got up from the bed. "You don't understand, Devin!" she said emphatically. "She has a history of depression and previous suicide attempts, and she was just diagnosed with a life threatening illness. Those three things alone are serious suicide risk factors. What the hell is wrong with me?"

"No one is perfect, Victoria." Devin tried to console her.

"I know that, Devin," she snapped, "but I should have done something. Damn it!" She grabbed a hair tie from the dresser and pulled her hair back into a ponytail. "I'm going to the prison. I don't know when I'll be back." She put on her coat and walked past the two steaming bowls of Gumbo on the dining room table.

Chapter 49

"GOOD MORNING, DR. Thomas," the front entrance officer greeted her.

"No, it's not," she wanted to say.

Victoria got her keys and walked to her office. This morning she was sipping a triple espresso, hoping it would keep her awake. She'd tossed and turned most of the night after arguing with Devin who ended up sleeping on the couch in their home office. Victoria unlocked her door and set her satchel down on the extra chair in her office and checked her messages.

"Hi, Doc, this is Lt. Williams, just want to let you know that Vasquez is being transferred to the Forensic Medical Center in Texas. Her wounds were so deep she needs full-time medical care and more intensive psych care."

She sighed and pressed two to listen to the second message. It was Scarsdale. "Victoria, I would have appreciated a phone call last night apprising me of the situation with inmate Vasquez. As you can imagine, I was a bit shocked this morning when I received a call from the Warden to discuss inmate Vasquez's transfer and had no knowledge of the suicide attempt."

"Shit!" She slammed the phone down. She wanted to throw up.

"Hi, Dr. Thomas, are you ready for me?" Bonnie Maldonado appeared in the doorway startling her. She completely forgot she changed Maldonado's session time because of yesterday's Christmas Program and wondered if Maldonado witnessed her slamming the phone.

"I'm sorry,..." Victoria tried to regain her composure. "Yes, please sit down."

Victoria tried to pull it together. She took a deep breath. It looked like Maldonado hadn't seen her lose her cool. She could feel her need to help Maldonado intensify. "So tell me how are things going for you this week?"

"Got a card from my mom."

"That's great. What did she say?"

Bonnie pursed her lips. "Merry Christmas. Love, Mom."

"What else?"

"That's it. That's all she says every year."

Victoria nodded. "How does that make you feel?"

Bonnie studied a loose string on the left pant leg of her khaki uniform. "Did I tell you Harris left?"

"Your roommate?" Victoria made a mental note to come back to her mother at a later time.

"Yeah, I got a new roommate."

Victoria tried to read her. "Is that good or bad?"

Bonnie looked up from her lap, but avoided Victoria's eye contact. "Not sure yet. I think it's good." Bonnie took a folded piece of paper out of her shirt pocket, carefully unfolded it, and handed it to Victoria. "Check it out, Sister Helen sent this to me a few weeks ago. She wanted to thank me for being a pen pal. Did you know that thirty-eight states have the death penalty and that California has the highest number of inmates on death row?"

Victoria took the letter and scanned it. "No, I didn't know that."

"Yep, California has 657 inmates on death row. Florida is the second highest with 398 and Texas has 392, but Texas has the highest rate of executions." Bonnie seemed proud of her new education.

"That's a lot of people on death row." Victoria shook her head.

"Sister Helen says a lot of them are innocent."

"I'm sure many of them are."

Victoria remembered reading *To Kill a Mockingbird* in high school and wondered how many of the men sitting on death row were black. Devin's mother had once confided in her that she never stopped worrying about Devin being pulled over by the police for *driving while black*. She'd also told her that she was relieved when he turned down a full scholarship to Morehouse, deciding to stay on the West Coast and get his undergraduate degree at Stanford, because she thought things would be worse in Atlanta.

"I've heard that if the victim is white and the defendant is a person of color rather than a white person, the person of color is more likely to get the death penalty than a white person who committed the same crime," Victoria said.

Bonnie shrugged her shoulders. "Maybe their crimes were more violent or something? Sister Helen says that the death penalty is wrong and that God is a forgiving, not a punishing, God. I've been thinking about putting in relocation papers to New Orleans so I could go help Sister Helen with her prison work."

"Hmm, that's an interesting idea, Bonnie."

"You think so?" Bonnie played with the loose string on her pants again.

"Yes." Victoria marveled at Bonnie. "That would be a very different path than the one you've been on."

"Yeah, I've never done anything like that before. In the past, when I've gotten out, I just go back to what I know."

"You've made so many positive changes since we've been working together." Victoria smiled at her. She looked at the clock. They had ten minutes left. "Bonnie, I want to tell you that I admire your courage and the woman you're becoming."

Bonnie grinned. "Thank you, Dr. Thomas."

"I think you've done a tremendous job in therapy." Victoria smiled brightly at her. "That's why I want to share your success and our work together with my colleagues."

"What do you mean?" Bonnie asked, shifting in her chair.

"I'd like to write an article about the work we've done together for a clinical psychotherapy journal. There would be no identifying information and it wouldn't have your name on it. How would you feel about that?"

"I don't know."

Victoria studied Bonnie's body language. It was clear from her folded arms and the creases she saw forming on Bonnie's brow that she didn't like the idea. "Think about it and we can discuss it more next week."

Bonnie got up and walked out of the office without saying goodbye.

Victoria stared at the wall. Her eyes were drawn to the pictures of her camping trip in Oregon. She thought about her first couple of sessions with Bonnie and about Bonnie's boyfriend who had been killed driving back from the mountain. At that instant, she recognized that her request must have felt like a betrayal to Bonnie.

Victoria slapped her hand against her head. *I can't seem to do anything right! Not seeing the signs right in front of me with Vasquez, the kittens, Joanne and now this!* She began crying. *I'm a failure as a psychologist. I can't help anyone!*

Victoria held her head in her hands and sobbed into her lap. Then, in desperation, she grabbed the telephone and called Peter.

"Hello, Dr. Murphy," he said. He sounded harried.

"Peter, it's Victoria." She turned her chair so no one could see her through the window in the door and swallowed hard trying to stop herself from crying.

"Hey, Vic, you okay?"

"Peter, I'm melting down."

"What's going on?"

"I had a client attempt suicide. I missed all the signs. I should have put her on suicide watch and I didn't. She sliced herself up really bad. It's a miracle she's still alive." Victoria sobbed into the phone.

"Victoria, that's awful. I'm so sorry."

"That's not all. Do you remember that client I mentioned to you back in April?"

"Yeah, what's happening with that?"

"The therapy was going well, but now..." She broke into sobs.

"Victoria, take a deep breath. It's going to be okay. Tell me what's going on?"

Victoria wiped her eyes with a tissue and tried to speak, "she opened up, Peter. It's unbelievable."

"Congratulations! That's amazing that you're making progress with a severe personality disordered Axis II client. No small feat, Victoria."

Victoria leaned on the chair handle, pressing the phone into her ear. "She's made such significant strides. But I screwed that up too. I wanted to share my experiences with colleagues, so I started writing this article about our work together. It helps me with my own process to be able to explore the treatment in writing. Anyway, I wanted to get her permission before I published it even though I planned on disguising her identity. I felt like I owed her the courtesy of letting her know that I would be writing about her. I'm pretty sure she feels totally betrayed by me. She walked out of our session. I feel horrible. I've been churning in my stomach acids ever since." Victoria leaned back hard in her chair and rubbed her temples with her left hand, the phone drooping in her right.

Peter was silent. She could hear his breathing on the other end of the line. "That's a touchy situation," he said softly. "What makes you think she feels betrayed by you?"

"I'm the first person she's trusted in a long time. I feel like I'm betraying her by putting her experience in print. At the same time, it's so valuable to me to document the treatment and get feedback on the clinical issues—I think it could offer other clinicians hope. You know how they tell us in grad school you can't treat Anti-social Personality Disorder. The diagnosis totally fits her, but Peter she is treatable! She's changed."

"You really think so?" he asked.

"Yes, I do Peter. It's amazing how much she's changed. I would have never known it was possible. I probably wouldn't believe it either, but I've witnessed it. We throw these people away, lock them up, and don't give them another thought. Think of all the people we give up on. We don't even give them a chance because seasoned professionals tell us we're wasting our time."

"You're really passionate about this, Victoria."

"Yes, I am."

"A client could feel flattered to know that they're a special enough case for you to want to focus more on their treatment. At the same time they could also feel objectified, dehumanized, and used."

"I really made a mistake, huh?" Victoria felt another wave of nausea.

"Do you think your client might feel like that?"

"Yes." Victoria looked at Bonnie's file and flipped through the pages of notes from their sessions. "I feel so at odds. I want to write this article, but I don't want her to feel like I'm just another person who has betrayed and used her. I don't want to be lumped into her category of victimizers."

"Ultimately, Victoria, you're not using her or betraying her. You're helping her heal. Part of your being able to help her heal is to work through your counter-transference, share your clinical experiences, and get feedback from your peers. Your impetus for writing the article is to help other women like her and clinicians working with similar types of clients. The article could even be redemptive for her."

"What do you mean?" Victoria perked up.

"She helps others by giving you permission to generically share her experience," he said reassuringly. "Isn't that redemption for what she's done?"

"Hmm, I never thought of it that way."

Peter cleared his throat. "I was wondering if I would hear from you again, I'm glad you called."

"I just didn't know how to respond after our last meeting."

"I want to talk about it, but my next client is here. Good luck, Victoria."

"Thanks, Peter." Victoria hung up the phone. She felt better after talking to Peter he always knew what to say to her. Still, she had an unsettled feeling in her stomach.

Chapter 50

BONNIE WAS LYING on her bed crying when Chico walked in. "What's wrong with you?"

"You wouldn't understand." Bonnie turned and faced the wall. She never cried in front of people and she never talked about her problems with any one except Dr. Thomas. Now she was furious with Dr. Thomas.

Chico walked over to the toilet and grabbed some toilet paper then sat down on the bed across from her. It squeaked when she sat down. "Try me," she said, handing Bonnie the toilet paper.

Bonnie rolled over to face Chico but refused the toilet paper. "I'm a fucking lab rat, a freak-show for shrinks." Tears streamed down Bonnie's face.

"What the hell are you talking about?" Chico gave up trying to hand her the toilet paper and tossed it on the bed next to her.

"See, I told you, you wouldn't understand." Bonnie rolled over again.

"Slow down. You're seeing a shrink." Chico gave her a funny look.

"Yeah, don't fuck with me. I started seeing her a couple of years ago. She helped me through some serious shit, but now she wants to write this fucking article about me because I'm her fucking trophy patient."

Chico stifled a laugh. "The shrink is showing you off by writing about you? Isn't the shit you say in there supposed to be private?"

"It's not fucking funny. She says she's not going to use my name."

Chico's brow furrowed. "Why would she want to write about you? Are you *loco* in your *coco*? Why do you see a psych anyway?"

"I must be some kind of serious freak-show, because she says I've done a 'really good job in therapy' and 'changed so much' that she wants to 'share our treatment with her colleagues,'" Bonnie said, mocking Dr. Thomas.

"Is that true or is that just smoke she's blowing up your ass so that she can get your permission to break your privacy?"

Bonnie started crying again, embarrassed that Chico was seeing her like this, but she just couldn't stop. "I don't know. I have changed a lot since I started seeing her."

Bonnie had never gotten the impression that Dr. Thomas's caring was insincere. But now, she wondered if this was the only reason Dr. Thomas was so interested in her.

"Man, I would never trust a fed." Chico moved over to Bonnie's bed and began stroking Bonnie's hair. "It'll be okay, Bonnie. Just let it go. You can't trust people. You gotta look out for yourself."

Bonnie pulled away.

Chico got up from the bed and opened her locker. She took out a plastic jar of Folgers instant coffee and scooped out some coffee into a beige plastic cup with "CHICO" stenciled on the outside in black capital letters. The letters had orange and red flames coming off them. She turned on the faucet and held the cup underneath.

"Here," she said, stirring the coffee with a plastic spoon.

Bonnie wiped her nose on the sleeve of her shirt and took the cup from Chico.

"Thanks."

"No sweat." Chico shoved the Folgers jar back into her locker.

Bonnie took a sip, spilling some on the wool blanket on her bed. "Motherfucker!"

"Damn girl, you're high strung. You need to chill out."

Bonnie slept hard that night. In her dreams she was shooting up. When she walked out of her housing unit that morning she found herself at unit D where Tennessee lived. If she went inside she risked getting another shot and ending up in the SHU. She saw Washington, a black woman she'd worked with at Maintenance back in Oregon, watering the plants in front of the housing unit.

Hey, Washington, do me a favor will ya?"

Washington looked her dead in the eyes. "You gonna do me a solid back?"

"Never fucking mind," she said, and started to walk off. Then she heard her name blaring across the loudspeaker in the center of the prison yard.

"Bonnie Maldonado report to the Psych Building." It was Dr. Thomas's voice.

"What does that bitch want now?" she mumbled under her breath, but even as she said it, the words seemed harsh. She stomped up the steps of the Psych Building and walked to Dr. Thomas's office.

Dr. Thomas looked relieved to see her.

"You rang?" Bonnie said, glaring at her.

"Please, Bonnie, come in and sit down."

"You want to study your lab rat some more, get some more data on me?"

"It's not like that. Please come in."

Bonnie sat with her arms crossed. She stared at Dr. Thomas.

"I know you feel betrayed by me. I'm so sorry, I don't want to betray you." Dr. Thomas looked like she hadn't slept much. She had bags under her eyes. "You've worked so hard. You've had tremendous success in therapy. I wanted to share it with others. You've inspired me and I really wanted others to experience that inspiration too. But I've decided that if you don't want me to publish the article, then I won't."

Bonnie was dumbstruck. She'd never even considered that she could have a say in the matter. No one had ever asked her what she wanted. She felt a lump in her throat.

"You really do care about me," she said.

"Of course I care about you, Bonnie." Dr. Thomas's eyes watered as she said it. "You are an inspiration to me. You've been through so much and yet you haven't given up, you've let yourself open up, and you've grown so much."

"I inspire you?" Bonnie smiled and wiped tears from her face with her hand.

"Yes," Dr. Thomas said and handed her a tissue.

"Does that make sense?"

Bonnie sniffed. "It makes a lot of sense now." She stared at the bookshelf, too embarrassed to look at Dr. Thomas. "If you really think publishing that article will help someone then do it."

"Thank you."

Bonnie got up from the chair. "Have a nice Christmas vacation, Dr. T. I'll see you next year."

Dr. Thomas smiled back at her. "See you next year, Bonnie."

Chapter 51

VICTORIA GOT IN her car and pulled out of the prison parking lot, free for two weeks. She was relieved Maldonado had given her blessing for the article. It seemed to re-affirm the progress she'd made.

The story of the man who walked the seashore throwing beached starfish back into the ocean came into her mind. *It mattered for that one.*

Her failure to save Joanne, those poor kittens, and Vasquez weighed on her, but she knew she'd helped Bonnie. *That, in itself,* she thought, *is a minor miracle!* She took a deep breath and exhaled as she merged onto the freeway towards home.

When she got home Devin was sitting in the leather recliner drinking a beer. There were two suitcases by the door. She felt sick to her stomach and stifled a gasp.

She set her bag on a chair in the dining room and walked over to the couch. She took a deep breath to steady herself. Her heart was racing. "How was your day?" she asked, biting her lip.

He shook his head. "Everything's been really stressful." He took another sip of his beer. "I need a break."

Victoria swallowed hard fighting back the lump in her throat. She couldn't believe it had come to this.

Devin put the can down on the end table and looked at her. "I packed you a bag."

Had she heard him correctly? "Okay," she said, trying to remain calm.

"Let's go," he said.

"I don't understand." Victoria wrapped her arms around herself. "I thought we we're going to talk?"

"We can do that while we're driving?"

"Driving where? I thought you were leaving me?" Victoria pointed to the suitcases.

"We're leaving." He smiled again. "Me and you."

"What do you mean?" she asked.

"I rented us a cabin on the Russian River. I figured we could use some time alone together away from family and work. Things have been so stressful for the both of us. I know how much you like being in the Redwoods and sitting by a warm fire."

Victoria got up from the couch, walked over to where Devin was sitting and sat down on his lap. She kissed his forehead. "You are so considerate, Devin. Thank you."

"I know," he joked. "Come on let's go. We'll see if we can beat the traffic."

Two hours later, they arrived at the rental house on the river. It was beautiful. Devin made a fire and brought her a cup of hot chocolate and sat down next to her to talk. She sipped from the cup and stared at the fire. "I need to tell you something." She turned towards him.

He looked up from the fire and met her gaze. "Is this about Peter?"

"What?" she asked startled, almost spilling the hot cocoa. "No, why do you ask?"

"I noticed you had dinner with him awhile back when I was in Seattle. You left a receipt out that you'd written 'Peter Murphy consultation' on. Sometimes you're really harsh on me about not being psychologically-minded. I know you and Peter had something going on before we met and I just wonder if you think you'd be better off with him."

Victoria was shocked. She didn't know how to respond. "No, this isn't about Peter," she paused. "It's about me. There's something I never told you about Joanne."

"Your roommate? The one who died?" Devin looked confused.

Victoria took another sip of the hot chocolate and set it down on the wooden table next to the chair she was sitting in. "I've never told anyone this." She swallowed and took a deep breath. "It's something I'm so ashamed of and can't forgive myself for."

He leaned back in the chair. "What is it, Vic?"

Victoria chewed on her fingernail and looked over at Devin. "It was…" Her voice broke. "It was my fault Joanne died."

Devin shook his head. "No, Baby, I know you're always blaming yourself for her death, but it wasn't your fault. You tried to get her into rehab. You did the best thing a friend could do. She wouldn't listen to you."

"No, Devin, she did listen to me." Tears began rolling down Victoria's face. "I was the one who talked her into doing cocaine the first time. She didn't want to and I begged her to just try it. We were at a party in the Hamptons and there was this guy. I wanted to be cool. It's a long story, but I talked her into it. If I hadn't, she'd still be alive." Victoria held her head in her hands and cried.

"Come here, Victoria." She felt his hand on her shoulder. He pulled her closer embracing her. "I do understand and it's still not your fault that she's dead. It was stupid to talk her into trying it, but you didn't force her to keep doing it. That was her choice."

She sobbed into his chest. "But I still blame myself."

"You always think you're responsible for saving the world and everyone in it."

"You don't know the half of it," she half-laughed, half-cried, wiping her tears on the sleeve of her shirt.

"Oh, I bet I do." Devin nodded. "You run around like it's your job to save the world. That's not your job, Victoria. Your job is to help people, but you can't prevent them from making mistakes, that's how we learn. It's like you're trying to defy Mother Nature, instead of allowing things to run their course. You're like *tikkun olam* on crack. Your job is to help pick up the pieces, not stop people from falling. You have to accept that not everything can be fixed."

"I'm learning that, Devin. I really am starting to get that." Victoria took a sip of her hot chocolate.

"Good, because you're going to make yourself sick if you don't."

"Did I tell you the nickname the inmates call me?"

"No." Devin gave her a funny look.

"Captain-Save-A-Crow." She smirked.

"What? I've heard of Captain-Save-A-Ho and I hate to say it but that one fits you to a T. What the hell does Captain-Save-A-Crow mean?"

Victoria shook her head. "I'm too embarrassed to tell you."

"C'mon, Captain, spill the beans," he said.

Victoria laughed. "Promise you won't call me that."

"I'll try not to."

"Promise, or I won't tell you."

"Okay, I promise, Captain," Devin said, trying to hold back laughter.

Victoria playfully smacked his thigh. "Last spring there was this fledgling crow and it couldn't fly."

Devin looked at her trying to keep a straight face.

"It's not funny, Devin. It really broke my heart."

"Okay, okay, I'm not laughing. Go ahead, I'm listening."

"The little crow kept hopping around on the prison grounds trying to fly, but it just couldn't. The worst part was there were these other two crows that flew down from the trees and started pecking at it, attacking him. I tried to chase them off. Turns out I was putting on quite an amusing show for the dozens of inmates watching."

Devin shook his head and saluted her, "My girl, Captain-Save-a-Crow."

"That's me," Victoria smiled and then was suddenly serious again.

"I wish I'd told her I was sorry for pressuring her that night. I was trying to be cool. I had no idea she'd get hooked."

Devin put his hand on her leg. "You were young, you..."

Victoria interrupted. "I wasn't stupid, I knew better."

"You were experimenting. People experiment in college."

"Did you experiment in college?"

"No, I didn't need to do that. I was already cool. That's more of a white middle class thing. We go skiing when we want to feel cool."

Victoria smiled. "I know you're trying to talk me out of blaming myself, Devin."

"Is that what keeps you stuck at the prison?" He asked, suddenly serious.

"What do you mean?"

"Is that why you're working in a punishing environment when you could be helping others and not exposing yourself to danger and disrespect. I mean seriously, the unpaid on-call, the correctional posts, the strip searches, and the firearms training. Victoria, you're a professional, not a cop. You didn't go to school to shoot M-16s and handcuff people. Why else would you force yourself to work in a prison and do things that have nothing to do with being a psychologist unless you're serving some sentence for some transgression you committed in your own mind?"

Victoria sat there stunned. "I never made that connection."

"That'll be $150." Devin smiled. "Wouldn't you prefer to work someplace where people valued you and took you seriously."

"You're wrong there, Devin, some of my clients do take me seriously and are working hard to change themselves."

"Okay, you're right, some of your clients take you seriously and you're helping them. But Scarsdale doesn't give you the respect you deserve and whoever heard of a psychologist handing out toilet paper and hair dryers to inmates so the government can save money by not hiring new staff? That's crazy! You think I'm insensitive, but that's not it. You can help without putting yourself in harm's way. I love you and I want you to be valued."

Victoria put her hand on Devin's cheek and kissed him. "That's the sweetest thing you've said to me in a long time. I love you."

"I love you too, but what am I going to do with you?"

Victoria got up from the chair and took his hand in hers. "I hope everything?"

"Really?" Devin raised an eyebrow and smiled.

"Really," she said and led him to the bedroom.

Chapter 52

Chico took off her work shirt to change into a T-shirt.

Bonnie lay on her bunk staring at Chico's back. "Where'd you get those trophies?"

"This guy stabbed me," she said, pulling the T-shirt over her head. "He was pissed off that a dyke was 'takin' ova his hood'. He and his buddies tried to take me out." Chico held on to the metal bunk frame and looked at Bonnie.

Bonnie regretted asking Chico about the scars. She knew how hard it was for her to talk about the stuff that had happened to her, but Chico didn't seem to mind sharing.

"They grabbed me as I was leaving a deal and started beating me and stabbing me. A car drove up and some people started yelling at them so they took off. The people were real nice. They dropped me off at the hospital. I'm not sure I would drive some punk kid bleeding like a stuck pig in my car. It's real hard to get bloodstains off of anything. I would've been pretty fucked up or dead if they hadn't come on the scene."

Bonnie was surprised by the way Chico talked about the event without any change in her emotions, and that she was calling herself a "dyke." She felt sad for Chico. She wanted to tell her about what had happened to her, but she'd never told anyone but Dr. Thomas. "You know, you should come with me some time to the meditation class. They're doing an all-day sitting on President's Day."

"Why?" Chico walked to the sink to fix her hair.

"I just think it would help you."

"I don't need no fucking help. I ain't into all that Buddhist crap." Chico combed water through her hair slicking it back. "If you're into all that Buddhist stuff, why you writing a nun? I was forced to go to church when I was a kid and I don't want nothing to do with those knuckle-smacking *penguinos* or any freaking monks neither." Chico grabbed a well-worn Maxim magazine out of her locker and started flipping through the pages. "This is all the help I need," she said showing Bonnie the centerfold picture.

"Whatever, I used to be a Billy Bad Ass like you once upon a time. Believe me, it gets old." Bonnie couldn't believe that sentence had just come out of her mouth.

Chico sat down on McKenzie's bed. "Making $5,000 a day doesn't get old."

"No, but it gets you caught."

"I got caught cause when the feds raided my place I had money and meth hidden in stupid places. Next time, I'll bury it."

"Bury it?" Bonnie gave her an incredulous look and sat up. "Chico, I know you started selling dope to help your mom out. You don't have to do that anymore. You could get your GED and...."

Chico interrupted her, "okay, *Mami*, thanks for the *sermón*, *pero* don't you have a meditation class to go to? *Vaya con Dios*, roommate!"

"Tease me all you want, Dolores, but you'll see."

Chico rolled the magazine into a cylinder and jumped up from McKenzie's bed. "You're gonna get a spanky from your Latino daddy if you call me by that name again. *Comprende?*"

"What the hell?" Bonnie laughed. She felt her stomach flutter as Chico hovered over her studying her with her dark brown eyes. "You're freakin' crazy, Chico."

"*Si, pero* I think you like crazy." Chico grinned.

The image of the Mexican kid from her high school flashed in Bonnie's mind. "I gotta go." She jumped up from the bunk and pushed past Chico into the hallway. It was close to open movement. She waited for the officer to unlock the unit door then she headed to the track.

Her mind raced. *Why am I letting a Mexican stud-broad get so close to me?* She thought about Cheryl. *That was different, Cheryl was for drugs.* Bonnie wasn't sure she could trust Chico, but she wanted to. Chico was complicated. She was strong and didn't care what other people thought about her, but she was also sensitive, always considering Bonnie's feelings, and bringing her soup or tea when she was sick or feeling down. *Tim and Gary would never have done those things for me!*

"Ouch! Oh shit! Ahhh!"

"What the fuck's going on?" Chico jolted up in the bed—it made a loud squeaking noise.

Bonnie sat up startled by the bed shaking. "Was that an earthquake?"

McKenzie writhed in pain. "My side hurts. It feels like it's going to explode."

Chico jumped off the top bunk wearing nothing but a T-shirt and a pair of shorts. "We need a PA."

"Chico, you stay with her. I'll go get help," Bonnie said, running out of the room barefoot towards the Officer's Station. She was glad that they hadn't locked the unit down yet, remembering how long it had taken staff to come when she needed help.

"We need a PA quick!" she screamed at the officer.

"Hey, slow down. What's the problem?" the officer asked.

"I don't know what's wrong! That's what the fucking PA is for. My bunkie is in some serious pain. She needs help bad."

"Don't get insolent with me." He pointed his finger at her.

Bonnie took a deep breath and tried again. "Listen officer, McKenzie woke us up screaming. She needs a doctor."

The CO slowly took out his radio and called for medical assistance.

When the staff arrived at the unit they packed into Bonnie and Chico's cell.

A Filipina PA wearing a white coat pushed her glasses up on her face as she peered over McKenzie. "Where does it hurt?"

"My side, my side is killing me." McKenzie grimaced. "Fuck, fuck, it hurts! It's like someone's stabbing me in the gut!"

"I hate when that happens," Chico snickered.

Bonnie playfully swatted at her. "Not cool, Chico."

"Yes, yes, sounds like appendicitis," the PA said. "She needs to go to outside hospital. Call Control and ask for an ambulance."

"Hang in there, Mac," Chico yelled as they carried McKenzie out on a stretcher.

Chico sat down on McKenzie's bed. "I guess if one of us dies, it's just one less inmate to count, huh?"

Bonnie sat on her bed her hands still shaking. "I think I'm too wound up to sleep."

Chico shook her head. "Me too."

Bonnie looked at Chico and then patted her mattress. Chico blinked her eyes at Bonnie. Bonnie patted the mattress a second time. Chico got up and climbed over Bonnie to the wall side of the bunk. Bonnie turned to face her.

"You're a beautiful woman, Bonnie," Chico whispered.

She looked into Chico's eyes. Heat rushed through her body. She wanted to tell her how badly she wanted to be close to her, but she didn't have words.

Chico put her hand on Bonnie's chin and lifted it up to meet her mouth. She leaned in and kissed Bonnie on the lips, then moved her hand down to Bonnie's breasts.

Bonnie trembled. She wanted to give herself over to Chico's hands.

"It's been years since you've been touched, huh?" Chico asked in a whisper.

Bonnie nodded.

"I want it to be perfect." Chico slipped her hand under Bonnie's gray sweat pants, through her government-issue white underwear, and slid her fingers inside her. Bonnie gasped and leaned back into her pillow. Chico bit down hard on her neck. She shuddered in a combination of pleasure and pain as Chico thrust deeper into her. Tears rolled down her face. She felt exposed.

"What's wrong?" Chico asked.

"Nothing's wrong," she said and grabbed Chico and pulled her closer, opening her legs wider to feel Chico deeper inside her.

Chico tugged at Bonnie's sweatpants. Bonnie lifted herself off the mattress and used her foot to help Chico free one leg from her sweatpants. Chico edged down the bed and began licking her, still thrusting her fingers inside her.

Her breathing quickened. "Chico," she moaned, unable to contain herself. "Oh," she cried out louder. She felt like she was going to explode.

Chico tried to quiet her with her free hand. Bonnie sucked Chico's fingers trying to stifle her moans. Her body shuddered with pleasure.

Chico gently slid her fingers out. "Was that good?"

"I didn't know it could be that good." Bonnie said, catching her breath.

Chico smiled. "I gotta get up or we're gonna get busted."

"No, don't let me go." Bonnie pulled Chico towards her and kissed her face.

"I'm not gonna let you go. I'm just gonna go back to my bunk so I don't get us both thrown into the SHU. Okay?"

Bonnie reluctantly let go of her and Chico climbed back onto the top bunk. Bonnie watched, still wanting her. She closed her eyes. She'd never felt this good.

The door suddenly burst open. An officer shined his flashlight into the room. "McKenzie needs her medication," he said.

"What's going on?" Chico asked, pretending to be awakened from her sleep.

"Your roommate says her blood pressure medication is in her locker and she needs it. Which one is hers?"

Chico pointed out the locker and then got down from her bunk to help the officer find the medication.

"That's enough excitement for one night," he said and closed the door.

Bonnie started laughing. "You have no idea!"

"Damn, that was a close call! Glad to see my instincts are still sharp," Chico said giving her one last furtive kiss before climbing back in her bunk. "Goodnight, Bonnie."

"Night, Chico."

Bonnie tried to fall back asleep, but her body ached for Chico's touch.

Chapter 53

BONNIE LOOKED AT the calendar on her bulletin board. She counted the days left in July. "I can't believe I'm going to be leaving in a month," she said aloud, then realized her mistake. She knew Chico didn't want to talk about it. She remembered how much it hurt Cheryl when she left state prison.

Chico nodded. "Yeah, it's coming quick."

"You know I'm going to miss you," she said, wanting to reassure Chico and sat down on the bed next to her.

"What else you gonna miss?" Chico bit at her nail.

"Besides you and Dr. Thomas—nothing. I'm not going to miss these people telling me what to do, what to wear, not getting to choose what I want to eat, not being able to go outside when I want to. Oh, and having to deal with some of these asshole guards, I'm not going to miss any of that."

"You afraid?"

Bonnie looked at Chico and then looked at the floor. "A little afraid of going back to dope. I always did before." She thought about Sketch and how he'd forced her to shoot up when she got out of jail the first time. "It's going to be weird to be around men again. I don't really like that idea."

Chico nodded. "I don't really like the idea of that either."

Bonnie lay back on her bunk with Chico. She thought about the past four years. Her mind wandered to the day she arrived at the California prison. She remembered the night she'd gotten the letter from Gary and how it had triggered memories of the guy she killed—that was the night she met Dr. Thomas.

As Chico held her in her arms she tried to imagine what it was going to be like without her on the outside. She couldn't. For the past six months she and Chico were together every night talking about their dreams and fears, walking the track, lifting weights. She even helped Chico step away from hooch.

"Chico you're my cell mate and my soul mate, if that exists," she laughed as Chico stroked her hair.

"I'm going to miss you, Bon," Chico said. "It's going to be hard as hell to be here another thirteen years without you." Chico bit her lip. "But I'm proud of you for releasing to New Orleans to help Sister Helen with the death row guys."

"For real?"

"I don't have to worry about you running off with them," Chico laughed as she said it.

Bonnie kissed Chico. "I love you," she told her.

She felt proud of herself too, but she couldn't imagine being without Chico. She knew if she caught a new case or just refused to cooperate with probation they would send her back and she could serve out the rest of her parole here with Chico which would buy them another year together.

Chapter 54

VICTORIA SAT ON a wooden bench in a Thai restaurant waiting for Peter. He was fifteen minutes late, which was totally unlike him. She started to wonder if he'd changed his mind. She'd heard the hurt in his voice when she called him yesterday. She thumbed through the menu even though she always ordered Eggplant Basil with sticky rice at every Thai restaurant she went to. Just as she put down the menu and readied herself to leave, the door opened and Peter walked in.

"Sorry, Victoria, Borderline in crisis." Peter's forehead glistened with sweat.

"What happened?"

"Some mild self-mutilation, but I had to do a suicide risk assessment and get her to sign a no-self harm contract to agree to call me before she cut again." Peter took a handkerchief out of his pocket and wiped the sweat from his brow.

A Thai waiter, dressed in a royal blue shirt with silver elephants, motioned for them to leave their shoes on a rack and led them up a platform to a table in the middle of the restaurant.

"I hope this is okay?" Peter asked, noticing that she looked a little uncomfortable.

Victoria sat cross-legged and scooted the wicker backrest snugly up to her back so she could sit closer to the table. "Yeah, it's really cute. Devin and I have driven by before and I always wanted to come here."

Peter took a sip of his water. "How are you?"

"It's been a hard year."

Peter gave her a quizzical look. "How's that client?"

"Like a different person. It's hard to believe she ever killed someone."

Peter stammered, "she killed someone?"

"Whoops, I wasn't supposed to tell you that." Victoria took a sip of her water.

Peter smiled. "Consider it consultation—everything in consultation is confidential, with the exception of..."

"Are you ready to order?" The waiter interrupted.

"I'll have the Basil Eggplant with sticky rice and a Thai Iced Tea."

"I'll have my usual." Peter handed him the menu.

"Green curry with chicken," the waiter smiled and jotted down the order.

"Where was I?" Victoria asked.

"You were telling me about your client who doesn't seem like a murderer."

"When you put it that way..."

"I can see why the client would be even more freaked out by the idea of you writing an article about her. What happened with that anyway?"

Victoria blushed. "I guess I left out a detail or two."

Peter cocked his head to the side and grimaced. "I guess so."

The waiter brought their drinks. Peter thanked him in Thai. Victoria marveled at his worldliness, for a white guy he'd always been thoughtful about other cultures and how he treated people. She admired his sincerity.

"Sorry, Peter," she apologized and took a sip of her water.

"Um hmm." He looked at her in a way that made her feel slightly exposed.

"After we talked I explained to her why I wanted to write the article. I told her if she didn't want me to write it, I wouldn't. I think when she saw she had a choice in the outcome she decided it was okay and gave me her blessing."

"So, it was a reparative moment for her."

"Exactly." Victoria nodded.

"Nothing in therapy happens by mistake. That's my theory anyway." Peter smiled and took a sip of his tea.

"It's a good theory That's just the beginning." Victoria stirred her tea with the straw. "I told you about my counter-transference with her."

"If I remember correctly you felt like if you could change her maybe you could get some mastery over the people who disapprove of your interracial marriage."

Victoria shook her head. "It sounds crazy, but yeah. I noticed this strange parallel process going on. I started to devalue Devin."

"What do you mean?" He looked perplexed.

The waiter delivered the appetizers. Peter picked up a spring roll and took a bite. Victoria put one on her plate and continued talking.

"I felt more distant from him. Maybe I felt like I was betraying him. How do you explain to your African-American husband why you're overly invested in helping a white supremacist? I don't think I could explain it to my grandparents either. It goes against the grain."

"Your grandparents were holocaust survivors, right?" Peter asked, still chewing.

"Yeah, but even when they got here it wasn't easy. My grandfather had a dry cleaning business in Manhattan. I used to spend time with him there when my mom was working. Once, when I about seven, this man came in with his laundry bag. My grandfather was pulling out his sweaters and shirts and I was counting them for him. The guy glanced at my grandfather's business license and he says 'Hyman Levine that's the most Jewey name I've ever heard.' My grandfather became so angry. He started throwing the man's clothes at him. He told him to 'get out' that he didn't need his business. It wasn't true. My grandparents were very poor. The man yelled at him about 'Jews taking over everything' and then he slammed the door so hard it broke one of the windows.

My grandfather was so upset. I'd never seen him that angry. He was typically a very kind, gentle man. He sat me down on the counter and told me that the world was broken and in need of repair, *tikkun*, he called it. He said what he and my grandmother went through showed how deeply the world was broken. He said that being a dry cleaner would never make him rich, but that it didn't hurt anyone. I understood later that he was referring to my grandfather Louis, my dad's father, and my dad, who'd spent their lives working for a company he said 'helped destroy our people.'"

"What company?" Peter asked.

"IBM. My grandfather, Louis, was a manager there and helped them activate the Poughkeepsie office and my dad's first job was as a lawyer for IBM."

"IBM, the computer company?" Peter looked surprised. "What does that have to do with the holocaust?"

"I don't know all the facts, but apparently IBM helped the Nazis by giving them discounts on some sort of counting machine, a punch card system, that helped them track the Jews." Victoria stopped and took a sip of her water. "It's weird to think about, but the profits IBM made on these counting machines helped Hitler kill Jews more efficiently and also provided capital to create the modern day computer."

"Damn, that is weird. I knew about Volkswagen, BMW, and Bayer, but I had no idea that IBM benefited from the Holocaust too. That's awful."

"There's another thing that's really strange and it's something else that's really haunted me, but I can't ask him, because he's dead now."

"What's that?"

"My grandfather Louis was from Germany. He and my grandmother came over before the war, but I remember him telling stories of going back to Germany for business. He once told me not to tell anyone I was Jewish. 'Rosenberg is a German name, if anyone asks.' But I've gotten off on to a wild tangent. Sorry." Victoria took another sip of her water.

"Victoria, you don't need to apologize. This is important. I didn't know any of this about you."

"Thanks, Peter, but I really am going on and on."

"I'll tell you when your time's up." He smiled.

"Ha! You asked for it."

Victoria took a deep breath and continued. "I remember being really confused about his telling me that my dad and Grandpa Louis were doing something bad like this man who had just hurt my *Zeide*, that's the Yiddish word for grandpa."

Peter nodded.

Victoria's eyes began to water. "I'm sorry," she apologized.

"Cut yourself some slack. Therapists are allowed to have emotions too."

She wiped her eyes and nose on the cloth napkin. "Anyway, *Zeide*, turned to me and said '*shayna maydala*,' that's what he called me, 'promise me that when you grow up you'll devote your life to *tikkun olam*, the repair of the world.' He was weeping as he looked into my eyes and he pulled up his shirtsleeve and showed me the number on his arm. I didn't know what it meant then, only that it had something to do with the bad place that he and *Bobe*, my grandmother, had to live at before they came to New York."

"Wow, that's a heavy story."

"I really let my *Zeide* down." Tears fell again. She blew her nose on the napkin.

Peter shook his head. "I disagree, Victoria. It's our job to find the best in people and then help them find the best in themselves. That's what you did with your client, white supremacist or not. How is that not repair?"

"You always have the right thing to say. No wonder you have such a long waiting list." She patted his hand. "I might as well tell you my other dark secret."

"There's more?" Peter leaned in and rested his chin on his hand.

Victoria put the half-eaten spring roll on the appetizer plate in front of her. "This is really hard to talk about. I hope you won't judge me too harshly."

"I'm your friend, Victoria. I don't expect you to be perfect. It might freak me out a little bit if you tell me you killed someone though."

Tears welled up in her eyes again. "Well, in a way I feel I did." She shook her head and wiped her tears with the napkin.

He gave her a strange look and waited for her to talk.

"One summer, my college roommate, Joanne, and I went to the Hamptons and I talked her into trying coke. It was the only time I ever did it, but Joanne got hooked. I tried to get her to quit. I even told her I would pay for her treatment so no one had to know about it. She overdosed on cocaine at the beginning of our junior year and died. That's when I changed my major from English Literature to Psychology."

"So that was the final defining moment. Seems like every psychologist has one. Not to minimize your experience, but when I was on the admissions committee at school and reading applicant essays, it seemed like every applicant described some pivotal moment in their life—a drunken parent, an anorexic friend, an abused neighbor kid, something happened that called to them to become a psychologist, sounds like that was yours."

Victoria felt like Peter's comment had trivialized her experience a bit, but at the same time it might have been Peter's way of normalizing it for her.

"Green curry with chicken and spicy basil eggplant with sticky rice," the waiter interrupted delivering the steaming platter to the table. "Can I get you anything else?"

"That's it. And so we don't have to fight about this later…" Peter quickly handed him his credit card.

"Thank you." Victoria smiled and took a bite of her food. "This is delicious."

"Thanks for meeting me." He smiled coyly and scooped some rice onto his plate.

"You're welcome." She smiled back. She felt the bittersweet of their connection. "So to bottom line this, I realized my client, who was a heroin addict, was bringing up feelings of guilt about not being able to save Joanne. On top of that, I had another client who had a serious suicide attempt I feel like I could've prevented, but missed the signs."

"That's putting a lot of responsibility on yourself," Peter said.

"Yeah, I learned that I am wildly co-dependent. Devin says I take *tikkun olam* to a whole new level. '*Tikkun olam* on crack,' I think he said."

"That's pretty funny," Peter chuckled. "What are you going to do about it?"

"My client finds meditation helpful in dealing with her emotions. Sometimes I think she's more balanced and centered than I am. Well, except the racism." Victoria shook her head. "Still working on that. Anyway, I'm going to go to a *Vipassana* meditation retreat and start meditating."

"Is that the ten-day silent meditation up in the Sierras?"

"Yes. Not sure I can go ten days without talking, but I'm going to give it a try."

"Is Devin going with you?"

"No. He doesn't have problems controlling his emotions and being detached. He could probably use a workshop on how to express his feelings a little more."

"Sounds like things are going better with the two of you?" Peter's tone betrayed his disappointment.

"Yeah, they are."

Peter looked crestfallen. "A guy can hope." He blushed slightly when he said it.

Victoria set down her fork. "You're an amazing friend, Peter. If things were different." She touched his arm. "Enough about me. What's happening with you?"

"Well, since you asked." Peter smiled. "I met this woman. She's a pediatrician at Oakland Children's Hospital."

"How'd you meet her?"

"At a reading a couple of weeks ago. Yalom was reading from his novel *Lying on the Couch* at Black Oak Books."

"Oh, I know how much you love Yalom."

"It turns out this woman—Christine is her name—really loves Yalom too."

"That's fantastic!" Victoria touched his hand. "I hope she knows what a treasure she's getting."

"Treasure, huh?" Peter cocked his head to the side and looked at her wistfully.

"Yep, pure gold."

Chapter 55

JULY FLEW BY and she was down to "seven days and a wake up." Thursday would be her last session with Dr. Thomas. Bonnie thought maybe she'd tell Dr. T about how it felt to be leaving Chico. She hadn't told her about their relationship.

When Thursday came, Bonnie walked mindfully to Dr. Thomas's office. It felt strange to be going in for her last session.

"So, you leave Monday? How does that feel?" Dr. Thomas asked, leaning back in her chair and smiling.

Bonnie nervously picked at the skin around her nails. "I'm looking forward to getting some new clothes. Beige is definitely not my color."

Dr. Thomas laughed. "Are you nervous? It's been quite a while since you were out there?"

"Yeah, four years. It's gonna be weird not going back to Portland. I've never even been to New Orleans."

"That's a big change. The West Coast is really different than the Deep South. Have you ever been to the South?" Dr. Thomas took a sip of her bottled water.

"Nope, before I got busted I'd never been out of Oregon."

"You know that there are a lot of black people in New Orleans? I thought that you didn't care for that sort of thing, based on your previous associations."

Bonnie looked down at her hands. This was the first time Dr. Thomas had ever said anything like that to her.

"I've been down a long time, Dr. T. Had lots of time to think and been around a lot of different people. When I was younger I fell into that, but it's not really who I am anymore. Now, I try to look at what people say or do, not their race. I mean, Harris, my old cellie, was a pretty stand up chick and some of the guys I've been helping Sister Helen with are black. I know I can't help them if I still believe that way. I just don't want to marry one, you know." Bonnie stopped and looked at her hands. *Whoops!* She hoped she hadn't offended, Dr. Thomas. She hadn't meant to. "It's fine if other people want to, I'm just sayin'…"

Dr. Thomas interrupted her, "that's progress, Bonnie."

"Thanks." Bonnie looked up from her hands and met Dr. Thomas's eyes. If the comment had offended her, she couldn't tell. Dr. Thomas was smiling at her and she thought she saw tears in her eyes.

"So, what kind of set up do you have out there?"

"Set up?" Bonnie asked, suddenly feeling defensive.

"I mean do you have a place to live or to stay?"

"Oh." Bonnie blushed. "Yeah, Sister Helen found these really nice folks who are letting me live in an apartment they usually rent out to vacationers. I'll move in there when the halfway house releases me."

"That sounds great. What do your parents think about this?"

Bonnie picked at a hangnail. "That I've gone off the deep end. They think Sister Helen is a cult leader. But they're glad I'm not asking for money or to live with them."

Dr. Thomas nodded. "Hmm, still no real support from them, huh?"

"Nah, but I have some good news I wanted to tell you."

"Let's hear it."

"A few months ago *Free At Last* published a letter I wrote about writing to death row inmates. They're out of New Orleans too. I told them I was relocating and they wrote back and offered me a part-time job with magazine distribution. They want to help me."

Dr. Thomas seemed genuinely surprised. "That's great!"

"They said I can write a few articles because they like my perspective on things and they don't do a lot for female inmates yet. I'm gonna help Sister Helen do outreach and write for *Free At Last*. Can you believe that? Almost seems too good to be true."

"That's amazing, Bonnie. You deserve this, you've worked so hard." Dr. Thomas smiled the biggest smile she'd ever seen her smile since they began working together.

Bonnie felt a warmth in her chest that took her by surprise. She sat up straighter and smiled back. "There's something else I wanted to talk to you about," Bonnie said, changing the subject. The session seemed to be going by so fast.

"What's that?"

Bonnie took a deep breath. "My roommate is really upset I'm leaving."

"Chico?"

"Yeah, Chico." Bonnie looked at Dr. Thomas trying to anticipate how she might respond to what she was going to share. "She's still got another thirteen years and we've gotten real close. I worry she might do something stupid when I leave. I feel guilty about being excited about leaving. What should I do?"

"It's hard when the people we care about go away. It's hard when they leave in a bad way and it's hard when they leave for good reasons too. If the shoe was on the other foot, and Chico was leaving and you were staying, how would you feel?"

Bonnie thought about what Dr. Thomas was asking her. "I'd be sad and pissed off I couldn't go with her, but I'd be happy for her and I wouldn't want her to come back."

Dr. Thomas gave her a questioning look. "Think she wants that for you too?"

"Probably." Bonnie nodded. "I mean...I'm pretty sure she wants me to be happy. It's just really hard for her because she still has a lot of time."

"I'm sure it's hard too because you can't stay in contact with her because the prison rules don't allow ex-inmates to write other inmates."

"We'll find a way to communicate."

"Maybe you can make more friends, meet new people. No one can replace your connection with your roommate, but you could bring other people into your life."

Bonnie chewed nervously on her nail. "That's hard, cause I don't really trust people. I trust Chico, but that took a long time."

"It's important for you to keep reaching out and connecting with people." Dr. Thomas looked at the clock on the bookshelf.

"Bonnie, I've so enjoyed working with you these past few years. You've worked very hard on yourself. You stopped using drugs, processed your feelings from the sexual and physical abuse you experienced, and you've taken responsibility for your crimes. And on top of all that you've started giving back and helping others."

Bonnie blushed. "Thanks, Dr. T. I couldn't have done it without you."

"Thank you for giving me the opportunity to get to know you. I've also learned a lot from our work together. I want to acknowledge your courage to come to therapy and work through your feelings and struggles. Even when you were mad at me about writing the article, " Dr. Thomas hesitated. "There's something I need to tell you. I don't like the idea of keeping secrets from you."

Fuck! She called the FBI? Bonnie eyed her nervously. Her hands started to shake.

"What?" Bonnie asked alarmed, the adrenaline filling her body.

"Let me just begin by saying this, therapists rarely disclose personal things in therapy unless it's extremely relevant to the therapy and will help the client."

Bonnie tried to calm herself. Dr. Thomas was going to tell her something, but it didn't sound like she'd called the police. It was something else.

Dr. Thomas looked directly at her. "I'm Jewish."

Bonnie quickly studied Dr. Thomas's features trying to see why she hadn't noticed. "You're Jewish?"

"Yes. Rosenberg is a Jewish German name. It felt strange to keep that hidden from you when you've been so honest with me."

Bonnie noticed that Dr. Thomas's hands were trembling slightly. "You know, Dr. T, before I met you, I didn't even know any Jewish people."

"That's what I figured." Dr. Thomas smiled.

"I don't believe those things anymore, Dr. T." Bonnie felt bad that she could have ever thought those things about someone as kind as Dr. Thomas.

"Don't feel like you have to say that Bonnie, I just needed to tell you. I didn't want that secret between us."

Bonnie looked at the ground. "I'm really gonna miss you, Dr. Thomas."

"I'm going to miss you too, Bonnie. I want you to know that you always have someone in your corner." Dr. Thomas looked at the clock again. "We're out of time."

"Thank you, Dr. T." Bonnie wiped the tears from her eyes and got up from her chair. "I know it's against the rules, but can I have a hug?"

Dr. Thomas stood up and gave Bonnie a hug and opened the door for her to leave.

"One more thing. If you need to talk, call. If I answer I can talk or you can leave a message, but I can't call you back. You can also write, but I can't write you back. Okay?"

"Got it. Thanks." Bonnie smiled.

"I'd wish you good luck, Bonnie, but you don't need it because you have the resources now to take care of yourself." Dr. Thomas smiled. "Maybe I'll see you walking out the front gate Monday morning in your civvies."

"I'll look for you." Bonnie waved goodbye and closed the door behind her.

Chapter 56

SUNDAY NIGHT CHICO came back to their room and told Bonnie she had a surprise for her.

"What kind of surprise?" Bonnie asked nervously. She had never liked surprises.

Chico lifted up the corner of her left shirtsleeve and showed Bonnie a new tattoo.

"Whoa, Chico, that tat must have cost you a fortune."

"Do you like it, Babe?"

Bonnie examined the tattoo closely. It was a heart with flames around it with Bonnie's name on a scroll that wrapped around the heart.

"Chico, I can't believe you did that for me. You always talked about how stupid it was to have a woman's name tattooed on your body and how you'd never do that."

"That was before I met you." Chico started crying. "I don't know how I can live without you. I can't imagine thirteen more years in this hell hole without you."

Bonnie wiped the tears from Chico's face. "You should talk to Dr. T."

"I told you," Chico said, suddenly angry, "I don't talk to shrinks!"

"I said that once too." Bonnie opened her locker. "I'm gonna make a cup of coffee, want one?"

Chico nodded.

Bonnie took her and Chico's cups and loaded them with several spoonfuls of instant coffee. "I'll be right back." She walked down the hallway to the microwave room, filled the cups with water, and waited for her turn at the microwave. *This is it.* She looked around the unit lobby at the shiny, waxed floors and the women shuffling back and forth from their rooms to the showers and the TV room. *No more lines.*

She looked over at the officer's station. The officer was in the office with the door shut talking on the phone and laughing. For a moment, she saw him as just a guy and realized how hard being a CO must be. *Three hundred and fifty to one, no wonder they're so uptight,* she thought.

"You gonna go?" the woman in line behind her asked.

Bonnie grinned. "Yeah, I'm leaving tomorrow."

"No, Bitch, I'm talking about the microwave. It's your turn."

Bonnie's face turned red. She clenched her jaw and gripped the cups in her hands a little tighter. *Let it go,* she told herself, *tomorrow this will all be behind you.* She shook her head, stepped forward, and slowly put the cups in the microwave.

She and Chico stayed up talking until close to the 4:00 AM count.

"I better get back up to my bunk," Chico said.

"No, sleep in my bed. I don't care if we get caught. There's nothing that they could do that would be worse than what's already happening."

"I'll come back down after the officer shines his flashlight in."

Chico got out of Bonnie's bunk and waited until the officer passed by, then she climbed back down and got under the covers with Bonnie in her bunk. Chico held Bonnie close in her arms. She kissed the top of her head. Bonnie felt Chico's tears as they streamed down her face and fell on to Bonnie's cheeks. Bonnie cried too.

"I hate leaving you, Chico. I'll never find someone who'll love me like you do."

Chapter 57

WHEN THE SUN rose Monday morning, she was still laying in Chico's arms.

"Bonnie Maldonado, report to R & D." The paging system blared in the housing unit startling them both awake.

"Did you hear that?" Chico asked.

Bonnie nodded, she had waited so long to hear those words calling her to the Receiving and Discharge office in the prison, but now as she heard them she felt deeply torn. She didn't want to leave Chico.

Chico held her tighter.

"I gotta go, Chico. It's time."

Chico looked into her eyes fighting back tears. "I'll never forget you, Bonnie. I'll always love you." Chico broke into deep sobs, her chest heaved.

"I'll always love you too, Chico." Bonnie bit down hard on her lip fighting down her own emotion.

"When I get out we're gonna be together again. I know we will."

"Chico, I gotta go now."

Chico released her and Bonnie got up from the bunk and took her socks and underwear out of her locker.

Chico watched as she dressed. She watched her slip on her prison uniform—the government issued pants, the work shirt, and the black boots—one last time.

Bonnie pulled her sweat suit off the hanger to take to R & D. She would be releasing in the sweat suit since no one had sent her release clothes.

Tears rolled down Chico's face as she watched Bonnie brush her teeth. It was unbearable. Bonnie reached into her jacket pocket and pulled out a sealed envelope and handed it to Chico. "Read this tonight before you go to bed."

Chico took the envelope.

"Here, Bonnie, I want to give you something." Chico held out a ring to Bonnie. It was a simple gold band. "I want you to have this. I want you to wear this and know when you look at it that I love you and always will."

"Chico, I don't want to know what you did to get this," she said smiling.

"No, you don't." Chico smirked and slipped the ring on Bonnie's ring finger.

"It's beautiful, thank you, Chico." Bonnie leaned in and kissed her again.

Just then the officer opened the door. "Ms. Maldonado, it's time to go home. R & D is paging you. C'mon now, time to go free."

"I'm coming," she told him. "Goodbye, Chico."

"Bye, Bon."

Bonnie walked out with the officer. She heard Chico weeping, but she didn't look back. She knew it would only make it harder and this time she was listening to the superstition that if you looked back you'd end up back in prison. So she kept looking forward as she walked out of the unit, towards R & D. She couldn't hold back the tears any longer, she'd waited for this day for so long, for a second chance.

Chapter 58

"MALDONADO?" THE CONTROL Room Officer asked as Bonnie walked into the sallyport and heard the door close behind her.

"Right here," she said.

"Bonnie Maldonado?" He asked again as she waited patiently in the narrow corridor behind barbed windows and the metal door.

"Yes, sir."

"Register number?"

"24827-056."

"Social Security number?"

"663-45-0971."

"Place of birth?"

"Portland, Oregon."

"Sally one."

The sallyport door released and Bonnie walked out of the prison dressed in the gray sweat suit she had bought off the commissary five years ago.

Officer Hopyard was at the front desk. She got up and walked towards her with a manila envelope in her hand. Hopyard was still wearing those stupid handcuff earrings.

"Be good out there, Maldonado." Hopyard smiled. She handed her the envelope and then patted Bonnie on the shoulder.

It felt weird to walk through the front door, past the barbed wire fences. She'd been through the door once for a medical trip, but in handcuffs and leg irons, escorted by two armed officers. Now she was walking through it and no one cared. Hopyard even held the door open for her.

She opened the envelope. Inside was a plane ticket and twenty-five dollars. She was to take the bus to the airport then get on a Southwest Airlines flight to New Orleans. The twenty-five dollars was supposed to cover meals since the flight didn't serve food. It was also supposed to cover the bus ride to the airport and a cab ride to the halfway house.

She had twelve hours to get to the halfway house. She had to be at the halfway house by 10:00 p.m. or they would consider her AWOL and she'd get an escape charge. This made her extremely nervous. She hoped she'd be able to find everything okay, but feared something would go wrong. She'd get on the wrong bus, or worse, miss her flight.

She waited at the flagpole for the inmate driver from the minimum security prison camp to take her to the bus station. She looked around hoping to see Dr. Thomas.

The day was cloudy, it looked like it might rain and she wondered if it was a bad omen. Already she was missing the safety of being on the other side of the fence and the warmth of Chico's arms, but she knew she had to go on. She'd made a promise to herself that she would try this time. She looked at the cars in the parking lot. They looked weird—the colors were unusually bright and they were shaped more like the futuristic cars she'd seen in sci-fi movies.

A white van pulled up. The driver, a pretty brunette with curly brown hair wearing a blue prison camp uniform, rolled down the window. She looked younger and softer than the women on the inside. She wondered what she'd done to earn her vacation at Club Fed.

"Going home?" the woman asked. She lit up a cigarette, blatantly ignoring the *No Smoking* sign on the dash.

"Well, sort of?" Bonnie replied.

"What do ya mean?" The woman looked confused.

"I'm getting out, but I'm going someplace I've never been before. So it's not like going home."

The woman took a drag off her cigarette. "Oh, where you going?"

"New Orleans."

"What's in New Orleans, boyfriend or something?"

Bonnie thought for a moment before answering. "No, some new friends."

"Okay, sounds complicated. I'll stop with the questions and just take you to the bus stop. Get in."

As they drove in silence Bonnie tried to manage her anxiety by taking deep breaths like the Buddhist books and Dr. Thomas had taught her to do when she got stressed. She looked out the window at all the signs and businesses. The barrage of noise and messages coming at her was overwhelming. *What if I can't find the right bus or I miss my flight?* She started to get superstitious that the Universe would make her pay her karma back by having her die in a plane crash.

"Here we are." The woman pulled the van over to the curb. "This here's the gateway to freedom," she said.

Bonnie looked at all the buses lined up. It made her stomach flutter.

"It's that one right there. See it says *Oakland Airport*." The woman pointed to the sign on the side of the bus.

"Thank you," Bonnie said relieved and got out of the van. She wondered why the woman hadn't just taken off with the van. She would have if she'd been in her shoes.

"Don't do anything I wouldn't do," the woman called out the window as she drove away.

Bonnie walked over to the bus and opened up the white envelope with the money in it. She hadn't seen money in years. She looked at the crisp dollar bills. It reminded her of the robberies.

"How much?" she asked as she boarded the bus.

"$1.50," the bus driver replied.

Bonnie looked through the envelope. She had a twenty and five one-dollar bills. "Do you have change?"

"Nope," he replied briskly.

She could hear people behind her waiting to board. She tried to put two of the one-dollar bills into the machine, but couldn't figure out how to do it.

"Here lady," the bus driver said, taking the bills from her. He gently slid them into the machine.

She could feel her face get hot with embarrassment. She worried that the people waiting behind her must have thought she was a complete idiot.

"Lady?"

Bonnie began walking towards the back looking for a seat.

"Lady?"

Bonnie turned.

"Your ticket!"

What a dumbshit! She heard her dad's words run through her head.

She returned to the front of the bus, grabbed the ticket and tried to control the emotions welling up inside her. Her ears were ringing. She took a seat. The door shut and the bus began to move. She reminded herself to breathe.

She spaced out on all the buildings they drove by. She saw some cows on the hillside. She couldn't remember the last time she'd seen a cow. Thirty minutes later, the bus pulled up at the airport. She tried to keep her composure as she walked by the bus driver.

"Have a nice trip, lady," he said as she walked down the stairs.

Bonnie didn't respond, she just continued walking. She wondered if he knew she'd just come from the prison. She stepped into the street and began walking, unsure of where she was supposed to go. A car honked and sped past her, another swerved to avoid hitting her. Then she noticed a crosswalk up only a few yards ahead. It was too late she was already in the middle of the street. Her heart raced with fear and embarrassment as she dashed across the street and through the airport doors.

She looked for the Southwest sign like the secretary at the prison had told her to do, and got in line. It seemed weird to see so many people wearing colorful outfits and so many men in one place. She felt uneasy. She was convinced people were staring at her.

After getting her ticket and clearing the security checkpoint, she walked over to a pizza place to get something to eat. They weren't selling pizza this early, but they had a few breakfast items.

She bought a muffin, a banana, and a bottle of orange juice. There were rows of plastic chairs. She found one with a table attached on the left side and sat down. She picked at the muffin. She hadn't eaten alone in months. Chico was with her at every meal. She felt lonely.

As she finished up her muffin and her last sip of juice she heard a woman's voice announce. "Now boarding Flight 65 to New Orleans- Flight 65 to New Orleans."

She got up from the chair, threw her trash into the garbage, and pulled the ticket out of her pocket. Then she walked over to the counter and gave the woman her ticket.

"Actually you were supposed to give this to us earlier," the woman told her, "so that we could give you a boarding pass."

"I'm sorry. I've never been on a plane before," she said, feeling embarrassed.

The woman looked shocked. "Really?"

Bonnie nodded.

"No problem. Here, come with me and we'll make sure you get a window seat."

The woman escorted Bonnie through the crowd and down the ramp onto the plane. "This is a very special customer," she told the flight attendant, a beautifully coifed blonde. "This is Ms. Maldonado's first flight ever and she chose Southwest. Please make her feel comfortable."

Bonnie was shrinking inside her skin. She didn't like to stand out and today she was wearing a neon sign that flashed: *fresh out of prison.*

The attendant smiled a perfect smile at Bonnie. "Welcome aboard!"

Since she had a choice, Bonnie picked out a seat near the wing. She'd heard that if a plane were to crash, the best place to be was near the wing. She took her seat and put on her seat belt. She looked at the ring that Chico had given her and wondered if she should order a drink on the plane and show up to the halfway house drunk. They would have to take her back to the prison if she did that. She played with the ring on her finger and decided to wait before making any rash decisions.

She looked out the window and saw planes taking off and landing. She leaned back and closed her eyes. She'd hardly slept the last four nights and was exhausted.

"Miss, Miss. Wake up." Bonnie opened her eyes and saw the blonde flight attendant looking at her. She expected to see a CO. "We're here."

Bonnie rubbed her eyes and looked around. The plane was empty. She'd slept through the entire flight.

She got off the plane and followed the other passengers towards baggage claim, then realized she had no bags to claim.

She went outside and immediately felt the sticky humidity in the air. It felt exotic and exciting to her. She walked along the sidewalk to the area where the taxis were lining up. She pulled the address out of her pocket. A gray-haired black guy, wearing a brown and white-checkered cap, approached her. "Where you goin' to, ma'am?" He asked.

She nervously read the address off the paper.

"Here, ma'am, I can take you there. Get in," he said. He opened the back door of the taxi for Bonnie and then walked around to the driver's side.

She slid in to the cab, feeling a bit apprehensive. She thought about Dr. T. She'd trusted a black guy enough to marry him. This guy looked harmless enough and she felt she could take him if she had to.

They drove in silence to the halfway house. Bonnie marveled at the ornate buildings. Everything looked so foreign to her.

The cab driver pulled over in front of a beautiful Victorian home with an immaculately landscaped yard.

"I don't think this is it," she said. She knew she must be in the wrong place.

"This is the address, ma'am," he said.

"Can you wait here a minute?" she asked, as she paid the cab fare.

Bonnie got out of the cab and walked to the house. She knocked apprehensively on the door. A young woman, with wavy blonde hair wearing a floral dress and tan sandals, opened the door.

"Um, is this a …? Bonnie stumbled over her words.

"A halfway house?" the woman finished Bonnie's sentence.

Bonnie nodded.

"Yes, it is. A lot of people find it hard to believe that a halfway house could be so nice, but it is. Are you Bonnie Maldonado?"

"Yes," Bonnie replied, relieved she was in the right place.

The woman waved the cab driver on. "Welcome to New Orleans, Miss Maldonado. Come on in and let's get you situated."

Epilogue

THE MONTHS SHE spent in the halfway house had gone by quickly. Bonnie was now living in a flat in the French Quarter, working with Sister Helen coordinating pen pals for death row inmates, and writing for the prison newspaper *Free At Last* like she'd hoped she would.

She continued to write Chico, who continued to talk about their getting together when she finally released. It didn't bother Bonnie. For now, she wasn't interested in dating anyone. She was enjoying her freedom too much.

Chico had taken Bonnie's advice and was seeing Dr. Thomas. Bonnie felt good knowing the two of them were talking, it made her still feel connected to Dr. Thomas.

Bonnie took a seat at her kitchen table and took a sip of her steaming mug of coffee. She was writing a new piece for the paper. The sun streaming in through the yellow curtained windows felt warm on her skin. She turned towards the window and looked out. She felt content, an emotion she was still trying to get used to. Everything around her was so beautiful. She could hardly believe this was her life.

She thought back over the years about all the important people her life. Chico, Cheryl, Chaplain Edwards, Mr. S, and Dr. Thomas they'd all made a difference. She wished she could tell them how she was doing. She wished they could see her. She smiled at the thought.

Ms. Masterson, the woman from the victim witness program, came into her mind. She wished she could tell her she hadn't forgotten their conversation and she'd forgiven herself, or at least started to. Now she was opening her heart and even beginning to let others love her.

She took a deep breath and exhaled slowly. This was what she was about now. This was the life she created for herself. It was almost too good to be true. Yet she knew it was. For the first time in her life she knew she deserved it. She took another sip of her coffee and turned her attention back to her writing. She felt lucky.

About the Author

Davina Kotulski, Ph. D., is a licensed clinical psychologist, motivational life coach, inspirational speaker, Agape Spiritual Practitioner, an internationally-recognized leader in the LGBT equality movement, and author of two books on marriage equality: *Why You Should Give A Damn About Gay Marriage* and *Love Warriors: The Rise of the Marriage Equality Movement and Why It Will Prevail*.

Dr. Kotulski received her Ph.D. in clinical psychology in 1996. For over 13 years she worked as a psychologist in a federal prison, leading empowerment workshops with female inmates, introducing them to the teachings of Thich Nhat Hahn, Napoleon Hill, and Tony Robbins. She currently has a successful private therapy practice in Los Angeles, California, an international life coaching practice, and leads in-person workshops and tele-classes on topics of spiritual growth and development, self-empowerment, and authentic self-expression.

Davina has appeared in over a dozen documentaries, *Newsweek magazine*, *USA Today*, and on CNN, and in mainstream newspapers throughout the United States and Europe. She has been interviewed on NPR and numerous radio shows. Her written work has been featured in periodicals, anthologies, online magazines, and blogs. Davina was the Executive Director of Marriage Equality USA. She has received notable awards for her civil rights advocacy, including the Saints Alive Award from the Metropolitan Community Church, the Michael Switzer Leadership Award, and Grand Marshal San Francisco LGBT Pride Parade. She was also sainted by the irreverent Sisters of Perpetual Indulgence. In 2011, she created a self-help audio program for LGBT people and their families, entitled "How to Come Out of the Closet and Into Your Power." Davina is passionate about helping all people live self-actualized and fully self-expressed lives.

Website: www.davinakotulski.com

Prison Facts

ACCORDING TO THE Women's Sentencing Project, between 1980 and 2014, the number of incarcerated women increased by more than 700%, rising from a total of 26,378 in 1980 to 215,332 in 2014. Carson, E.A. (2015). Prisoners in 2014, Washington, D.C.: Bureau of Justice Statistics.

According to the Correctional Association of New York, "The overwhelming majority of women in prison are survivors of domestic violence. Three-quarters have histories of severe physical abuse by an intimate partner during adulthood, and 82% suffered serious physical or sexual abuse as children." http://www.correctionalassociation.org/

According to a Bureau of Justice Statistics 2003 Report, "Correctional populations report lower educational attainment than do those in the general population. An estimated 40% of State prison inmates, 27% of Federal inmates, 47% of inmates in local jails, and 31% of those serving probation sentences had not completed high school or its equivalent while about 18% of the general population failed to attain high school graduation." http://www.bjs.gov/content/pub/pdf/ecp.pdf

Acknowledgments

THANK YOU, CREATOR, for waking me up in the middle of a hot summer night in August 2000 to begin writing Bonnie Maldonado's story. I remember how easily those first twenty pages flowed on to the page. I knew then that writing this book was a part of my spiritual calling, I just had no idea how long the journey would take and how the story would unfold. Thank you for the invitation to co-create with you.

I also want to thank and acknowledge: Martivón Galindo, Ericka Lutz, Terri Fabris, Shefali Tsabary, Tara Zampardi-May, Lisa Fowler, Jessica Colp, Jennifer Amir, Gerald Wright, Regina Gibson-Broome, Tunde Illone, Bianca Peters, Phillip Eisner, Diane Schroder, Charmaine Colina, Colin Watts, Shannon Kenny, Parvine Kangarlou, Jennifer Sookne, Christine Allen, Stephanie Rosenbaum, Sarah Lamb, James Hanna, Brian Walton, Roberta Conroy, Audrey Borunda, Colin Tipping, and my father, Richard Kotulski. Thank you all for your support in the unfolding of this book.

I want to acknowledge the following people who contributed to my personal evolution: Debra Simnitt, Margie Gordillo, Sandy Dibbel-Hope, Karen Saeger, Ann and Ken Yabusaki, Ruth Palmer, Howard Pollack, Tara Zampardi-May, Kristen Valus, John Turberville, Gina Meyer, Rachel McLaughlin, Stormy Gale, Rachel Robasciotti, Becky Robbins, Cary Little, Alice Lancefield, Pan Sammons, Lynne Bartz, Deanna Gaige, Joe Racklin, Mike Aanavi, Robin Beringer, Kathy Mayglothling, Stan and Mary Durst, Robert Jay Green, Valory Mitchell, Carol Huffine, Anita Fitz, Rev. Joan Steadman, and Michael Bernard Beckwith.

Thanks to my family for their love and support; Janice Duchon, Ray Parker, Barbara and Charles Whitman, the Kotulski family-Absalom, Amy, Chloe, Dylan, Levi, Richard W., Louann; Vicki McKay, Elaine Smith. Thanks to my former wife, Molly McKay, who provided me with priceless editorial assistance with this novel and who was my confidant during the thirteen years I worked at FCI Dublin. Thanks to the McKay family who were my extended family during my prison years.

Thanks to those who unknowingly contributed to this novel by inspiring me with their teaching, writing, and life's callings: Thich Nhat Hahn, Claude Brown, Edward Albee, Bill W., Dr. Bob, Goenka, Ghandi, Norman Lear, Garry Marshall, S.E. Hinton, Dr. Martin Luther King, Simon Wiesenthal, Anne Frank, Elie Wiesel, Alexander Key, Judy Blume, Ernest Holmes.

I wish to thank Myla Young who offered me my first job working for the California Department of Corrections at Vacaville State Prison and Sue Sabol who hired me fresh out of graduate school to work for the Federal Bureau of Prisons. Thanks to my correctional colleagues, especially Scott Barrett, Tracy Henderson, Kuma Deboo, Heather Martin, Stephen Formanski, Sue Feder, David Crago, Kika Pellegrin-Enriquez, Laura Friedeberg, Earlene Durio, Bill Marek, Wayne Aune, Linda Young-Miller, Sara Garcia, Hans Hoch, Carol Louie, Teresa Graciano, Ba Tiba Jones, Paula Ferguson, Bill Adams, Tina Stocking, Pedro and Maria Saenz, Robert Gonzales, Carol Reed, Stacey Terrell, Karen Beckles, Charles Gilette, Susan Samaniego, Victor Turkan, Phil Magaletta, Valerie Stewart, Ann Ma, Wardens Reese, Schultz, Benov, and Clark and Associate Wardens Jeter, Gordon, Avalos, Roberts, Nelson, Jones, Butt, and Newell.

Special thanks to my psychology interns who kept me grounded in my profession in an environment that was often at odds with the intention to provide healing and hope in a dark place. (Nancy, Aida, Jerome, Karen, Richard, Joanne, Mimi, Carey, Tanya, Teresa, Tanda, Tone, Jei, Suzanne, Rick, Olivia, Tracy, Cory, Kaho, Maureen, Elizabeth, Sethlin, Aparna, Karen, Lisa, Alexander, Jason, Sonia, Kaire, Dave, Camellia, Clemencia, and Elizabeth).

I want to thank my clients at FCI Dublin who taught me more about the human spirit than I can possibly express. As Jody Foster once said, "You know who you are."

Thank you Carmen Goodyear and Laurie York for providing me with a lovely cabin to write in when I desperately needed a writer's retreat. Thank you, Jane Tucker and all the wonderful people at the Dairy Hollow Writer's Colony in Eureka Springs, Arkansas.

And last, but not least, I want to acknowledge my girlfriend, Diana Leone, and her boys, Luca and Dominic, for bringing joy into this new chapter of my life.

Red Ink Press

RED INK PRESS was founded in 2016 to give voice to authors, characters and topics that are underrepresented in mainstream media.

The mission of Red Ink Press is to uplift our readers with fiction that is inspirational and educational while still being entertaining; and with non-fiction that inspires, enlightens, and empowers our readers to move beyond fear and perceived limitations to be their best and highest selves and create a world where love prevails.

Red Ink Press fiction focuses on inspirational fiction. Red Ink Press non-fiction focuses on personal growth, self-empowerment, spirituality, and mind-body-spirit. Red Ink Press is committed to supporting authors who have a powerful message to share with stories of transformation, inspiration and redemption.

We publish books and provide inspirational online courses and in-person events.

To find out more, please visit our website.
www.redinkpressbooks.com